The
Witch's
Assistant

The Witch's Assistant

BITCHCRAFT BOOK ONE

A. T. NAPOLI

Podium

Cover design by Lisa Marie Pompilio

ISBN: 978-1-0394-6927-3

Published in 2024 by Podium Publishing
www.podiumaudio.com

Podium

To you, who has ever felt like a Clark.

CONTENTS

The
Witch's
Assistant

"No tree, it is said, can grow to heaven unless its roots reach down to hell."

— CARL JUNG

PROLOGUE

The Tower

Darlings," said the woman with copper hair. She spoke in a lisping Queen's English, soft yet menacing, and with venom on her tongue: "There is a spoiled, rotten apple in our bunch . . ."

The women amongst her candlelit circle, dressed in black like her, held on to her every word with bated breath. The room was still save for their peroxide strands swaying in the whisper of the opening in the roof. The jewels on their necks pulsed with their stiff heartbeats.

"We have a traitor in our midst."

For a moment, even the night sky around them splashed across the glass floor seemed to be leaning in, watching, listening. Slowly, the hollow-eyed women followed her forbidding gaze, until all came to rest upon a single member. The young witch's face fell from smug, smirking satisfaction into a bewildered look of pure terror.

"No . . . !" she gasped. "It wasn't me! I swear! I— I didn't do it!"

Lip curled, voice even, the copper-haired woman hissed a single, merciless word: "Liar."

"No! I would never! I love you! I've always loved you!" the witch said. "You've got it all wrong!" Her desperation hung in the air, echoing in that round glass tower.

"When one bad apple spoils and rots," the copper-haired one continued, speaking to the members of her circle, "the others will surely follow. That apple must be disposed of."

"No, please! I'll do anything! Anything you want! Anything, I promise! *Please!*" the witch begged. Mascaraed tears began to line her cheeks in sooty, black runs. Uncontrollably, she began to tremble.

But the copper-haired woman simply stared down at her from atop her long, straight nose. Unmoved, she said, "One does not suffer a traitor witch to live."

"No!" cried the other woman. "I didn't mean to! I'm sorry! Please don't! *Please!*"

The other women of the circle dared not look away. They watched, statuesque and still, thrown into severe relief by the pentagram's quivering candles. All knew what was to come, what they could not stop. Far below them, New York City carried on sleepless and none the wiser, late-night business as usual.

The copper-haired woman hissed, "And what is a witch to do about her traitor sister, my darlings?" Sparks like lightning pulsated from her aura, a glowing black halo that seethed all around her with electric rage.

The frantic woman broke the circle and carefully backed away, step by step. She shook her hands and tear-streaked face in helpless protest. "Leave me alone! *Leave me alone!*"

At this, the copper-haired woman's face broke into the most peculiar and dangerous of smiles. It stopped just short of the apples of her cheeks, and failed to reach her seething green eyes.

Her answer was simple: "She fires her."

"No! Stop! Don't! Leave me alone! LEAVE ME ALONE! NO! NO! *NOOO!*"

First came the quivering smoke billowing from her nose, ears, and mouth. Then, in a flashing instant, the woman erupted into screaming flames, a human bonfire from head to toe. Her shrill cries filled the air and reverberated against the round tower windows, while her flames licked the tall glass ceiling. It could not be determined whether the betrayer was engulfed by the fires of her own anxiety or by the power of the copper-haired one's mind, but it happened all the same.

The other women hardly flinched. They stared, the light of that magnificent golden fire dancing in their alabaster eyes.

"Do not break the circle," the copper-haired woman commanded.

Wailing, the woman on fire hobbled away on high heels, and after only a few steps, came down hard onto her knees. She fell onto the glass floor and crawled towards the iron banister staircase. She did not get far. Eventually, after what felt like a lifetime, the fire came to die as abruptly as it had started. Smoking and smoldering, the whimpering witch opened her encrusted eyes and gasped with a shaking, rasping, heaving breath. She tried to utter a word that would not sound—and with her blackened arm outstretched, reached for the young man watching behind that iron banister that descended into the black-as-night glass floor. Then, her head slumped over, her whimpers subsided, and a single bloodstained tear escaped her eyes, menacingly affixed to his. Her smoke escaped the opening in the ceiling, and she lay silent and still.

"We have one more rotten apple to tend to," the copper-haired woman said, even calmer and more forbidding than before. "Ladies, please, open the circle for our little guest." As she turned her gaze, her circle followed, and suddenly, to the young man's complete and utter horror, all the hollow eyes in that glass room tower had been aimed at none other than him. He had been discovered.

"Come here, my darling," she said with a murderous smile. Her leering green eyes locked onto his, glassy-eyed, brown, and full of fear.

His stomach dropped, his blood ran cold, and with a jolt as if he had suddenly missed a step at the bottom of a staircase, the young man startled himself awake. He was tangled in his sweat-soaked bedsheets in his home.

It had all felt so real. He could swear there was a lingering malodor of dread in the air: the smokey vestiges of scorched skin and hair mingled with the metallic taste of blood in his mouth. There was a prickling itch in the middle of his forehead too, and a shrill, high-pitched ringing in his ears, like an echo of the screaming woman. Worst of all, he had the uncanny feeling that someone was staring at him, that someone had taken notice of him who shouldn't. Burned into his mind's eye was the acidic gaze of the copper-haired woman, as if it had been wrenched into reality with him, unblinkingly affixed, gapingly open, and looking straight at him.

Huh . . . the young man thought to himself. *Weird!*

A glance at his clock showed it was just after three in the morning. Unable to make sense of it all, he chalked the dream up to indigestion and an exuberant imagination, and after some moments, fell back to sleep.

When he awoke again, the uneasy feeling of being watched remained.

Still, he put the entire ordeal out of his mind, and by the afternoon, forgot about the feeling of being watched altogether.

CHAPTER I

The Interview

Once upon a time, in a magical land far, far away called New York, New York—the city so good they named it twice—there lived a twenty-three-year-old boy . . . Clark Crane put his novel down for the umpteenth time. *There, we find our noble hero on the most elusive, daring, and stupid of quests: a job hunt in the middle of August . . .*

If only the interviewer would show . . . Clark thought to himself.

He rubbed his sleepless brown eyes with a yawn and another check of his watch. Clark had arrived over half an hour early after a sleepless night. The interviewer, he noted, was over half an hour late.

He had been waiting in the back of a dark, empty café, sheltered away in the shadow of a tall Sixth Avenue building a couple of blocks off Central Park. The café was so small and tucked away, in fact, that he had somehow walked past it two or three times before noticing it. Looking around, he found the café to be as sleek and as sterile as his cold linoleum chair and the table he had been seated at. In the time he had been there, and much to his curiosity, Clark had been the only patron.

Maybe I missed the lunch rush . . .

Whatever the reason, Clark was just happy to be somewhere with air-conditioning and so thought nothing more of it. To him, it was a welcome reprieve from the one-hundred-degree city day outside. He sat listening to Midtown Manhattan bustling beyond the café doors: tires on potholed asphalt, honking cabs and wailing sirens, jackhammers on concrete and their catcalling hardhats, the patter of passersby in conversation, the bumble of business calls on cell phones and the bass of air traffic above. New York City was a soundtrack he never tired of hearing.

Of course, being the sole customer did not stop the waiter from throwing him a few disapproving glances now and again for taking up his table. Clark's smudged glass of water had been left unfilled for quite some time, collecting condensation and sweating on his tabletop, party of one.

If he was being stood up, Clark decided he could live with that. If he was being *bamboozled*, however, well, that just wouldn't do. It was all happening suspiciously fast anyway. Just the day before, his mother's friend had rung him up with the news:

"*Clarky!*" Patricia had chirped in her sitcom-nasal Queens accent he so adored. "Are you still looking for a new job? You free tomorrow? Oh, good! Listen, I have a friend of a friend, someone very important looking for an intern of sorts, and quick. I thought of you right away! You would be great at it. It could open many doors. A million girls would kill for the job—*literally!* I'm gonna set you up for an in-person with her personal assistant—they're a little 'old-fashioned' like that. A year there would change your life, Clarky."

But what kind of internship, and for whom exactly? Despite his curious pressing, Patricia would reveal nothing more.

"Don't worry about all that! Just be your sweet self, do exactly as you're told, and they'll love you like I do. Promise! I see big things in your future, Clarky . . . By the way, have you talked to your *mutha?*"

All Patricia forwarded him was a time and address, and that was that, so there he found himself, waiting for who he wasn't so sure. Was it normal to be this late for an interview? Had something happened? Had they found someone else? What had Patricia told them about, he ruminated, and why did it have to be something bad about him?! Clark resisted the urge to bite his nails, to no avail.

"Trust me," she said . . . "It'll be great," she said . . .

Despite all the résumé-sending that summer and not landing any leads, none whatsoever, Clark was grateful to have lucked out on his current job in the first place, truly he was, even if it was a meager one; dead-end even. When job listings were calling for a degree and two to four years' experience minimum, how was he or anyone else to compete, let alone survive? In this job market . . . ? In this economy . . . ? *Maybe a city internship is too good to be true after all, a fairy tale; shame on me for dreaming . . .*

Just as he resolved himself to the fact that this was why he hated interviewing, right as he was beginning to pack up his things, a woman arrived, dressed in far too much black for summer in the city.

She breezed in through the heavy glass door, wearing a curtain of long, straight dark hair that spilled over a smart black blazer and a cleavage-baring little black dress. A black snakeskin purse hung off one arm, and those impossibly long legs on which she strode landed in heels that clacked with every step—until, that is, she saw that it was only Clark inside. She stopped dead in her tracks and her face fell as she looked around.

"Hello," he said, standing up and extending his hand. "I'm Clark. It's nice to meet you."

Ignoring him, the woman removed her sunglasses from under a heavy fringe. For a moment, those piercing gray-blue eyes rimmed in cat-like kohl and thick mascaraed lashes narrowed in on his. He smiled back.

"You were the one . . . referred by Patricia Hartford?" she asked, her accent properly, undoubtedly English.

"Yes, that's me!" he said.

"Strange," she began, pulling up her phone. "I could have sworn I was looking for a—"

"I, um, prefer to go by my middle name, Clark, if you don't mind."

A terse half smile flashed across her face. She placed a manicured hand in his for a shake that was polite and prissy yet limp. *"Pleasure. Monica Chase-Whiteley. I was going to say, I was looking for a woman."*

"Oh haha . . ." Judging by the look on her face, he had the impression that he wasn't the only one Patricia had failed to prepare. Clark smiled back at her anyway. He noticed how her smile didn't quite reach those blue-gray eyes as they took their seats. "Well—thank you for meeting with me!"

Monica pursed her lips.

Here we go, starting off on the wrong foot . . . Clark "like Kent" Crane, saving the day already . . . Way to go, nerd . . . The waiter approached their table.

Slightly hunched over, his deep walnut skin lined with age, the waiter held his arms behind his back in feigned modesty. "Can I start you off with a drink?" he asked in a monotone, looking only at Monica, leaving no doubt it was a question he couldn't care less to hear the answer to.

"Coffee—iced, black, no sugar—and sparkling water."

Clark watched almost amusedly how she spoke without looking up from her phone.

"I'll have the same, please," Clark added. Both Monica and the waiter turned to look at him. "Thank you!" The waiter frowned, turned on his heel, and left.

Monica asked, "How did you become connected to Patricia?" She hardly hid the skepticism in her voice when she said, "You seem to come with the . . . *highest* of recommendations."

Clark surmised Monica was in her mid-to-late thirties, maybe younger, judging by her smooth, blemish-less skin, and cheekbones high as a skyscraper. She was styled in clothes likely worth more than Clark's entire rent twenty times over, and those peculiar, unblinking gray-blue eyes under arched brows . . . Monica was gorgeous, wealthy, and cool. Clark—gawky in his big-boy clothes of well-worn Oxfords, secondhand slacks, a white button-down, and mousy brown hair and eyes—was not. She surveyed him in return and let out a deep, reluctant sigh.

"Oh, Patricia, she's a good family friend, almost like the aunt I never had," Clark replied with fondness, then kicked himself for using the word *friend*. "I'm really grateful she thought of me." Truthfully, he had seen more of Patricia in the last few years than he had his own flesh and blood.

Monica flatly replied, "How lovely."

As the waiter returned, Clark scrounged up a toothless smile back again. The waiter set their glasses down and poured their coffee over ice. "I will give you a minute to look over the menu."

Monica said, "That's all."

The waiter cut her a look and turned away. When he disappeared behind the kitchen doors and they were alone once more, she put down her phone and continued.

"So, *Clark*, who are you, and why the hell should I hire you? Clearly, I haven't heard of you before."

"Ah, well . . ." Clark began, "I was born and raised in the city. Actually, I was raised in Astoria, just over the bridge in Queens where I, uh, live now. Have you ever been?"

Monica smirked. "No, I can't say I have . . ." Judging by her manner, her words almost seemed to imply, *And I never will.*

"Oh," Clark said, plowing on. "Um, well, I moved from home right after my freshman year of high school, and I've been on my own ever since. I rent a studio for chips from the landlord's wife, a kind old Greek lady I know. Um, what else . . . I was an English major; I'm an avid reader. I've always loved books and a good story," he said, holding up his well-worn copy of *The Great Gatsby.*

"*Wow*, that's so cool," Monica said. "You don't sound like you're from New York."

"Haha, thanks, neither do you," he replied. She stared blankly back at him. Clark took a sharp inhale. "The uh, the accent never took hold," he quickly added, "but sometimes it likes to make an appearance." *Abort mission . . . !* he thought. *Monica ordered one girl-interview, hot and fresh, hold the sarcasm, and I am* not *delivering . . .* He shifted in his chair. "How about you? Where are you from, Monica? The UK?"

She narrowed her eyes at Clark. "London," she replied, lifting a manicured finger and giving a haughty toss of her hair with a roll of her eyes. "I mean, *obviously.* We have homes in Paris, Ibiza, in many cities the world over, really. Although, I am nothing if not a London girl at heart. I attended an all-girls boarding school, studied Business Fashion at uni, and after I graduated, traveled throughout much of my twenties with my husband and my kids." She held up her hand and flashed a wedding ring the size of a rock.

"I devoted myself to my charity work until, of course," she continued, "I began working for Charisma. She was the one to introduce me to my husband. She is all about empowering women, after all . . ." Monica paused to contemplate her ring. Was it wistfulness that registered on her face? If this was her with strangers, Clark was afraid to imagine what she was like in private.

With a small pop, the air pressure at the table changed. Clark wiggled his ear. He figured the waiter must have turned the easy-listening down but . . . He perked his head up: was there even music playing to begin with? Had the noisy street outside gone still and quiet? Monica didn't seem to notice.

"Charisma is a long-time friend of the family. We are a long line of prominent and highly influential witches, and we are *very* well-connected, in this city and more. It's been a few years now that I've been in New York. We live just over there, on the Upper East Side," she said, pointing northeast.

Clark was beginning to feel all kinds of naive. *Nice one, telling someone like Monica my big bad hobby is reading . . .*

"Do you work? Actually," she asked, sizing him up and down, "let me rephrase that: what do you do for work?"

Then again . . . Clark thought to himself, *the two of us, we're not really cut from the same cloth . . . Wait . . . did she say "witches" . . . ?* They regarded one another from across that cold table, him in his white hand-me-down shirt and her in her black designer wardrobe.

"Yeah, I, um, I work at a . . . *café,* kinda like this one," he said, waving his hands and motioning around the modern, dim, customer-less space they were seated in, "but I'm looking to explore other opportunities."

The honest answer was that by "café" he meant more an old-timey relic of a coffee shop in Astoria, the last of its kind. It was a brick-and-mortar situated between two new developments, a community institution. There he served bridge-and-tunnels their donuts and *cawfee* on their way to their office jobs in the city or out to *Lawn Guyland*, watching the sun rise and set out the front window.

Did he hate it? Not exactly. At least, he wouldn't say that. Most days, he liked the regulars and the routine, the neon sign, the familiar homey atmosphere and the aroma of their roasting Mexican coffee. They were long, early shifts, but there was free caffeine at hand, he could go to school in the evenings, and sometimes, in his downtime, he could even sneak a page or two of his reading.

The pay wasn't much, however, not much at all: after New York City bills, rent, and groceries, Clark had just enough left to treat himself to something here and there—a new book or two perhaps, or maybe a matinee at the movies, but little else. It was a means to an end until something bigger and better came along. Nevertheless, Clark was smart enough not to give away that he was desperate for change and better pay, and that this could be his one-way ticket out. *Don't fuck this up, nerd . . .*

As he sat there, a thought crept up on him: What if this was it? What if he didn't get this internship? What if bigger and better never came and there he remained, watching life go by all around him, stuck behind the counter of that tiny little Astoria coffee shop, until the day he died?

"I brought a copy of my résumé!" Clark produced a printout from his backpack and slid it along the cold table.

Clark Crane
rclarkcrane1024@gmail.com
718.640.5555
2640 30th St Apt 5E
Astoria, NY 11102

*Native New Yorker useful for cawfee, books, and cavalier
humor. Aspiring to honesty, empathy, and authenticity.
Professional dork and storyteller.*

At this, Monica looked up at him. Clark sheepishly smiled back.

EXPERIENCE
*Barista at Astoria Coffee Shoppe (7 years to present), Astoria,
NY—*
- Day-to-day tasks include inventory, shopkeeping, and
maintaining customer service and food-and-beverage
excellence, in service of a community cornerstone.
- Long-standing record for perfect attendance.

*Tutor at Grade Smart Tutoring (1 year to present), Astoria,
NY—*
- English Literature, and Lang and Composition Tutor for
grades K-7.
- Highly rated across GST's grading scale. Great with
parents!

Boarder at Catsitty NYC (4 years to present), Astoria, NY—
- Private, in-home cat sitter through agency.
- Trustworthy. Lifelong pet lover. Strong predilection for
playtime.

EDUCATION
Hunter College, New York, NY (4 years)
English Literature Major

References available upon request.

She checked the back of the printout before saying, "You tutor as
well as"—Monica almost stifled a laugh at this—"cat sit?"
"Yes," Clark said.

"Why?"

"Why? Um, I like reading and writing, and it's something that doesn't require I exchange my body for." Quickly, he added, "Like physical labor! And I love animals."

Jesus, Clark . . .

"No, why on earth do you work three jobs? This 'café' doesn't pay you enough?"

"Oh!" Clark turned a bashful shade of pink. "Tutoring gets slow this time of year. I really want a cat of my own, but I figure it's better to make money on them for now. Cat sitting doesn't happen often enough though, and they chew at my plants. I couldn't do contract work like my father, I just wouldn't fit in. The coffee sh—the *café*, I mean—is my steadiest gig but, no, it doesn't pay what I want to be making." Come to think of it, Clark didn't know one person his age who didn't have a side hustle or two. He wondered, *Why am I telling her all of this . . . ?*

Monica put down his résumé. "How old are you, exactly?"

"Twenty-three," he answered automatically, immediately kicking himself for it. *Is that even legal to ask . . . ?*

"I see," Monica said. "And, it says here that you haven't yet graduated?"

"I'm . . . currently on a break." *Hey, Clark . . . ?* he thought. *Shaddup . . . !* He wasn't about to tell someone like Monica that he had dropped out to survive the city. What was he going to do with a boatload of debt and a BA in English anyway? A girlfriend of his was selling pictures of her feet for good money—*and honestly . . .* he thought, *that's looking more and more like a lucrative endeavor . . .* At this, Monica shot him a look with those gray, hollow eyes, and for a moment Clark almost worried that she could read his mind.

"Right . . ." she said. "Well, I'm afraid the position is for someone who can commit to full-time—*preferably female.* The job is demand-ing, to say the least, with some physical labor. The ideal candidate would wear a lot of hats."

"I can commit to full-time!" he said in a hurry. "Physical labor is A-okay with me." *Can I . . . ? Is it . . . ?!* Clark's palms were clammy, and as he wiped them on his pants, he pushed the worry down and away that he was not winning her over. Before he could continue, however, the waiter reappeared.

This time, Clark watched as the man inhaled a reluctant breath, summoned a smile, and asked, "Can I get you anything else?"

A commendable attempt at pleasantness . . . Clark thought. *Will it work . . . ?*

"No," Monica said, without looking up or removing her eyes from Clark, who could read the disdain all over her face. She waved the man away.

With a roll of his eyes, the waiter disappeared once more through the kitchen door. Clark couldn't be sure but he had a hunch Monica might have always been a woman of privilege: here she sat, clacking her manicured nails on the tabletop, a spoiled little girl sighing with boredom and contempt. Clark imagined she had been gorgeous and popular growing up, but maybe not well-liked on the playground.

He cleared his throat. "About the position," Clark began. "Patricia mentioned you were looking to hire an intern. Something about an extra hand? She didn't really explain much at all, to be honest."

Monica narrowed her eyes yet again. She asked, "You don't know who I am, nor what I do?"

Clark shook his head.

She sat back in her chair and crossed her legs. The city outside had gone completely silent, and the café was still and quiet too. To Clark, it was as if all the world seemed to turn to mute. Monica's every word punctuated the air, like her upturned nose she spoke through as she slowly said, "I am Charisma Saintly's fourth assistant. I am her Keyholder, manager of her estate, and a member of her coven."

Is she serious . . . ? So she did say "witches" . . . He asked, "Her . . . fourth assistant?"

"Correct," she smartly replied. "We are an intimate team of about five or six. Charisma doesn't like too many personalities around, and she is a very private person. There are four assistants on her team and coven, myself included, and a booker—that is, her sister. With the exception of her financial advisor, all of her companies are female led and run. The rest are in and out: her personal chefs, her photographers, her designers and stylists, and her many brand supervisors, managers, and handlers. The other assistants and I are all too busy juggling the needs of Charisma and her clients, a roster of *very* important people, and we are indeed looking for help. Somehow, the responsibility of hiring and conducting interviews always seems to land on me, so . . . here we are. And the interns, well." She sighed, sizing him up and down once more. "We've had a hard time finding the right fit for the job."

Clark nervously *haha*ed. "Oh, right!"

Monica raised an eyebrow from under that heavy fringe. Clark gulped. He wondered what she meant by witches, who the last intern was, and how that all might apply to him.

"What happened to the previous intern?"

"It's a fast-paced work environment. Some can't seem to keep up, or for that matter, last."

This sounds insane . . . Clark thought. "What would my responsibilities entail?"

"An intern's work is an assistant's work—the same as any other witch's assistant," she said in a snit of irritation, as if he should've already known. "A junior's responsibility—junior assistants, we call the interns—is to make our lives easier. Delivering, clienteling, organizing, preparing Charisma's kit, maintaining her home and accounts, making sure all is running smoothly, etcetera etcetera. We require someone bright, reliable, and trustworthy, who is task-oriented, efficient, and can anticipate our every need. Charisma Saintly runs the tightest of ships, as do I. Your discretion would be of top priority."

Anticipating their every need . . . ? More like reading their *minds . . .* "I'm dependable!" Clark said. "I'm discreet!"

Ignoring him, Monica glanced at his résumé and asked, "And you? How far along are you in your practice? I don't see anything about it here."

"My 'practice'?"

"Yes."

"Of what?"

"*Of the Craft?*" Her eyebrows were so dubiously raised under her bangs they had all but disappeared.

Clark nervously *haha*ed again. "Oh, that!"

Monica rolled her eyes.

"Um, well, I guess you could say I've always been kinda 'spiritual.' Actually, I've always had dreams that somehow seem to come true; insight I can't explain; things happening around me—to me. I guess I've always been a bit *intuitive*, maybe since I was li—"

"I highly doubt that," she said flatly. "Your mother, she isn't a witch?" Incredulous, she asked, "You *were* brought up as one, were you not?"

"My mother? A witch? Um . . . I'm not so sure about that. My grandmother, my mom's mom, maybe? She was a fiery woman, a figurehead to her community in her time, but I only know her through stories, of her—"

"So you haven't assisted before?" Monica asked, cutting him off again.

"Assisted? Oh yeah, lots!" Clark could feel himself beginning to flush pink.

"Whom have you assisted?"

"Um, well, Patricia."

"Patricia?" She narrowed her eyes, and the air seemed to become charged around her. "*Really?*"

Clark gulped. "Yeah. A ton."

Monica enunciated every syllable and held herself very still. "And what have you assisted Patricia with?"

"Um, uh, well . . ." Clark stammered. He trailed away. Without a sound, the waiter appeared through the kitchen doors. He hurried to the landline on the wall, and Clark froze in disbelief at what he was witnessing: the phone was raised to the waiter's ear, except his lips were moving and there was no sound emanating, none whatsoever. Clark realized he couldn't hear a thing outside their table, nothing at all. His throat having gone dry, Clark took a gulp of water and, almost inhaling it, coughed and sputtered. "Is it just me or—"

"So let me get this straight," Monica said, cutting him the deadliest of looks. "You don't have a client book."

He thought, *A client book . . . ? Am I supposed to . . . ?!* "Um, well, not really but—"

"You are not a practicing witch . . ."

"I think that depends on your definition of—"

"—you were not raised in the witching community—"

"Well, not exactly, but—"

"—and before today, you had not heard of me, nor Charisma Saintly."

Clark blinked back at her. Suddenly he wasn't so sure about any of this, and judging by the look on her face, neither was she. Clark could feel his cheeks and ears burn, and a prickling itch in the middle of his forehead.

"*Seriously?* What, do you live under some kind of rock under the 59th Street Bridge? You must've crawled out from one to come here and waste my time, no doubt!"

Clark's stomach just about fell into his groin. He backpedaled: "I'm sorry! The name rings a bell. Is she . . . a designer? I honestly don't pay much attention to fashion or celebrities!"

At this, Monica's lips slowly broke from pursed disdain into a gleeful smirk, one that did not quite reach those icy eyes and high-arched brows. This time, it was as if the entire world had stopped to listen to her speak, and as if everything was leaning in, even the walls.

"*For your information*, Charisma Saintly is not only a megastar with a billion-dollar empire, but also the High Queen of All Witches, the Number One Witch in the World, and the most powerful of us all. She—along with *us*, her coven," Monica hissed, "is behind the most powerful names alive today. If wealth could be measured in influence, she is certainly the richest woman in the world. Literally, she *is* the richest woman in the world, bar none, a gazillionaire, *a goddess on Earth.* Women and men alike worship the very ground she walks on. The Coven is one of her many businesses, and her most treasured. Under her rule, we lead an empire of witches around the globe, and most importantly, her throne here in New York, where I was somehow led to you. How you have not heard of her, let alone me, is beyond!"

Clark's eyes were wide, his mouth sand, and his shirt clung to the small of his back in a cold sweat.

"Right now, as Charisma and her family are away on holiday, we are preparing for her return. September is a busy month, and upon that return, we, her team, will be meeting to discuss the rest of the year ahead. This is the job that a million girls would kill for—*literally*—and, well . . ." She stared dead at Clark, who stared back, mouth slightly agape, hanging on to every word. "We need someone quick."

She waved her hand and snapped her fingers at the waiter, who reproachfully put the phone down.

"Yes?" he hissed once at their side.

"One coffee, iced, to go," she said, "and a splash of milk." She shot a look directly at Clark and added, "This coffee's left a bad taste in my mouth."

The waiter's top lip curled and he appeared to be most displeased. "Certainly, Mrs. Chase-Whiteley." As he left for behind the counter, Clark glanced at the untouched iced coffee, sweating onto the table.

"It is not an easy job by any means," she said. "But it is the opportunity of a lifetime, one that could open many doors and change one's life. Charisma changed mine. She launches stars. She could turn a rube into a ruler. You would be giving yourself to something bigger, something greater than yourself. Charisma knows what she wants when she wants it, exactly how she wants it, and she accepts nothing less than perfection . . . If you were right for the job, of course, which you most certainly are not."

Clark gulped. *A rube into a ruler . . .* He had so many questions. *Quick . . .* he thought. *Sell it.*

"I love witches!" he blurted out. This time Clark's mouth moved quicker than his mind. "Uh, I mean, women! I mean, witches! I mean—you know what I mean. I know all about them! I was practically raised by Hermione and the Sandersons! I know witches in books and in movies. I grew up collecting candles and crystals, and girls—around girls, not collecting them." Clark was pretty sure there was spit collecting in the corner of his mouth. Monica was certainly giving him the most contemptuous of looks, knowing that this time he wasn't lying: he was deranged.

Clark took a deep breath. "I might not know who Charisma is, or who you are, or much about how this whole . . . business works, for that matter," he said, waving his arms around. "But I'm a hard worker, I'm a quick learner, and I'm never, ever late." If life was a bunch of negotiations, Clark was not about to go down without a fight. It was this or the coffee shop.

Monica, however, had had enough. Seeing all that she needed, she swiveled around and grabbed her purse.

"It seems like a great opportunity!" Clark fawned. *Something feels off about this . . .* Still, Clark said almost reflexively, "I'd love to be in the run!"

Monica held up his résumé. Speaking slowly and enunciating every word as if talking to a fool, she asked, "Is this your phone number? Can you receive text messages at this number?"

"Yes, but . . ." he replied, looking down at his hand-me-down cellular and then up at her.

Monica folded the sheet crisply down the middle and stuffed it away. She stood.

"When would I start?" Clark asked, standing up with her.

"I'm all out of time for your silly questions," she said, giving a curt half smile and a tilt of her head. She clasped up, and with a haughty toss of her hair, shouldered her purse and made for the exit.

"Okay, well, thank you for meeting with . . . me," he called out, but it was too late. Monica had already sauntered away, muttering something about how some people should "sharpen pencils for a living." She snatched her coffee from the waiter on her way out of that glass-front door and disappeared into a black town car that Clark realized had been lurking outside, all along.

The overhead lights flickered and the ambient noise of the city came rushing back like a wave crashing all around him. It was as if they had been sitting in a soundless vacuum the entire time, and it had been carried out in her huff.

The waiter appeared once again, watching the car drive off. "The bill, *sir*," he said in a cold, mocking English accent. He dropped it on the table and walked away. Clark's face fell as he looked down.

Monica had left him to cover the check.

Clark stepped into the city heat wave. The blinding 58th Street sun bounded off its beige buildings, and, lost in thought, he made his way homeward. In the sweltering underground of the Fifth Avenue–59th Street Station awaiting the Astoria-bound N train, Clark did a quick internet search of Charisma Saintly. Just an hour ago, he'd had no idea big business around witchcraft could exist, let alone a network of witches and their witch queen. Was this for real?

"Designer 'darling' Charisma Saintly celebrates her 42nd birthday on the French Riviera with her family," a headline read from just the day before, August 13. It was one of many.

One article from a couple of years prior proclaimed, *"Charisma Saintly to divorce from second husband, Edgar Dortier, billionaire media proprietor and investor."*

Another read: *"Charisma Saintly acquires one-of-a-kind, mega-million 'air mansion' of New York City's Billionaire's Row in heated divorce settlement."* A photo displayed a multilevel penthouse atop a skyscraper, complete with a giant deck and a mirrored glass tower, and flanked by *"gothic stone gargoyles imported from an abandoned cathedral on the outskirts of Bucharest."*

One major publication caught Clark's eye: *"Charisma Saintly and the Renaissance of New York City."* Charisma was the cover star for the magazine's latest publication in the coming month. *"The Brit has invaded, and she's taking over the world"*:

Thanks to her successful empire of New York City-based, critically acclaimed restaurants, bars, and nightclubs—even her own church—Charisma Saintly, touted "Queen of the City," is championed for bringing the return of glamour to New York, New York.

But that's not how she got her start.

Just a decade ago, the beloved mother, billionaire, and multi-media mogul launched her namesake fashion line with a collection of twelve LBDs (that's *Little Black Dress* to the rest of us) designed after her signature style, to a record-breaking debut.

Today her brand portfolio also spans home goods, beauty, and the launch of her first-ever fragrance—all of which continue to break sales records for women across all categories. There is no glass ceiling she can't shatter, and nothing this woman can't achieve.

"I love empowering women," the style star emphatically shared during a sit-down at her posh, five-level penthouse. "I want to help all women look and feel their best. I love what I do, I've worked *bloody* hard for what I have, and I'm not going to stop!" We love a girl's girl—read: a woman's woman—who is unafraid to be ambitious.

For years, Saintly has been the name on the tongue of the rich and the famous the globe over, helping to style, brand, and market some of the biggest names of our time. Now, the tastemaker hopes to bridge the us-them club of celebrity and the everyday woman.

As she tours me through her living room, I'm quick to point out the many photos of her and her clients, the who's who of politics and entertainment, all of whom call Charisma their best kept secret.

"Friends, my darling," the trusted confidant corrects me. "These are all my very good friends."

The five-level mega-home coined "air mansion" is the first of its kind in the West. It sits atop the tallest residential building in the world, overlooking a panoramic of the Tri-State area: a throne fit for a queen perched high above her queendom.

The penthouse spans approximately 18,000 square feet, with a whopping twelve bedrooms, seven baths, six fireplaces, three elevators, and a primary suite that takes up the entire top floor—a space off-limits to guests and cameras, the only part of the celebrity's life that is, in fact. Fans can only hope to catch glimpses of the extravagant private quarters on the enigma's social media, an insider's view Saintly almost teasingly seldom features. Some secrets a woman just has to keep to herself.

The apartment even comes complete with a private spa, an entertainment center, an indoor swimming pool, two chef's kitchens, and a 1,450-square-foot terrace—"For my parties, darling! I love to entertain."

Want to be invited? Invitations to this queen's parties are extravagant, coveted, exclusive, and infamously sent by private couriers for personal delivery to lucky attendees.

One of many homes, planes, yachts, and businesses spanning the globe, the apartment was awarded to Saintly in a heated and very public divorce settlement with her former husband, media tycoon Edgar Dortier.

Her most prized possession, however? Her children, of course.

"What matters first and foremost is always the children, keeping them safe, and keeping them happy," she says, sharing a photo of Noble, 6, and Grace, 14. "They are my everything. The rest, like the penthouse, is just a bonus."

Charisma Saintly's life has splashed the public eye for much of this decade and more, and yet there is (still) so much myth and legend surrounding the icon and her namesake brand. Luckily for us, the curtain is steadily rising with the birth of social media, and Saintly is at the forefront.

Sure enough, her accounts draw in a following by the mega millions of well-engaged and dedicated fans across the globe. They dole hearts to photos of her and her fashion, her restaurants, and her sensationally glamorous work and travels.

"Your name has become so synonymous with glamour and empowerment and womanhood," I point out, "it's like we've always known you!" It's true: Saintly is in the mind and heart of the modern woman, all around the world.

"I've always been here, darling!" the social media darling replies with a playful smirk. Saintly was surely the first to capitalize on style-to-celebrity-to-commerce, a feat both unparalleled and somehow, dare we say, so American. From her unmistakable style and golden-copper hair, to her emphatic, infectious way of speaking, Saintly can only be described as, well . . . charismatic! Simply put, she is famous for being famous, and for being Charisma.

"Like I always say, *'Give a woman a little Charisma, and she can conquer the world,'*" she shares with an infectious laugh. "We all need a little Charisma in our lives!" The social media darling adds, "The fans have been so special, really. I only hope to give back all the love."

I ask the star, "What can we come to expect next?"

"First, it's New York and fragrance," she teases, holding up her debut luxury perfume, *Charisma the Eau de Parfum.* "Next, the world."

It's Charisma's world, and we are all lucky to be living in it.

Clark's train charged into the station in a gust of wind and creaking metal. "This is an Astoria-Ditmars-bound N train. Next stop, 59th Street–Lexington Avenue," the crackling intercom announced. At the unmistakable *ding-dong* of the closing doors, Clark bookmarked the interview to finish later.

The captions on Charisma's photogram gave Clark pause: big, splashy photos, all with a smile. With my friend so-and-so celebrity, they read. Clark did not have to keep up with celebrity culture—which he, of course, did not—to know that these A-list "friends" were the choicest of the A-list. Even Felicity, the sellout pop star-turned-actress Southern American he grew up idolizing, tagged her in a happy birthday post. The photo's caption of the two read, "Charisma changed my life. I owe this wonderful woman so much. Happy birthday, my friend!"

Clark scratched at the middle of his forehead, which wildly itched. There was such familiarity about Charisma, and it wasn't just her conspicuously copper hair that made Clark wonder if he had seen her face somewhere before. If only he could place where . . .

The next thing he knew, Clark was receiving advertisements for her first celebrity fragrance and her eponymous cosmetic range. Clark's head was abuzz, swimming with words like "coven" and "internships" and "always cruelty-free."

Nowhere, not in one article or caption or website, could he find the word "witch."

But are they actual witches . . . ?

The train dipped and Clark lost service, rushing into the sloping tunnel under the East River, the great divider of the haves and the have-nots. On the other side, the train climbed above ground to Queensboro Plaza.

Even before rush hour, the platforms were packed with commuters, and every year increasingly so. With its easy proximity to the city, its relative affordability, and its access to the diverse foods of the World's Borough of Queens, his hometown of Astoria was going gone: another victim, Clark reflected, lost to gentrification, commercialization, and transience, and quickly becoming the newest yuppie hot spot. The secret was out; the jig was up; and if he were being honest, maybe things had always been headed this way. Maybe he just wanted to keep it all to himself.

Even the air was different on his side of the tracks. There was a palpable taste of desire that flavored the hustle and bustle of New York City's atmosphere—a polluted appetite, a wanting, a yearning that was never satiated. Here, however, the desperation of Manhattan and its fast-paced lifestyle was almost absent. Astoria, with its old-school, European charm and its longtime residents, had a slowness about it, an easier way of being. Still, New York was not a city for the soft.

Some minutes later, as Clark hopped off the train and down the stairs, passing a freshly burglarized laundromat swarmed with police and dancing lights, he noted that not even Astoria was immune to the growing tension of the times. Pandemics and super-weather, food shortages and a heating globe, the rising cost of living plus the onset of civil unrest and war: one could feel it all.

Down Newtown Avenue, past the bodega and up his sloping, tree-lined street, Clark bounded up the stairs of his prewar five-floor walk-up, into the respite of his tiny studio apartment. The quiet stillness and shrill ringing in his ears were drowned out with the push of a button on his ancient window air-conditioning unit. His interview attire, spotted in sweat, found itself on the hardwood floors.

To Clark, the studio was less of a "studio" and more like a bedroom. Even so, it was home. Its tall ceilings hugged exposed brick and drywall, coated over so many times over the years in thick, dripping paint that he sometimes called it his "papier-mâché home." The plants that filled the available floor and ceiling thrived under all the natural northern sun. It bounced off the neighboring buildings and storybook rooftops and in through the studio's large windows, exposing an almost uninterrupted Astoria blue sky. Inside, Clark barely had enough space to stretch his arms.

To the left was an outdated white-refrigerator kitchenette, stove, and sink. In the middle of the studio sat his full-size bed, and next to it a bedside table holding the lava lamp his mother never let him have, the light switch of which he reached down for. It illuminated the single picture frame next to it: a mature woman with graying hair and an earnest smile. She was reading "The Frog Prince" to a little boy tucked into bed, beaming up at her with his stuffed animal frog cradled in his arms.

On the wall above the bed were posters of his favorite three witch sisters and girl-group pop stars (that part of the interview he at least hadn't faked, he mused). To the right was a hand-me-down wooden dresser, and in the corner lived his wall-less, exposed "bathroom" of a clawfoot tub framed in old white subway tile, a toilet, and a pedestal sink.

As he peered into the mirror above the toilet, Clark thought, *What just happened . . . ?* The entire ordeal had been so odd. No talk of scheduling, nor pay, just a desperate downward spiral. *Boy, did she like to hear herself talk . . .* He felt like he'd let Monica drive the entire conversation. He felt like he'd failed to impress. He felt like he'd blown his chance at something big.

The way she just walked away . . . Why hadn't he just told her the truth from the get-go instead of fawning over her and playing along? He would email her a follow-up the next day—"Thank you for your time," he would write. "I look forward to hearing back from you." *But what good would come of it . . .* he questioned. *Way to go, Clark . . .*

In that mirror, he saw himself staring back just as he was. His five o'clock shadow, he reflected, came in patchy; his chest hair was sparse and scant. Clark stood just an inch shy of six feet, on the cusp of many an "almost": tall, but not broad; cute, but not sexy; thin, but without much definition—and if he were being honest with himself, soft, owing to his proximity to coffee-shop pastries. Clark's sallow olive skin cried out for a day off, out in the sun. His dark brown eyes were, well, brown, unless the sun hit his golden irises at just the right angle, framed by eyebrows he always thought a little too thick for his face. His jawline could have been sharper, and his shoulders could have been broader—they were narrow from a lifetime of playing small, he figured. Beauty marks freckled his entire body like stars he would draw constellations of as a child in marker and in pen. He would do anything to feel special, much to the distress of the adults around him. Mostly, Clark thought himself ordinary, or dare he even say "average," one of his least favorite words after "boring." Staring back in the mirror was a boy, not a man.

Looking into his eyes, Clark thought, *Could be better . . .* He just wasn't sure what to do about any of it. He wanted to muster up a smile, but instead, he broke away. At the microwave, Clark fired up a lunch—frozen chicken taquitos from the dollar store—trying his best to drown out his ruminations in the hum. He was so damn tired of living on those dollar-store taquitos.

Exactly a week before Halloween, Clark would turn twenty-four on the 24th of October, his golden birthday, an age he thought he would never reach. By that age, all of his high-school classmates and college peers had graduated and moved on to their high-powered careers, or gap years traveling to foreign beaches and overseas countries, or to marriages and babies and first-time mortgages—and otherwise onto their August vacations he could never afford, leaving him on his own in the big city for yet another summer in a row. That feeling crept up on him again like tears that wouldn't come: Clark couldn't help but feel behind in life. He felt so stuck.

He approached his bookcase, the shelves crowded with spine-cracked novels, tattered comic books and memorized fairy tales, and the creative chaos of many a tchotchke. Everywhere he looked, in fact, there was a memento, like a stuffed animal frog donned in a wizard's hat and cloak. Clark picked him up and gave him a kiss.

"Hey, Froggie," he whispered as he set him back down. "I tried."
I'll get 'em next time . . . Promise . . .

His plushie sat a hero among many, in the company of the many stories he had amassed, of escapist adventures in faraway places, of school-going witches and wizards and the magic they wielded, of battles against evil villains and savage monsters, of brave souls and superhero underdogs who would face all the odds and rise to victory. They were reminders of his lack, beyond a wish, as much as they were of his dreams. Clark pulled a diary from the shelf.

Go to work, pay your bills, his pen seemed to write on its own.
Poor in money, rich in spirit. Sometimes I wish it were the other way around.
Eat, sleep, rinse, repeat.
Nothing is different.
Nothing changes.
You pay your rent and then you die . . .

The microwave beeped, the din of the refrigerator buzzed down, and the AC switched off to energy saver. Clark stood there in the stillness, listening to the commotion of his neighbors in the hallway, and the aboveground subway blowing by some blocks away. As he looked upon the little that he owned and the little he had accomplished since leaving home, he contemplated his own life story written. What would become of him?

Clark scarfed his meal and, once finished, sprawled over his bed for a nap.

Nightfall came slowly at the end of those long, hot August days.

Still, after he awoke, Clark pulled back his curtains and opened his window to the surprise of a mourning dove roosting on his fire escape. On evenings like these, when the heat had died down, he liked to climb up the banister to the rooftop. As Clark sat on the building's ledge, he would catch those delicate moments of the sun setting behind New York's long cityscape, a glittering horizon of light and labor, iron and glass, for miles north, south, and all around. The yellow fluorescent windows, and the LaGuardia airplanes in the blue sky above, were the city's only visible stars. Watching them come out was his own private ceremonial.

That Thursday evening, Astoria was alight with the proletariat returned from their nine-to-fives, settling into their evenings. Clark was a voyeur to the all-too-familiar back-buildings and alleyways he peered down into, watching alley cats darting between parked cars while stray old ladies tended to their gardens and balcony plants. Flitting birds and squirrels ran across the branches and powerlines that lined those alleys and numbered streets, filled with rows of Tudors and prewar brick and modern homes. Their contemporary inhabitants did what those before them had always done: perch on their stoops and hang from their windows, or otherwise gather in their kitchens and at their tables or on their string-lighted patios, cutlery clinking, music streaming, family gathering. Here, he imagined what it would be like to be them. They were too preoccupied with their own immediate worlds to notice anybody else's, never mind Clark's watchful presence from high above.

The moon was out early that night, Clark reflected. *Waxing crescent* . . . It sat just beyond the liminal white-and-blue Robert F. Kennedy Bridge, some few blocks west on the East River. Its double-red eyes stared back at him as if the bridge were aware of Clark's presence too: the ever-impenetrable watchtowers of Manhattan.

All seemed to remind him that even in a place like New York City, one could be surrounded by people above and below and yet still be very much alone.

Poor and purposeless, living in the best city in the world with little to no money to enjoy it, no prospects for better, no real plan, no real direction, no real skill or talent, as a single, housebroke, college dropout: Clark asked himself what the point of any of this was. *Will I ever amount to anything . . . ?* The light of day waned and dimmed.

Blue summer sky turned to orange, pink, and violet, giving way to the velvet cusp of twilight until the sun had descended behind the city and all was a melancholy "Astoria blue," as he called it:

periwinkle, indigo, and gray, like the bugleweed at Astoria Park some blocks away. He let the buzz of the world wash over him, its shadow swallowing him up in a daze of despondency. Some evenings, he would lie there, just staring up at the sky, letting the night fall onto him and the rooftop turn black as the Earth spun without him. Maybe in his dejectedness, he was the most alive. Nowhere to go but up, nowhere to be but now. A nobody. A nothing . . .

Clark looked up to those shimmering towers he was on the outskirts of, of the world he so longed to be a part of. He wiped his eyes, and a single dark eyelash came away, resting on his finger amongst the salty wet. *Make a wish, dork* . . .

On that moon above him, on that starless sky and the city's lights that twinkled in their stead, on all those stories at home below, on all the joy and the pain he had lived through, with all his heart and soul, under the watchful eyes of the RFK Bridge, Clark made a wish that he was going to do whatever it took to make it, to change, to rise to the occasion, to his highest potential, no matter what the cost or the sacrifice, to make a life worth living. He knew he wanted more than to just survive, and more than the taste of freezer burn on his dollar-store taquitos. Clark wanted so desperately to be free of the trappings of his working-class life.

He inhaled, poised to blow, when a gust of wind lifted that eyelash clear off his finger. It vanished in an instant, gone to the night air.

Awesome . . . Clark thought to himself. *Love that* . . .

Curiously, one of those blinking city lights somehow buzzed up over the ledge and onto the roof. Slowly it began to meander toward him. The light landed on Clark's outstretched palm, a solitary firefly, before flying into the air and disappearing up and over that ledge again. Clark wiped his cheeks and hoped that nobody could see.

Once the crickets were chirping and the roof had plunged to dark, when the cloak of night had been well lowered, Clark stood up and dusted himself off. Down the ladder of the fire escape and through his open window he climbed, into his papier-mâché hideaway. A long hot shower washed away all the dismay the day had brought.

He didn't pick up a book or write in his journal that night. Instead, he put on that show about that vampire slayer he had seen a million times and crawled into his cool sheets, where an early, deep, dreamless sleep came fast.

The next day was Friday, and Clark's second day off from the coffee shop.

He lay awake in bed, staring up at the ceiling. His circadian rhythm was telling him he should already be on his millionth pour of coffee into those blue-and-white disposable cups that proclaimed, "We are happy to serve you."

Instead of rolling over and falling back asleep, however, he checked his phone. It was a quarter past six. There, a text message made Clark's stomach drop in shock. A text message that would forever change his life as he had come to know it:

(3:03 a.m. unknown number): 2 W 57th Street. 7:00 a.m.
Be on time. —Monica.

CHAPTER II

First Day

$\mathcal{C}$lark had never in his entire life jumped out of bed as fast as he did that morning.

One piece of toast and a subway ride later, Clark had miraculously arrived ten minutes early. He gave his name to the doorwoman at the desk in a grand marble lobby, so excited and nervous he was short of breath:

"Good morning! My name is Clark Crane, I'm here for Monica Chase-Whiteley?"

At his mention of Monica, the doorwoman held her gaze at him in surprise, but nodded. With a few clicks of the computer, some shuffles of paperwork, and a phone call upstairs, however, she informed him that they had no note of his arrival, no knowledge of his being there, and as such, they could not let him up.

"I'm supposed to start at seven. Are you sure?" he asked, checking his watch. He showed her the text message from Monica, but the doorwoman shook her head.

"Sorry," she said. Until someone from upstairs could confirm, there was nothing else she could do. "Them's the rules, kid." Clark ended up on one of the lobby's black sofas reading a book, to the noise of the giant waterfall opposite and the odd phone call to the desk.

As it turned out, that certain "someone" responsible for securing his entry was Monica.

It was almost nine a.m. by the time she finally sauntered in, her heels echoing across that marble lobby, muffling the sounds of Clark's grumbling stomach.

The doorwoman said flatly, "Good morning, Mrs. Chase-Whiteley." Monica moseyed on without a pause and without an answer, and Clark made haste to catch up with her. She wore giant sunglasses, and had her purse in one manicured hand, coffee in the other, dressed in all black like the day before. Was she wearing the same clothes?

"I just *loathe* mornings, don't you?" she asked. She was chewing gum and had bathed in copious amounts of fragrance. Judging by her sunglasses, Clark wondered if she was covering up a late night, or otherwise nursing a hangover.

In a private elevator, no manicured finger was raised nor a key-card swiped for the electronic sign above them to light up "PH" for penthouse, and for the doors to draw to a close. Up they wordlessly went, 131 stories high. They were up so high that Clark's ears popped.

The elevator doors opened to a grand foyer, with tall ceilings and portraits, columns and chandeliers, and the morning summer sun streaming in through a ceiling of skylights and mirrored walls. To the right were gold kitchen doors and leafy houseplants. Down the hall, a white marble fountain stood in its center; at the end was a spiral marble staircase, flanked by a room to the left and a hallway to the right. "Where are we?" Clark asked.

"Charisma's," Monica said.

To Clark, it felt more like a museum or white-marble palace than a home, or maybe more like a place of worship, sheltered on its perch high above the city . . . Clark could not remember seeing a more luxurious space. Maybe some of the summer mansions he had visited on outings to barbecues in the Hamptons with his parents' as a child, but none as extravagant as this. He fought hard to hide the look of discovering a technicolor Oz on his face.

"Wait there," Monica commanded, pointing to a crimson velvet loveseat on the right and disappearing around the corner, heels clacking on marble.

The mirrored walls were embellished in cream and gold leaf, with mural depictions of goddesses etched in white, in various scenes. Towards the stairs were portraits of ladies in all their regality from bygone eras. Clark tried to imagine what their stories were. *Family portraits,* he wanted to imagine. Sitting beside him was a marble bust of the goddess Tanit, in her curled bob and robe, staring blankly through him.

In the mirrored wall directly opposite, Clark observed himself seated among the refinery: dressed in a cheap blue button-down, khaki pants, and thrift-store shoes. His ungainly legs seemed to move him out of his seat as if a mind of their own. He wandered down the corridor.

The portraits he came upon depicted women of power and prestige in various poses. They wore their lace and silk, cashmere and fur, and were dressed, Clark noted with curiosity, all in black. Set around them were backdrops of natural sceneries of forests, hills, and seasides, and ornate thrones fit for monarchs, all of which seemed to delineate—was it their hometowns? Or maybe it was something else . . . *Their queen-doms,* Clark thought. It was as if they were iconography. He discovered upon second glance that their pets, seated in their laps or on pedestals, or on leashes close at hand, were not just small poodles and wild-eyed cats *(like their owners . . .)*, but foxes and tortoises, and snakes and birds. One had a frog, and another a red-eyed white rabbit.

Clark followed the portraits around the corner and to the left, into another grand landing room. Here the floor-to-ceiling windows overlooked the west and south sides of Manhattan, so high above it all the city was soundless. The usual white noise of sirens and honks and the city's millions of inhabitants were eerily mute and insulated. From Charisma's tower, the miles of unattainable city were well within Clark's grasp and at his feet, the cars below a personal ant farm, the veins of the city teeming with life and possibility. He became dizzy from the view and so drew away.

The decor inside was again in cream and gold, elegantly decorated and tastefully minimal, with well-lit oak shelves just behind him, displaying various vases, figurines, and star-studded photos, just like the article the day before had mentioned. One sculpture was of a pair of intertwined hands, almost touching. There were two blue velvet Art Deco couches atop a freshly vacuumed and untouched rug that led up to a smart marble fireplace. Opposite to this was the room's only portrait, the grandest painting of them all and the clear focal point of the space. Clark drew up even closer.

It was less portrait and more a tall, full-bodied spectacle, almost as high as the ceiling, unmistakably of Charisma Saintly, dressed all in black. One of her legs stepped out of the slit of a long dramatic gown, whose train exited portrait right. Her arms were slipped into black velvet gloves, and her bust was on full display. Her fiery copper hair lay in cascading waves around her shoulders, complete with fringe, a backcombed bouffant, and a diamond tiara.

More like a crown . . .

She stood on a spotlit gray canvas and shadowed background, and just within the frame to her left was a tree, the leaves and trailing branches of which bore a single raven and many red, round apples. Their color, like her copper hair, punctuated against the contrasting, monochromatic palette. Level with or just above the artist's eyeline was Charisma's kohl-rimmed gaze of yellow-green, feline-like eyes staring back, leering out across the room at Clark from her perch. He had that telltale feeling that her eyes were following him around the room, watching him. Clark wasn't sure if the entire thing was gaudy or extravagant and wondered why he found it to be so arresting all the same.

Clack clack clack went a pair of heels creeping closer, a landing above. Figuring that Monica would not like to catch him on his own private tour, and surely not wanting to wait around to find out, he took the lightest, most deft tiptoe of steps back towards that loveseat in the foyer so as to not make a sound, just in time for Monica to appear on the landing and clack her way down. *Clack clack clack.* She took forever to reach him.

"Here," she said, none the wiser, handing him a pen, an NDA, and an envelope made of fine stationery.

"Is this for me?" Clark said, turning it over and reaching for the lip. She swatted at the top of his hand.

"Of course it's not for you. Under no circumstances are you to open this," Monica said exasperatedly. He looked up and flushed. "Sign this NDA, and then take this envelope to the address I am sending to you now via text. Await further instruction there. Hand deliver it, delete the address when you are done, and most importantly, *guard it with your life*. Do you understand?" "Yes," Clark said with a nod. Silently, he read through the form.

> *Nondisclosure Agreement . . . Recipient shall not disclose confidential information or permit the disclosure of confidential information of CHARISMA SAINTLY INC., for any purpose except to evaluate and engage in yada yada yada, blah blah blah. The term "confidential information" means uh-huh uh-huh uh-huh. Upon signature, this Agreement shall bind, blind, mute, and inure to the benefit of CHARISMA SAINTLY INC. and their respective successors and permitted affiliates. Yeah yeah yeah, whatever that means. Huh, that's funny. This Agreement will be interpreted and construed in accordance with the laws of the 'American Witches Tribunal' in Salem, MA. Seriously; they've got to be joking.* He signed the bottom with his name and the date.

Inside the elevator, when the doors closed, Clark peered up. A security camera and its blinking red eye stared back at him. He turned the envelope over in his hands to examine it anyway: the envelope was small and squarish, made of thick, rich paper that was blank on both sides and sealed in red wax, with an emblem stamped in the symbol of an eye. Curiosity welled up inside of him.

As instructed, Clark set out into that sun-drenched summer morning, to the address he received via text. His journey took him up Fifth Avenue past the tourists at the infamous windows at Bergdorf's, and the equally infamous legless, armless panhandler in front. He walked by the Plaza Hotel and the telltale smell of the horse carriages at Central Park, past the museum and the zoo, twenty or so blocks north. There, the doorman seemed almost surprised to hear who he was sent by.

"First elevator on the left," the doorman said. At the landing on the sixteenth floor, there was a single apartment door, and no sooner had he arrived did he receive a text message from Monica:

(9:59 a.m. Monica Chase-Whiteley): Where are you?

What in the . . . Clark thought to himself. He typed:

(10:00 a.m. Clark Crane): Hi Monica, I just got here.
Delivering the envelope now.
He rang the doorbell. Had she really expected him back that fast?

A short woman appeared and Clark could almost not believe who was standing in front of him. Elegant and poised, her blonde hair in a messy bun, she was dressed all in black *(of course* . . . he thought). The woman peered out at him and simply said, "Hello?"

"Good morning! How are you today?" he piped back.

"Oh, I'm fine, thank you."

"Delivery from Charisma Saintly," Clark said, presenting the envelope to her with both hands.

"Thank you, sweetie," she said, not taking her eyes off him.

"You're welcome," he said with a smile. She smiled back.

"You must be new, I haven't seen you before. What's your name, pumpkin?"

"It's Clark."

"Aw, hiya, Clark! Aren't you just the cutest, most handsome thing!"

Clark blushed. "Pumpkin" was the pet name his mother used, his favorite.

"Would you like to come in for some water or lemonade?" She opened the door, beckoning him in. "It's freshly squeezed, just made it," she encouraged.

As they stood on the landing of her sunny, air-conditioned home that smelled sweet like jasmine and vanilla, a voice in his head echoed the old adage *never take candy from a stranger* . . . He wanted to say, "thank you but I have to get going!" and make his way back to Charisma's. As she smilingly stood there with the door ajar, however, and said "I won't bite," another thought came to mind.

"Sure! I'd like that very much, thank you."

She showed him to her kitchen and poured him a glass of crisp lemonade, which Clark drank down almost in one gulp. The next thing he knew, he was being toured around her three-story Fifth Avenue penthouse with homemade cookies on a napkin. There was a wall of shelves displaying her many Grammys and awards, but mostly she waved those away. They glided past the magazine covers and the portraits of her glossy editorials. Instead, she talked animatedly fast about the photos of her daughter and her family, beaming up at the camera, the candids on the beach or on safari, in nature, or at home, and about how she so wanted to have grandkids ("How old are you?" she asked him, one question of many). She showed him her gorgeous garden terrace with a view of Central Park, and a giant library with thirteen-foot-tall ceilings that could make any reader salivate. In the end, she sent him off with a couple more cookies and a tight hug. Clark thanked her profusely.

"Have a good day," she said from her doorway, waving and smiling before the elevator closed. "Good luck, sweetie." Clark was too charmed by her to think anything ominous.

When Clark returned—with a cheery wave to the doorwoman, who only stared back at him—Monica was already in the foyer.

"What in the hell took you so long?" she demanded. "Who did you leave the envelope with?!"

"Wow, was she nice," Clark said, clasping his hand to his cheek. "I can't believe I just met—"

With a wave of her phone, Monica said, "Bette just called me to tell me how *adorable and precious* the new guy is. You actually *spoke* to her?"

The glow on Clark's face came crashing down.

"You know what," she said, "I thought you might be a psycho the first time I laid eyes on you yesterday, but now I know for sure that you are. Do you even know who that is?!"

"We only exchanged a few words!" Clark said defensively. "She offered to show me her home. It happened so fast, I couldn't say no!" But not even Clark bought his own lie.

Monica took a couple of steps toward him, narrowing her eyes on him. Sharply, she said, "I don't care if she offered to pluck your impoverished little ass from Queens and adopt you. You are not here to make friends, you are here to work for Charisma! Never, under any circumstances, are you to speak to a soul. Do you understand me?"

"Oh, okay. I didn't know . . . Yes," he said. "I'm sorry," he added.

"Good." She tossed him another envelope. "Be back here, and quickly."

Clark nodded. "Okay."

By the time the elevator doors closed, those gray-blue eyes were just about burned into Clark's retinas. *Did I just make a big mistake on my first day . . . ?* He thought to himself in the quiet, *How was I supposed to know not to engage . . . ? She was very engaging . . . !* In spite of that, Clark reasoned he hadn't been fired yet, and that he had the rest of his shift to redeem himself. As he landed on the main lobby floor, a smile crept back onto his face, the awe of who he had just met and who he was working for having dawned on him. He did a little dance before stepping into the noise of the city.

This time he walked south, twenty or so blocks to the address sent on Park Avenue, running the envelope and its stamped eye wax seal over in his hand and in his mind. On his way, he bypassed the longest soup kitchen line he had ever seen, spanning around the long avenue block, with a preacher shouting a sermon on the corner.

"Isaiah warned the Devil would hide in plain sight. The witches are here! Your blood will be on your own hands! Leviticus 20:27 . . ." he shouted. Clark was so distracted, in fact, that as he stepped off the curb and into the street, a food deliverer on a bicycle almost ran him over. The man let Clark know about himself with a couple of choice words in Spanish before continuing on.

The doorman at this residence looked at Clark at a slant too—his blue button-down was spotty with sweat, and he had gotten warm fingerprints all over the parchment envelope. Clark gave the doorman a sheepish smile, but this one spared no words, and not a glance more. Clark tried not to take it personally.

When he arrived on the landing, a maid bade him enter and disappeared, into an apartment even grander than the last. Clark received another text:

> (10:21 a.m. Monica Chase-Whiteley): Leave the envelope with the maid.

As Clark looked up, a woman entered from a hallway to the right and gave him a dubious look.

Clark said, "Hello, delivery from—"

The envelope was almost snatched from his hands, and quickly she walked away, disappearing down the hall.

"Thank you, ma'am. Have a nice . . . day," he said aloud to the empty landing. Had she taken a single look at him and run?

On his way back, Clark was too hungry to wait a second longer. He stopped at a lone deli, disappearing from the commercial streets of the city, for a quick breakfast sandwich— "*Baconeggandcheese*, please," he said, laying on a New York accent thick—when he received another text:

> (10:25 a.m. Monica Chase-Whiteley): Where are you???

Clark fumbled with his phone from hand to hand and almost dropped it, before typing a white lie he regretted immediately after clicking send. *Shit . . . !* he thought. *Am I late already?!*

> (10:25 a.m. Clark Crane): Hi Monica, I'm on my way back now.

Clark, being at least smart enough to know he couldn't possibly show up with food in hand, not on his first day, tore down the street while scarfing his sandwich. He dodged tourists and bag-ladies-who-lunch, and jumped around pigeons on the sidewalk *(flying rats . . . !* he thought). Twice he almost spilled his coffee crashing into a tourist who short-stopped on the sidewalk to look at their phone or look up at a building, and at one point he almost gagged and choked.

With a cramp in his side and a scalded tongue that would take three days to heal, Clark made his way back up to Charisma's sky mansion, just in time for Monica to meet him at the door once again. She cut him the most severe of looks.

"What took you so long this time?" she asked with her hands on her hips. "Stop for a tea and a chat, and to braid each other's hair?"

"I caught every red light," Clark said, lying through his teeth, which he hoped had no visible remnants of food.

Monica's eyes narrowed in on him, her heavy-lined and shadowed eyelids contrasting against her blue-gray irises. "I thought you said you were never late."

"I'm not," Clark said, his cheeks turning pink.

"Allow me to spell this out for you, because I don't think you get it," she hissed. "Many, many girls would kill for this job. *Literally.* It is a privilege to be here. Everyone is replaceable. And here I thought you wanted to work for Charisma. Are you a lazy little liar, Clark?"

Clark wanted to shrink and disappear. "No," he said.

Monica advanced on him, and leaning in, she spoke dangerously lower than before. "Then listen to me very, *very* carefully, so that you don't fuck this up, for my sake: a good assistant—and that includes *you*," she said in a hiss just above a whisper, hovering over him closer and closer, "is seen and not heard. One must always be on time. *Always.* One must speak only when spoken to; one must do exactly as they are told; and one must always look busy. Actually, don't just look busy. *Be* busy. Don't laugh. Don't smile. Don't even so much as *breathe* out of turn. Never save the day. Never forget your place. Your one and only function, your sole purpose here, is to serve Charisma, and by extension, *me*. Got that? Everyone has a role; this is a well-oiled machine; and when one steps out of line, one gets cut. Do not step out of that line. *Do you understand me?*"

Clark gulped. He looked her in those gray-blue eyes, hollow and wild. He replied, "Got it."

She handed him a third envelope. "Be back in thirty minutes, or this time, don't even bother coming back." She said nothing more, no other energy expended or spared, and walked away. Clark just about hightailed it out of there.

When he reached the lobby downstairs, his phone vibrated and he did a double-take in disbelief: this location was even farther than the last. He triple-checked it, hoping he had maybe mistaken the address. Then he set off in a hurry, dodging passersby and darting in between cars slowed at traffic lights as fast as he could.

"Delivery from Charisma Saintly," he said when he had arrived, panting, to the doorman, who had an elevator already waiting. It let him out on a landing, with warm yellow light in a bright foyer where a maid was standing at the ready.

Swiftly, Clark swapped the envelopes and grabbed the elevator doors that had not yet closed, on the elevator that had not yet left, sprinted through the lobby past the doorman, who did not look up, and out the doors to the street outside.

Damp, uncomfortable, and out of breath, Clark returned to Charisma's lobby in record time. Only, this time the doorwoman had words for him: "Go through the back, kid," she said, catching him before the elevator. "Up the freight elevator, to the employee entrance. You'll see it." She pointed him down the block and around the corner. "Just ring the doorbell," she said, eyeing his sweat-dripped shirt up and down. She didn't wait to hear any of Clark's questions before disappearing.

At the numbered entrance to the freight elevator, Clark rang the doorbell as instructed. He looked up at the blinking camera. The red light on the door flashed green and buzzed open. He stepped in, clicked PH, and up he went. Clark checked his watch: it wasn't even noon yet.

Clark wound up in what appeared to be a storage room lined in boxes and shelves. Around the corner was a small landing room with hooks and cubbies. It was lit by fluorescents and a small window, and so quiet his ears were ringing in the soft hum of the air conditioner.

Opposite him was a set of double doors. He stepped up to turn one of the handles: locked. *Shit . . .* he thought. *Now what . . . ?* He felt the buzz of his phone. *Probably Monica . . .* He wondered if being sent to the back entrance meant he was keeping his job, or if he was, in a way, demoted. The middle of his forehead prickled and he reached up to give it a scratch.

"You lost, baby?" a voice behind him said. Clark was startled so badly that he let out a gasp and spun around. Behind him, sitting in a chair at a table with a paperback in hand, was a small, slim, mature woman he had somehow failed to notice, taking deep rasping breaths, slapping her hand on her knee. Clark realized she was laughing, and he couldn't help but laugh too.

"Sorry," he said. "I didn't see you there."

"That's okay, sweetie," she replied in a nasal alto. Clark thought it endearing. "I'm sorry to laugh, and I sure as hell am sorry to scare you like that, but, my gosh, it was as if you had seen a ghost!"

He smiled. "That's okay."

"What are you doing here, baby? You know you shouldn't be here." Clark's face fell. He wasn't sure how to answer. Had he gotten off on the wrong floor?

"Isn't this the employee entrance?" he asked.

"Here, we like to call it Hell's Entrance," she said matter-of-factly. Clark looked back at her, perplexed.

"That's what we like to call the help's entrance. *Hell's Entrance.* And you sure as hell found it, baby." They regarded one another from across the room, her with a smile in her warm, brown eyes that conveyed a motherly softness, while Clark stood there, damp and dehydrated, envelope in hand, and deeply confused. Clark considered her, with her short hair, reading glasses, dignified posture and crossed legs. She was dressed in a matching blue-gray top and pants and clean white sneakers: a maid's uniform. The book she was reading was still open and aloft in her hands, one finger holding her page like a bookmark.

"What I mean to say is," she continued, removing her glasses and dropping them from their beaded-chain lanyard, "what is a boy like you doing here, mixed up with a crowd like this?" There was a slight twang to her voice that Clark imagined could only be from the south.

"Oh," Clark started. "Um, well . . ." He held out his arms and shrugged. He was at a loss for words. *What* am *I doing here . . . ? Is this what I really want . . . ?* "I guess I'm the new junior," he answered.

"Ha!" she exclaimed. "What is she having you do, run notes around town like some kinda errand boy? 'Intern,' my ass. More like a carrier pigeon."

"Yeah," Clark said, "she is actually . . ."

"Mmhmm, I see. These people, they've got no trust in the mail system. No, better to hand deliver their important communications. Who would suspect an intern like you, anyway? But just you wait, baby. First, it's letters, then she'll have you running boxes, so much so you'll think you should be wearing brown and driving a truck. You watch out for that one, you hear me? Evil, that one is. You see it in her face, don't you?"

Before Clark could help himself, he said, "Now that you mention it, she's got the most villainous eyebrows. And her smile—"

"—doesn't reach her eyes," she finished with a nod. "Yep, they're all like that. Nothing good behind those eyes to find. I've been here a while, baby, seen lots in my time. Lots of *interns* and *juniors*, whatever you wanna call 'em, come and go. None of them are like you, though. I can tell. You've got a heart of gold and a light—a big, big light out of that gold heart—and a soul that's worth more than all of these bitches combined. Don't you let 'em have it, you hear me? Don't you let them! You just keep your wits about you, just keep to yourself." She leaned in, unable to hide the desperation in her voice. "Keep to yourself, and don't show fear, but don't be too sweet either—*or these witches will eat you.* You hear what I'm sayin'? They'll chew you up and spit you out, a little snack like you," she said, "just for the fun of it." There was a ferocious sparkle in those warm eyes of hers, gleaming up at Clark, that told him she meant what she said.

"Me, I like to mind my own," the woman continued, flashing her book and leaning back into her seat. "They're in there, by the way," she said, pointing to a cubby on the shelf nearest the door. "The other envelopes. I saw her put them out."

Clark turned and read the labels: on one cubby, "Inbound," and the next, out. He opened the latter and sure enough, there was a stack of small envelopes waiting inside, with red wax seals and an eye stamped on each.

Clark looked up to the corner: a security camera stared back at him, blinking red, and another blinked by the elevator. He quickly examined the envelope he had been holding: this one was blank and unaddressed like the others. For all of the effort, he thought it all unceremonious, and a little disappointing. He switched the deliveries and turned around.

"Thank you," Clark said. "Hey, can I ask you something?"

"Sure," she said.

Clark asked, "What's in these envelopes?" He hoped that the cameras didn't pick up sound.

"Hmm," she began slowly, admiring him with an inquisitive eye. "You're a reader, huh? I can see it. Your granny was a cunning woman, too. She used to read to you. Helped develop that curiosity, that *discerning* eye of yours."

Bemused, Clark watched her tap the middle of her forehead with her free hand. He thought it odd and tried not to wear it on his face.

She said, "Yeah, I fancy myself a reader too."

Clark could see the title of the book in her hands, *The Master's Tools Will Never Dismantle the Master's House* by Audre Lorde. He thought fondly of that photo next to his bed, of him and his grandmother. Sometimes at night, as he was falling asleep, he could almost remember her voice, almost hear her reading *Grimm's Fairy Tales* to him just before bed like a dim echo. She was the best storyteller.

"Yeah, I've seen 'em," she said, "handwriting those notes by candlelight like it's feudal Europe up in here. I've seen 'em reading those notes too. Snuck up on 'em once or twice. They just need a little light. Can't read them otherwise. Sometimes they're just invitations and little 'thank you's, but other times . . . I say throw it in the mailbox and forget about them. Don't spare this lot another thought. Hear me? Take yourself on home and don't come back."

In his head, he parroted, *They just need a little light . . .* "I'm not sure what you mean," he said aloud.

"Secrets, baby," she said, straightening her posture. *"Witch secrets.* And take it from me, baby, with witches like these, the fewer questions you ask, the better. Did you sign anything?"

"Sign anything?" Clark parroted.

"Yes, baby. Anything in writing?"

"Oh. Yeah, an NDA, I think."

She tsked. "Never sign a witch's contract, baby. Everybody knows that."

Clark wasn't sure what to make of it all. *Can I trust her . . . ? What kind of "witches" does she mean . . . ?* "You think they're actual witches?"

"Doesn't matter what I think," she said quickly. "What do you think? What's your gut tell you? You really wanna wait around and find out?"

Clark chewed his cheek. After a moment's consideration, he said, "I'm sorry, I don't think I caught your name?"

She paused for a moment herself before answering with a smile that was as warm as a hug: "You can call me Miss Honey."

"I'm Clark," he said, smiling back. "Thanks, Miss Honey."

"You're welcome, baby," she said.

Clark checked his texts: they were a series of addresses from Monica. "Guess I'd better get to pigeoning." He waved his phone and held up the stack of cards. "It was nice to meet you."

"It was nice meeting you too, baby," she said, opening her book and crossing her other leg. Clark made his way around the corner and to the exit.

"Oh, and Clark?" Miss Honey called.

"Yes?" he said, turning around in the arch of the doorway.

"If you're smart—and I know you are—you'll listen to Miss Honey and get the hell out now while you still can." The way she leaned in and the earnestness in her eyes, Miss Honey wasn't kidding. With that, she gave him a wink and returned to her reading.

CHAPTER III

The New Guy

$\mathcal{I}$t was around seven p.m. when the sun began to set on Clark's first day at Charisma's, casting shadows on the stone and glass of New York City. Or, at least, he could see that it was, judging by the sky outside the window of Hell's Entrance. Clark had sat there for a couple of hours, at the same table as Miss Honey earlier that day, idly sighing, unsure of what to do with himself. Monica had given him no further instruction, no envelopes to run, no coffee to pick up, no mail to sort, no other menial tasks. No further word. His battery was low; putting his phone down, Clark's gaze plunged over the window-sill to the streets below. The city's skyscrapers, which looked so tall from the ground up, seemed so far and away from Charisma's tower. After the high of his first day, those same buildings that shimmered with the hope of possibility just that morning were once again a glade of concrete and needles.

So much for a successful first day . . . he thought to himself, when *(finally . . .)* his phone buzzed with a message:

(7:20 p.m. Monica Chase-Whiteley): You can go.

On the ground, he took a long, deep breath of relief of the city's familiar, unclean air. Being in the commotion of midtown post–work hours, he almost smiled.

By the time Clark arrived home, both his body and clothes were salty and tired. He stood in the tub for a shower, only to discover that the hot water was indeed out again. Such was life in a pre-war Astoria building. He left that shower with goosebumps.

Eventually, he fell onto his bed, wrapped warmly in his towel— and fell fast asleep with the lights still on.

The entire evening, Clark failed to notice the pair of yellow-green eyes watching him from outside his apartment window.

The next morning, Clark groaned at his five thirty alarm.

It was Saturday at the coffee shop when Clark submitted his change of availability with the owner. He explained that a new opportunity had presented itself, suddenly and without warning, one that he couldn't pass up. One that could "open many doors," he said. He babbled to the owner that, while he was really grateful for all that she had done for him all those years, he would only be available for doubles on weekends—if she would ("please") have him. Clark reasoned it was the middle of August, that business was slow while New Yorkers were out of town anyway, and that weekends were their busiest days all year long.

"Congratulations! Of course, *guapito*, no problem. You sure this is what you want?"

Clark sighed with relief. Gloria, the owner, was a stout woman with a Mexican-American accent. She had lots of questions for Clark, who had been there for so long, had never missed a shift, mostly kept to himself, and was great with her two little girls, whom she so happened to have brought in that day. What was this "apprenticeship" about? Gloria asked. Whom was he working for? "Are they good people?" Clark didn't know how to answer that last one. Mostly, she was concerned if Clark would be okay with money.

"I'll be fine," he said. But Clark wasn't sure that was true.

Payday was every Friday: after taxes, he would barely have enough money for rent, utilities, a fraction of his groceries, and nothing more. He'd pray for tutoring and cat sitting gigs (and maybe selling foot photos) to make ends meet, that August having been unusually bleak and barren. Clark figured he'd sneak a leftover pastry or two on the weekends . . . and would figure out the rest.

It's just a sacrifice for a short while . . . he told himself, but not even he was sold.

"I want to do this," he said. "I *need* to do this. Thank you for your under—"

Gloria embraced him in a bear hug. Her eyes were swimming.

"We are all rooting for you, Chico," she said. Clark gave her a big hug back and welled up a little too. Her two little girls, Erica and Beatrice, joined in, hugging their legs. To Gloria, Clark was like a little brother whom she just so happened to employ, and to Clark, she was the closest thing to a big sister apart from his own. It made the decision all the more difficult.

There's no turning back now . . . he thought.

"You can always come back to fulltime," Gloria said. "There is always a home for you here. Just say the word." But Clark would not hear of it. How could he return after this? And disappoint them? Prove to everyone that he was incapable of finishing what he started? He would only disappoint himself in the process.

Nevertheless, in Clark's eyes, it was as if he had left the nest for the second time, like he had taken a step to make a change and grab life by the reins. He was happy to graduate to something more, something bigger.

Sure enough, something bigger meant that by Monday at Charisma's, Clark had moved on from small envelopes to small boxes, and after Monica could see how much he could carry, smaller boxes to bigger boxes. He schlepped them all around the island of Manhattan, just as Miss Honey had predicted. For the next two weeks, that was his life: Clark had become an errand boy.

"Charisma is due back at the beginning of the month, where she hosts a gathering after every Labor Day," Monica had relayed to

Clark when she met him at Hell's Entrance with a few more packages. "It's a countdown to Fashion Week, and our biggest party and the event of the year, Halloween. That means we are now deep in preparation for her return."

Once, Clark had gone on a run with a stack of boxes from the five-mile span of the Upper East Side to Tribeca and back, almost within an hour—no talk of transportation reimbursement or otherwise ("Bore someone else with your questions"). He just had to figure it out himself. Dress shoes quickly turned to high-tops (*Wish I could afford running shoes right about now . . .*), and he did the best he could.

What's more, Monica began to request her personal responsibilities be taken care of on top of Charisma's: dry cleaning, grocery shopping, her daughters' school-supply shopping in the crowded back-to-school market lines—a horror Clark was unexcited to revisit—and a run to Tiffany's with Monica's black-metal credit card that ended in him being escorted to the back by security. All this was due to her being the "only assistant holding down the penthouse and New York affairs" while Charisma and her family were away.

Monica had even asked Clark to proofread her daughter's summer essay, which meant not so much "proofread" as *write*. A week into her term, her daughter would go on to receive a 100, naturally, and would even be asked to present it to her class. At this news, Monica would tell Clark, "next time," not to make it look so good, and to make it look more like how her daughter would write it ("I'll try," Clark would tersely reply, swallowing his words).

The only thing more absurd, even more intense than Monica's demands, were her coffee orders—so ever-changing, in fact, he got to thinking she was testing him. "Mochaccino, extra shot, light foam, with space," "Blonde espresso—the other espresso was absolutely disgusting—and three cubes of ice, only," "Don't forget the whipped cream, you did last time," "Piping hot, and I mean piping." When coffee and its complicated orders had already been such an everyday part of his world, why should he think her requests would be any more out of the norm, or taken personally for that matter?

Still, the oddest thing to Clark was that at every location he had been, not one person would engage with him. They were all reluctant, and most of his interactions were wordless at the mere mention of Charisma Saintly. Doormen and the help alike could hardly meet his eyes, never mind reply to his hellos and how are yous, and he had little idea of why. It was as if Charisma's name, and he by association, put the fear in them.

He spent most days saying so little, thinking he might die from going unheard, that one late-August day he actually came down with a touch of tonsilitis, a sore swelling at the back of his throat accompanied by a fever that took a few days to go down. Clark was a ghost, anonymous on the streets of the city and hungry to be spoken to, acknowledged even.

He was all alone . . . until one morning.

His train had arrived on time that day, and so he turned up to Hell's Entrance just a little earlier than usual when, oddly enough, an impossibly handsome, bearded man walked in on him from inside the penthouse.

"These chicks are wild, bro," he said with a big smile to Clark, who noticed a smudge below his lip a shade of pink too shimmery and saccharine to be natural. He wore a black T-shirt and was as wide as a tree.

"Yeah, tell me about it," Clark said.

The man gave a booming laugh. "Have a good day, bro!" He walked out of Hell's Entrance with a bounce in his step.

Why is he in such a good mood this early in the morning . . . ? "You too . . . bro," Clark replied, amused. What was a man like that doing walking out of the employee entrance of Charisma's, when she and her family were out of town, and the penthouse was occupied by just him, Monica, and the help? He tried to put the encounter from his mind but couldn't help but revisit it often.

By the time the day before Labor Day weekend arrived, it had been an even longer week of errands and envelopes—running what, well, he couldn't be so sure. Working seven days a week had taken its toll fast, and Clark felt at his wits' end. He craved a day off and it was written all over his face, etched into his under-eyes, his tear troughs grooved and shadowed. Truthfully, Clark worried about how long he could sustain this. He was beginning to lose track of his eating, often having no time with Monica's scheduled runs and demands, and if he were being honest with himself, sometimes he skipped lunch altogether just to get his tasks done, not wanting to feel sleepy or slowed down by digestion and using the restroom. All he had to show for his big life change was a pair of well-worn Chucks and the early onset of an eating disorder.

On this—his fabulous, anonymous, party-of-one tour of Manhattan, with its millionaire inhabitants and all of their avoidant little helpers—Clark's errands had taken him not just to Gramercy Park townhouses and the Village's modern lofts, but to NYC landmarks like the Upper West Side's Apthorp, the city-block-long residential building of the Belnord, the Empire State Building, Grand Central Terminal and Lincoln Center, SoHo boutiques and Rockefeller department stores, and Midtown hotel bars like the St. Regis. On that cloudless Friday morning, Clark's first run took him to a Midtown rooftop restaurant called Northlight, not yet open for the day. He was to drop off a medium, label-less box, taped and tightly bound, and with the most peculiar rattle. He gave it a shake. *Is that the sound of . . . beads . . . ?*

"Leave the box with their manager, Louis," Monica had said. "Do not leave it out of your sight." Name-dropping Charisma Saintly at the desk had gotten him upstairs, but no farther. The manager wasn't in yet, so Clark sat at the bar on a leather-and-chrome stool and waited, just as he was told.

He looked up Northlight online, a grand mid-century modern spectacle that was the Swinging Sixties and space-race American Googie all in one, transporting its patrons into the past and the future at the same time. It was one of the city's swankiest and most exclusive, appointment-only, reserve-way-in-advance establishments, and Clark would have never set foot in it had it not been for this job. He discovered that it was, of course, owned by Charisma, building and all. She spoke so emphatically on an interview at the grand opening, so passionately and feverishly with her hands, that Clark had never seen anything quite like it before. By the end, he had lost count of how many times the pet name "darling" was said—certainly more times than what should have been permissible. Clark was curious about her, if not even beginning to resent her.

All I hear lately is "Charisma this" and "Charisma that" . . . Clark thought to himself. *Who even is she and why is she so important anyways* . . . *? Why is everyone so obsessed with Charisma* . . . *and why is everyone so afraid of her* . . . *?* He had no idea what he was doing working for her and Monica, nor if the doors that would await him at the finish line would be worth opening. *Will I even last another month of interning here* . . . *? Is any of this worth it* . . . *? Maybe I should just* . . . *quit* . . .

Miss Honey's words had not left him: "Get out now while you still can."

Clark looked out that rooftop restaurant window at the East River and Central Park, contemplating how long he would need to be an intern before dining at a restaurant like Northlight and having his piece of the patriarchy pie, when a nagging thought overrode all the others.

What Clark really wanted to know was if they were all an actual, real "coven" of witches. That's when a voice came from behind him.

"What can I get you?" the voice asked. "Witch's brew?"

"What . . . ?" Clark asked, caught unawares. He swiveled around. Standing behind him was a young man who, to Clark, was . . . incredibly handsome. He had a charming smile, and dark, slicked-back hair straight out of a black-and-white film, right down to the suspenders he wore over his broad, triangle-shaped torso. Was he younger than Clark? Older? Clark couldn't tell. He surely looked more mature: handsome in a debonair way, more well-developed than Clark. His sharp jawline was freshly shaved and a touch of chest hair peeked out from his button-down. He flashed Clark a smile.

The guy raised a black, conical witch's hat he held in one hand. With a shoulder and a nod, he gestured to a few open boxes by the window, full of what Clark realized were Halloween decorations.

"Oh!" Clark said. He laughed. "Isn't it a little early for that, even for a witch?"

"What, doesn't everyone put their Halloween decorations up in August?" he replied sarcastically.

"Actually," Clark said, "mine went up last week. It's my favorite."

"Mine too! Halloween comes early here, boss's orders. Which is fine by me, since it's my favorite and I love witches."

Clark wanted to reply that he loved witches too, but, *these days, I can't be so sure* . . .

The guy whipped around the bar, polished a glass at lightning speed, and filled it with water and ice. "We're just taking inventory for now," he said, sliding the glass to Clark with a wink and a smile. Was that a smile breaking on Clark's face too?

"What are you gonna be this year?" Clark asked.

"Oh, just a heartthrob bartender," the guy said with a wink. "How about yourself?"

"Hopefully still employed," Clark said. The guy chuckled.

"So you're the new intern, huh?"

"What, you a psychic or somethin'?" Clark teased. "Could you tell?"

"I don't gotta be a psychic to see that," the guy said, glancing at the mystery box on the bar next to Clark. "Except I almost couldn't tell, seeing as how you're not dressed all in black in the dead of August. Nor are you a female, which . . . either way, is fine by me." He extended his hand for a shake and flashed his big, charming grin. "I'm Joey, by the way."

Like the answer to his wishes, here he was, someone who wasn't just willing to talk to Clark, but who also happened to be handsome and . . . *Is he flirting with me . . . ?* After all the apps and the string of unsuccessful flings and serial first dates, not to mention the new gig and the lack of time—just when Clark had all but given up—something inside him clicked into place. "Hi, Joey." He reached for his hand. "I'm Clark." He discovered Joey's hand was wide and strong, and his shake firm.

"It's nice to meet you," they both said at the same time. They chuckled.

"Are you from the city, Joey?"

Joey answered with that same delectable smile, "Yeah, how'd you know, youz psychic or somethin'?"

"That and the Brooklyn in your voice," Clark replied. "How you talk with your shoulders might've given you away, too."

Joey chuckled. "Oh, *a wize guy over 'ere*," he said. "I guess the jig is up. Where you from, Clark?"

"I'm from Astoria."

"*Queens in da house*," Joey said. "Very nice. I love Astoria! I'm from Bay Ridge, and . . . not usually this dorky. Or maybe I am, I dunno."

"A dork from Bay Ridge," Clark said. "It's nice to see one out in the wild this time of year." Immediately he blushed.

"For sure, especially in these parts," Joey mused.

Clark smiled and stifled a giggle, when another thought occurred to him. "So, you said the other interns were girls?"

"Yeah," Joey said. He leaned in, and gravely this time, he said, "but these were no regular girls. These were a different breed, my dude. Mean and cagey as fuck. Most of them would barely utter a word to me—those were the nice ones. Some of them would look at me like I was shit under their nose, and treat me like it too."

"Yeah, I'm not surprised by that, 'my dude.' I'm sorry, that's, um, all kinds of terrible," Clark said.

"Yeah . . . But it's cool! Mostly they'd just pop in and out of their black town cars. They'd get me to pick up whatever box or two they were delivering, and drive away, and I'd never see them again. For a second there, it felt like there was a new one almost every week."

Clark almost gasped. "Wait, they took *cars*? And here I've been huffing it on foot."

"*Yeesh,*" Joey said. "They're workin' youz hard, huh?"

"Yeah, tell me about it . . ." *That explains a lot . . .* Clark thought, taking it all in. *No wonder Monica questions why I'm away for so long . . . "A new one almost every week . . ."*

"Guess you just gotta keep at it and smilin' that pretty smile anyways, huh?" Joey said.

Clark's stomach did a flip. *My smile . . . ? Pretty . . . ?* "Yeah, I guess you're right . . ."

Joey threw his arms out. "And I love to hear it. " He leaned in again, chest forward over the bar, and added, "Lucky for me, though, none of the others were as nice or as cute as you." The tops of Clark's cheeks turned a bashful shade of pink.

Clark cleared his throat and said, "Well, fortunately for you, I'm not a bad witch. I'm a good witch—you know, depending on the day, and if I've had my *cawfee* and if my train cart has AC."

"Well, in that case," Joey said, "maybe I can *ax* you out for a *cawfee* sometime soon and see how good of a witch you really are." With all he could muster, Clark refrained from checking if his ears were red in the mirror behind Joey.

"Yeah, I'd like that," Clark replied. "On just one condition though."

"What is that?"

"You don't go telling everyone that I'm good. I've got a reputation to uphold." *Hey, Clark . . . ?* he thought to himself. *Shattup . . . ?*

He and Clark smiled for a moment, regarding one another from over the bar, when a man entered from the front of the restaurant. They broke eye contact and turned around.

"'ey, boss, good morning," Joey said.

"'ey, Joey, how you doin'?" A bald, middle-aged man came up to the seat and grabbed the box. "This for me?"

"This is Louis, my manager," Joey said.

"Hi, good morning, Louis," Clark replied. "Yeah, yes it is." Louis took the box and disappeared behind the kitchen doors.

Buzz buzz: Clark's phone lit up, another text from Monica. He sighed and stood up. With a sad smile and a wave of his phone, he said, "That would be *my* manager. Duty calls I guess, when you're a lowly intern like me."

Joey put down the glass he was polishing and walked around to meet Clark at his bar chair. Clark stepped down to meet him. Joey was about Clark's height, maybe an inch or two shorter. "Can I get your number?"

"Sure thing," Clark said. Instead of pulling out his phone, Joey produced a napkin and a pen with not a second wasted. Amused, Clark wrote his number down, taking extra care to write it legibly. He could almost feel Joey watching him do so, could feel his eyes trace him from his mousy hair, down his neck and back . . . Joey folded the napkin and tucked it into his breast pocket, which made Clark's ears blush all the more.

"I'll see you soon, Clark from Queens," Joey said. He extended his hand, this time a little closer to his body, and pulled Clark in towards him. Clark stepped so close he could catch the cologne on Joey's shirt. There was a fragrance just under it, too: an air of fabric softener, like the smell of home and a mother's love. Clark thought it cute. Their hands locked, as did their eyes. Clark could feel a case of the butterflies coming on.

Clark said, "Yeah. I hope so too, Joey from Brooklyn."

Downstairs in the lobby, Clark's ears burned as he read Monica's text:

(10:45 a.m. Monica Chase-Whiteley): We need to talk.

Am I in trouble again . . . ?

(10:48 a.m. Clark Crane): Okay. Is everything alright?

Monica did not respond.

At Hell's Entrance, Clark didn't have to wait long for one of the double doors to open. It was Monica who beckoned him inside. Something felt amiss.

"Charisma is back," she stated.

"Okay," Clark said. "Is that bad?"

Monica scoffed. "Yes." They paused in front of a pair of swinging, industrial kitchen doors. Through the windows, Clark could see a handful of cooks busy at work. "Some things are about to change: we have a meeting this evening. Charisma's sister Lorena wants to meet with you personally," Monica said. Clark's stomach churned. "But first things first: meet the girls."

With a push, she swept through the swinging kitchen doors, which Clark caught just before they hit him in the face. He hurried to catch up with her.

"Fresh meat coming through," she announced without stopping. Clark gave his pleasantries, and although one or two of the cooks looked up at him, none could be bothered to pause. He could tell they were preparing quite a volume of food. How many people would be attending this meeting?

Opposite the kitchen in another corridor, they walked into a silver elevator. Monica pressed Main, where one floor up, they followed a reverse path through a set of tall, white-and-gold doors across that marble floor, into a white, windowed, and brightly lit kitchen.

Inside were two cooks, one moving trays of food off a cart, the other preparing plates. Seated at the countertop were three young women dressed all in black, one on their phone and the other two deep in conversation. Their makeup. Their nails. Their hair. Their jewelry. These were no vanilla-beige fashion girls: these women dripped in beauty, each more impeccably styled than the next, adorned in, like Monica, designer clothing probably worth more than Clark had ever owned in his entire life. Though they were individual in their style, the throughline was the same: Heels. Curves. Cleavage. Legs. Just like Charisma.

"Ahem . . . ?" Monica began. "Ladies?" The three women stopped in mid-sentence to turn and stare at Clark, who had the sudden, acute feeling he hadn't experienced since high school of what it was like to be sized up by a group of girls. Their eyes started at his mousy combed-over hair, and traveled to his traitorous cheeks, which flushed deeper and deeper. From there they moved to his dorky button-down and tie, down to his thrift-store khakis, until finally, they came upon his well-worn high-tops, where all eyes came to a stop.

Monica introduced them from left to right: "This is Alicia Henceley, Charisma's first assistant and personal manager, as well as her niece and right hand." The leftmost of the group gave no gesture, revealed no emotion, and only looked back with her sharp green eyes and copper hair, the same as her Aunt Charisma. Her style was the most uncomplicated of the women, dressed in a black lacey button-down top and business-casual bottoms.

"Melissa Silvestri, second assistant to the Coven, Charisma's second personal manager, and event planner," Monica said, eyeing her up and down. Swarthier and older, maybe closer in age to Monica, she wore a tank top under a designer suit with power pumps that ended in the sharpest of points. Melissa's heavy brunette curls fell over her shoulder as she cocked her head to the side, staring at Clark, and looking at him like he was good enough to eat.

"Emily Manitis, third assistant to the Coven, coordinator of Charisma's social diary, family affairs, and team of personnel," she said, pointing to the blonde amongst them in a romantic top and mod miniskirt. Emily gave Clark a little wink.

"As for me," Monica said, her voice perking up in her self-indulgent way, "I am, of course, Charisma's fourth assistant, Keyholder, and manager of Charisma's many residences around the world, her yachts, cars, and private jets." Seeing her with the others, Monica's LBD looked almost lazy. "Alicia's mother, Lorena, is Charisma's sister, and booker and manager for the Coven, whom we all report to, and—"

"Aw, look," Melissa interrupted, her head still cocked to the side. "Monica dragged in a stray. What's your name, little gayby?"

Monica rolled her eyes. "This is, uh . . ."

"Clark," he interjected. *Does she honestly not remember my name . . . ?*

"Like Kent?" Melissa asked. *"Aww!"* She snickered and his hair stood on end. Melissa brushed her thick dark curls to the side, and peering at Alicia and Emily, said, "Told ya." Melissa let out a boisterous laugh that could only belong to an American, her accent decidedly northeastern.

"I was going to say, the new junior," Monica said, giving Melissa the side-eye.

"Welcome to the fold," blonde Emily, also American, said to Clark. Clark blushed something fierce, and all the while his forehead had that telltale, tingling, prickling itch. Alicia sat with her arms folded and her legs crossed, quietly watching.

"Monica," Alicia began, "are you actually serious?"

A hush fell over the room, even for the help. Melissa watched with glee.

"Serious about what?" Monica asked, putting one hand on her waist.

"About *this*," she said, nodding towards Clark.

"Yeah," Melissa added. "You know Charisma doesn't employ boys."

"For your information, he's not some stray off the street. He was a *referral*, and I was conned. I thought he was a girl, something about his name . . ." she said matter-of-factly, giving Clark the side-eye and turning up the tip of her pointed nose. "I didn't expect him to last this long. Anyway, he's been useful for carrying boxes at least. I haven't had to call down to the lobby for help, not once. And besides, *Alicia*, your mother is going to interview him herself shortly."

Clark's stomach churned, the feeling of dread slowly creeping up on him.

Alicia shook her head. "Yet another one of your messes for us to clean up, as usual," she said, her accent English like Monica's. "You couldn't have brought in Amanda or Milly Noble? Roxanna Champion or Sofia Winston? Those girls already know Charisma and the Coven and would absolutely murder to be here."

"They didn't get back to me . . . on time," said Monica. For a moment, the room was so tense one could cut the air with the looks they gave each other, sharp as daggers.

"Monica," Emily interjected, breaking the silence, and the tension, "um . . . are you feeding him?" All of the women present, even the maid and the cook, stopped to lean in and survey Clark once more. Why did he have the peculiar feeling he was being looked at like he was their own next meal? The kitchen smelled of rich cooking, and Clark's stomach uttered a loud garbling. His face turned a shade of pink.

"Oh, he's fine!" Monica exclaimed, rolling her eyes.

"That's what you said about the last one," Alicia remarked testily. "Then she collapsed of heat stroke and exhaustion and ended up in the ICU, which is how you got us into this mess in the first place."

Melissa stifled an inappropriate laugh. Playfully, Emily slapped her shoulder, mouthing, "Melissa . . . ! Oh, my gawd!"

Monica pursed her lips. Was this a Monica in submission he was witnessing? Had she met her match? Clark was sure to commit it to memory so he could recall it later.

"If this one goes, that would make it our third *since July*," Alicia said, without breaking eye contact with Monica.

"Yeah, *Monica*," Melissa said sarcastically, "hiring a boy was a stroke of genius. I bet after the last one, everyone's heard and no one wants to work with her."

"Oh please," Monica snapped. "At least no one will suspect his deliveries are from us."

"Yeah—because we don't hire boys!" Melissa snapped back.

"Exactly!" Monica said.

"Word is going to travel fast that there's a boy, and a non-witch at that," Alicia said.

"I bet they're already talking," said Emily.

"They are," Melissa said. "I heard he shows up *on foot*." All present looked down at his sneakers again.

How else am I supposed to show up . . . ?!

Alicia turned to Melissa and asked, "Remember the junior who disappeared on Halloween last year? What was her name again? That was fun . . ."

"Oh yeah," Melissa said excitedly, "the one whose head was sent to the penthouse in a box, with her eyes gouged out of her—"

"Ladies?" Emily said, nodding to Clark. "Please? Mind our guest?"

Clark could feel his eyes were as wide as the plates being prepared.

*So nobody actually wants "the job a million girls would kill for" . . . ?
More like to be killed for . . .*

"Carolina, could you be a doll and fix one up for our new friend,
too, please?"

"Sí, señorita," one of the cooks said, "of course."

Monica shot her a reproachful look, but said nothing. Clark got
the sense that, in the order of things, Monica was low on the totem
pole, or at the least, dared not challenge Alicia. He wasn't sure if he
liked these girls, but he thought, *Anyone that doesn't take shit from
Monica is good in my book . . .*

"Carolina, bring it along with Lorena's," Monica demanded.
"That's where he is headed now. You," she said to Clark, "come."

Emily waved goodbye, Alicia returned to her phone, and Melissa
watched him walk away wearing a hungry smile that did not reach
her peculiar eyes.

Clark was led down an adjacent hall, walking in silence except for
the sound of Monica's heels clacking on marble. They passed an enormous living room with a tall vaulted ceiling and gold chandeliers,
a waterfall, and a giant terrace. A left turn took them into another
hallway, ending in an oak panel door, on which Monica knocked
three times.

An imposing voice barked from within the word "Enter."

As Monica opened the door, Clark turned to look at her. She gave
him a wave of her hand, mouthing, *"Get on with it"*—and pushed
him in.

The door shut behind him with a *click,* sealing him inside.

CHAPTER IV

Human Resources

Clark was standing inside a high-ceilinged office buttressed by marble pillars, wood panels, and floor-to-ceiling windows with the blinds drawn. To the left was a cognac leather bachelor-pad couch, and two matching armchairs. As he scanned the shadowed room through a cigarette haze, Clark's eyes came to rest on a handsome wooden desk, flanked by a marble fireplace left cold, in front of which Lorena sat under an acid-green lamp, looking right at him.

"So," she said, her voice a gravelly English soprano, "you're the new guy." With all the lamps on and the dramatic lighting, he thought she looked like a detective straight out of a film noir movie.

Clark replied, "Guilty as charged."

Lorena sniggered, staring at him as he stood by the door. Clark couldn't tell whether she was amused or put off. She popped a cigarette in between her teeth, produced a silver lighter, and fired it up. After a deep, deep drag, and with the cigarette still hanging on her lips, she muttered, "Have a seat." She motioned to the chair in front of her desk.

"Thank you," he said, doing as told.

"You don't mind, right, darling?" she asked, puffing smoke into the air above her. Clark's eyes watered and he was already green at the gills.

"Please," he said.

Whether Lorena was younger or older than Charisma, Clark couldn't say. Lorena had intense green eyes like her sister and daughter, but dark auburn-brown hair that spilled over one shoulder in waves, voluptuous and thick. She wore a plunging neckline that exposed a sun-drenched chest, and her curves fit snugly into a fitted black dress. On her desk was an empty coffee mug with plum lipstick prints on the rim, and a picture of her and her daughter, which she moved to the side.

Lorena leaned back in her chair and popped off her pumps with a couple of thuds. She propped up her feet. Her pantyhose, Clark mused, made her small feet look toeless and clubbed. Lorena was pretty, he decided, if a little sordid. In a way, she reminded him of some of the crass northeastern women he had grown up around, except with Lorena, he had no idea what to expect. He smiled politely, hoping to deflect that he was a touch scared of her.

An echo came to him then, of Miss Honey's voice, saying, *"Don't show fear, baby . . ."*

Easier said than done . . .

"Tsk tsk. She hasn't been feeding you, has she . . . ?" Lorena stated, her eyes surveying him up and down.

"Who, me? Oh, I'm fine." His stomach growled loudly again, giving him away. "Really!" he said. Instantly, Clark succumbed to nerves: he didn't want to cause any more trouble, lest he be on the receiving end of more of Monica's perverse demands.

Lorena uttered a wheezy cackle. "You're cute," she said, "but you're a bad liar." She took a drag and slowly blew it out.

There was another knock on the door. "Come in," Lorena barked again.

It was Carolina who opened the door. "Hello," she chimed, rolling in a cart carrying two large trays and drinks. "Here is your comida, ma'am."

Lorena slammed her fist on the desk and snapped, *"I told you never to call me that!"*

Both Carolina and Clark froze in place. Seeing this, Lorena broke into a sheepish laugh, and with a cloying smile, said, "'Ma'am' is for my mother, Mrs. Saintly." She added, "Please, be a dear and set it down over there."

Carolina did as instructed. "Okay, Miss Lorena."

Yeesh . . . This one, he decided, was not to be crossed.

"You," she said, pointing at Clark and then to the couch. "Come. What we don't need is yet another one of Monica's juniors landing in the bloody ICU." They moved left to the couches, where Clark took the armchair and Lorena lounged on the sofa, stretching her toes like a contented housecat. "Eat," she commanded. This was not a request.

Carolina lifted the lids off the trays, revealing two fine cuts of filet mignon, with garlic mashed potatoes, peas, and a side salad each. It smelled so decadent, Clark's stomach let out yet another unruly grumble. He barely uttered a "thank you" before digging in and taking a bite so delicious, it almost seemed to melt in his mouth. It was so delicious, in fact, *he* almost melted himself, into that leather armchair. Clark could not remember his last big, warm meal. Between the slices of buttered toast he hurriedly scarfed on his way out the door in those early mornings, or the pizza rolls he nuked in the microwave at night, he realized that he had been absolutely famished to the point of exhaustion. Lorena watched with amusement as Clark could not help but follow bite after bite almost without stopping to chew. He reminded himself to slow down, so as not to appear too needy.

"The closed mouth does not get fed, darling. Do not be shy to ask for what you need," Lorena said. Clark seriously doubted whether that power had been within his grasp all along. Who was he, a junior, to ask for the bare minimum with a boss like Monica?

Carolina poured a glass of top-shelf vodka and soda over ice, with a single lime wedge on the rim and another squeezed in. Lorena mimed with her lips and her bejeweled finger *"one more"* to Carolina, who procured another glass for Clark. Clark dared not turn down free food and alcohol on the job, let alone something offered by a woman like Lorena, and so he obliged. Lorena lifted her glass in a small gesture of cheers. Clark did the same, and they both sipped. It was strong. Clark grimaced: too strong. He let out a sputter and pulled at the tie around his neck.

"Tut tut, darling. Maybe it'll put some hair on your chest, ay?" She let out a small cackle. Clark laughed nervously back.

Lorena waited until Carolina closed the door behind her, and for Clark to be well on his way through his plate, before digging in herself. "I am just positively *famished*," she said, eyeing him while slicing her knife back and forth on her steak. "Traveling, am I right?" She chortled. "I'm sure I need no introduction: my name is Lorena. I am booker for the Coven, manager of the assistants, and Charisma's sister. Consider me HR . . . and your boss. Everything under this roof goes through me. I am the direct report for you and the girls. Is that understood?"

"Got it," Clark said. "I mean, yes. Understood." He was careful to not say the M-word.

"Excellent," Lorena said. "I know Monica has kept you busy these past couple of weeks. Usually, we interview our juniors a little more . . . *thoroughly*. But, given the short notice and the need for the position to be filled, not to mention that we were abroad for the month, I am sure you understand why I have brought you in myself. What you are doing here is a very integral part of our operations."

Clark paused to wipe his lips. *Is it . . . ? What have I accomplished that could be so important . . . ?* He decided, "Thank you for having me," would be safe enough to say.

Lorena spoke slower this time: "Tell me, Clark. You are clearly not a woman. You are not a witch. You were not born into the witching community. How then, my darling, did you happen upon Monica and our open position, and infiltrate our midsts?"

Infiltrate, Clark thought. *A choice word . . .* Clark explained how Patricia had caught wind of the position and arranged for an in-person with him and Monica. One thing led to another and the next thing he knew, he had found himself the new junior. He had spent the last couple of weeks running errands around the city and getting things in order for the arrival of Charisma and company, which was how he had ended up sitting in front of her then.

"I see," Lorena said. She took a drag and observed him through slanted, smoky eyes. "And, tell me, what is a boy—*a man*—like you hoping to gain by being here, in a place such as this?" The ice in her glass clinked as she raised it to her lips, watching him from over the rim.

"To gain by being here?" Clark parroted.

"Everyone wants something," Lorena said, eyeing him curiously. "What is it that you want?"

"Well . . ." Clark began, taking a moment to chew, think, and swallow. *What* do *I want by being here . . . ? Pay, but I dunno if I can say that yet . . . Opportunity, but I definitely won't say that either, at least not yet . . . So what do I want . . . ?* "I was in school part-time, and now I'm not. I was working full-time, but now I, um, work on weekends, so I have the availability to commit to here . . ."

The way she was studying him, scanning him, there was something behind that smirk that Clark couldn't place. Was she not so convinced? Lorena pursed her lips and took a sip.

"I guess what I'm trying to say is, what I want by being here," Clark said, "is to do something that matters. I'm looking for a career. I know I could be great given the chance. If I could just be more involved, have the experience of—"

"'Experience'?" Lorena interjected, setting her glass down. "My darling, what kind of 'experience' were you hoping to gain, exactly?"

Clark knew then that he had said something wrong. "Um, well, all I'm doing is running errands and letters. If I could just do something more . . ." But what could he say? Be given more responsibility, this early on? She gave him the side-eye, and Clark knew he was in trouble.

"My dear boy, don't you realize," Lorena said, "a million girls would kill to be in your shoes? A million *witches*, in fact. The experience to be gained is in working for Charisma, period. You of all people should be so lucky to work for us. Anything more is, well, up to you."

Clark took a sip and wished it were water. The question he had been burning to know suddenly rose up to his lips, and he asked it almost automatically: "Are you all . . . actual, real witches?"

After a moment's pause, Lorena finally answered. "Oh yes. As real as any other." Her face broke into a guileful smile.

Clark gulped, his throat gone dry.

These people are so self-important, it's nuts . . . And they actually think they're witches . . . "How does one become a witch? Were you taught?"

Slowly, Lorena's smile fell. Clark watched as she put out her cigarette. "My naive boy," Lorena said, "a queen is not made. She is born. One does not become a witch: one simply *is*. The very essence of her nature is her homecoming; the prowess she reveals, the Gifts she possesses, the innate Potential her inheritance handed down from generation to generation. A witch might acquire a skillset, sure, a trick or two, under the appropriate guidance. But to a witch, the Art lives in her heart, simply because it is her preordained destiny. What is it that you think we do here, exactly? *This isn't 'ogwarts, darling!*" She laughed, a gravelly chortle, and popped a piece of steak crudely into her gaping mouth. If he were honest, the way Lorena loudly chewed with her mouth open made Clark a little sick.

Wouldn't that be nice . . . Clark thought to himself. "Sorry, I uh . . . some of this is still new to me," he said. He wished he hadn't. *This whole thing is a sham . . .*

Lorena asked, dangerous and low, "Do you think what we do here is some kind of a joke . . . ?"

"Oh . . . no," Clark said quietly, "of course not."

Without removing her eyes from him, Lorena produced a fresh cigarette, popped it onto her lips, and inhaled through her open lighter. She took a big, long pull, and exhaled its smoke towards Clark, whose eyes watered and nose burned. He dared not cough to give her a rise.

"Indeed," Lorena said. "Allow me to inform you: witchcraft is a women's realm and a women's sport. And quite frankly, *sweetie darling*, the position of junior assistant is traditionally given to a woman.

Always has been. Always will be. And yet, here you are. Here you are, when the truth is, you should be grateful to work for Charisma, and by extension, me. A good assistant never forgets their place, and a good assistant never asks for more. *More* is a gift one is bestowed when one is deserving of such an honor."

Clark tried his best not to reveal his dismay, and his fear. *I'm getting the feeling I might have to Charlotte my way into Judaism . . .*

"So, be that as it may," Lorena went on, shifting on the couch, "why should we—that is, I—keep you here, when a million other girls would absolutely kill to be in your . . . shoes, for nothing in return, absolutely nothing at all?" At this, Lorena looked down at his crossed ankles and on to those well-worn high-tops, which squeaked back as if in indignation. Clark chewed her question over.

Why should *they keep me . . . ? What do I want, and why should I stay . . . ? And how many times has she used the word "darling" already . . . ? They could find any girl for the job . . . So why me . . . ?* By then his plate had been finished; he had just a few peas left and a couple of sprigs of arugula, so he put down his cutlery so as not to look completely starved. Clark watched Lorena push her plate to the side too, her half-eaten steak sitting in a pool of its own red runoff. He almost wanted to ask if he could finish it.

"I think I could be of, uh, of use to you, if I stay," he said carefully. "I can lift boxes. I'm quick on foot—" Clark made sure to hide his shoes under the table and out of sight. "I already know the job. I just met the girls. You wouldn't have to interview or train anyone else. I would really like to be here. To stay." *"A year here could open many doors"—change my life even . . . Be brave and get through this in one piece, Clark . . .*

"Maybe some . . . testosterone would be good for you ladies," he added with diffidence, puffing up his chest, however unimposing it may have been. At this, Lorena laughed, a small, shrill cackle, and Clark, in turn, erupted in a small, warm sweat.

"Yes, that's true," she said, "I do wish sometimes that we had a . . . *man* around here." Her body undulated with the punctuation of every word, and she bit her lip as her eyes trailed him up and down.

"Ideally one who is, oh, I don't know, easy on the eyes, muscular, a skilled masseuse, and *completely mute.*" At this, Clark's mouth, which had been held agape in suspense, snapped to a close seemingly against his own volition. Lorena threw her head back, cackled again, and took a swig. Clark meant to laugh but grimaced and let out a half-hearted *hahaha* instead as he rubbed his jaw.

Lorena got up off the sofa and, still barefoot, slowly slinked towards Clark until she sat on the arm of his chair, only inches away from him. She was sitting so close, in fact, that Clark could smell the lady perfume radiating off her body, and the vodka on ice and cigarettes cold on her breath. "But," she said, crinkling her nose and looking straight into Clark's eyes, *"wouldn't that be nice."*

The hair on Clark's arms stood up on end as he found himself, yet again, with the acute feeling that his thoughts were being listened to. Lorena smiled that smile that didn't quite reach her eyes, and Clark reached up to scratch the middle of his forehead.

"If it is experience that you seek, that much is up to you." She sighed and stood up to face him, this time with one hand on each arm of the chair. Lorena leaned in with her hair cascading over her chest, heaving forward, and her voice dangerously low. "You have to prove yourself worthy to us, not the other way around. Certainly, you know too much by now, too much to replace on such short notice . . . for the time being. That said, a keen insight as to who we are and how we work is crucial for the job, which you seem to be rather slow on. Consider yourself lucky that you are here—on a mere *technicality.*"

"But, what do you mean?" Clark asked. "What do they do, the assistants? How does it all work? How can I prove myself if I, to your point, don't know how things . . ." He waved his hands around. "Work around here." Clark was in over his head, like he was careening straight for a collision. His brain was mush from the vodka, flowing right through him.

"What we do,'" Lorena said, rising as tall as she could above him, "is sell witchcraft. Think of it as life insurance policies, or, say, financial advising—but for your karma, your career, your love life—whatever. Whatever our clients want: status, riches, power. Like Charisma always

says, 'Give a woman a little Charisma, and she can conquer the world.'
Charisma need only say the magic word and guide them to their ulti-
mate desires . . . for a price. Her success rate is unmatched. Her word is
the only word that matters. And when Charisma cannot be in two or
three places at once, the assistants are called upon in her stead."

"Oh, okay . . ." Clark said. "Whatever the clients want? Can you
really do that?"

Lorena scoffed. "Witches don't just wiggle our noses or wave
around a magic wand, boy. Witchcraft is more than, oh, I dunno,
turning cards for pennies like some commoner in a street side shop!"
Lorena was so crazed Clark could see the whites of her eyes. "That's
why we are paid the big bucks."

"The 'big bucks' . . . ?"

"Oh yes . . . royally. Clients will pay big money for raw talent.
The assistants have their own VIP clients around the world as well
as handling Charisma's, and in turn, have large fanbases themselves,
who worship the ground they walk on. Haven't you seen their socials?
I think Alicia is at, what is it now, twenty-five million followers?"

If she thinks you know too much, Clark, you have leverage . . .
he thought to himself. With some trepidation, Clark asked, "Can
juniors be paid?"

Lorena stared back blankly and took a drag. "Only the assistants
are paid here, boy."

Dare he press on? *Be brave, Clark . . .* he thought again. Lorena
was a hungry jaguar pacing her prey, one that could pounce at any
given moment. He spoke carefully. "Then, how does one become an
assistant?"

A devilish smile slowly broke onto Lorena's face. She took another
swig of her drink before speaking. "We do not proselytize. Assistants
come to us. First, hopeful candidates must bring something to the
table, like a proposal, an offering of sorts—a *sacrifice*, if you will. But
that alone is not enough. What are their talents? Whom have they
assisted? Who are their clients? Can they work with the Coven in
tandem? Even then, there is no guarantee one can be initiated into
our ranks. Here, we are a family."

"Oh, I see," Clark said. "And, forgive me, are you . . . a part of 'the Coven' too?"

"Of course," she said, folding one arm over the other and taking a puff of her cigarette. Clark was deeply bothered by her smoking, and having to endure his first meal under her scrutinous sparring. He was thirsty, the middle of his forehead was prickling something fierce, and he desperately wanted to leave.

Clark asked, "What was yours?"

"My what?' Lorena asked, taken aback.

"Your sacrifice."

"My . . . sacrifice?" she asked distantly, trailing off and looking to the left of him. Scenes seemingly unbelonging to Clark flickered across his mind's eye one by one, like scenes on a film reel, a daydream he couldn't help but be carried away by:

A small girl with brown hair bounded up a beach on an early morning. She reproached, "Sissy!" to a copper-haired young girl, who turned to look at her. Behind them, just over the dune, civilians and news cameras approached a row of whales, sharks, and dolphins. These animals lay beached, dry, and dead under the morning sun, as far as the eye could carry.

Like a flick of the remote on a television set, the daydream shifted and changed: young girls in a schoolyard taunted, *"Witch! Witch! Witch!"* They threw rocks and trash at a young Lorena and that same copper-haired girl, who looked back at them in seething indignation.

Another flicker: on that same cobblestone yard, covered in snow, one of those taunting schoolgirls lay writhing and screaming, crying out in agony as if being electrocuted by some invisible force. There was a circle of girls backing away as Lorena pushed and shoved through the crowd. In the center, the copper-haired girl stood over the writhing girl on the ground, with those dangerous, menacing green eyes. Lorena grabbed her by the arm and pulled her away.

Then, a more mature Lorena had been cornered by a sharp-eyed, traditional-looking woman. The woman's tight, red lips moved, saying she must give up her life "in the service of a higher good." The words "why can't you be more like your sister" seemed to ring in Clark's ears, and somehow, Clark knew that Lorena called this woman Mama. Those high, arched eyebrows and hollow eyes gave him a case of déjà vu, as they turned to look at none other than Charisma herself, standing by her side.

"Never mind that," Lorena said, coming to. She put out her finished cigarette. When Clark snapped back too, his body had run cold and there was an unusual taste in his mouth: one of foreboding entrapment and blackmail, mingled with the metallic taste of blood. What he had just come to understand, or see in the eye of his mind, he wasn't so sure. Was Lorena bullied into the family business? Or did he come to imagine it all?

Lorena leaned down and in close to Clark once more, but this time, Clark's heart began to race as she smoothed his tie, and traced it with a single finger. "Charisma hates men in ties. So stuffy . . ."

He almost lost the will to speak.

Be brave . . . Don't panic . . . "Right," he said nervously, sinking in his chair under her. "No ties, got it. Thank you, ma'—*Lorena.* Um, but, while I greatly appreciate the experience of being here, I really do—"

"'But'? What's the matter, boy?" she barked, raising an eyebrow. "And here I thought you wanted to work for us."

Clark flushed red. "Yes—no! I do! What I mean to say is, I'd really like to continue working here, and, um, I know the juniors before had town cars, which might've helped them get things done more efficiently—more quickly, I should say—and, um, well, it's just that, with the errands, things add up, and . . . being paid would help tremendously. If I could even have—"

"*How much?*" Lorena snapped flatly. Surprised that she entertained the thought at all, Clark uttered the first hourly figure that came to mind, the same as at the coffee shop. Lorena grunted. He regretted it instantly and wished he had asked for more.

"Those were their own cars," she said. "No one asked those girls to take cars." She raised herself up tall as she could be and looked down on Clark from the tip of her pointy nose. "Something does not come from nothing. If that's what you want—to be more involved, to be paid—I'll make sure you get put to good use. I don't want to hear any complaining, nor any complaints. Got that? No drama whatsoever. Zilch. Not a word. No one likes a drama queen. If you do well and stay out of the way, well, we'll see. *But I make no promises.* Know this: under this roof, we all answer to Charisma, even me. No one is above her. You are replaceable. We all are. Is that understood?"

They had their own cars . . . Clark felt particularly small and powerless in a workplace like this, negotiating with a woman like Lorena as she hovered over him. "Yes," he replied. "Thank you," he added.

"Good," she said, standing up and leaning back. "Don't let Charisma see you. At least not yet. We'll have to break this to her gently." Then, licentious Lorena took a long drag of her cigarette and blew it in his face. "You may go."

Clark becoming better acquainted with the team seemed to give Monica license to kill, and she quickly made sure Clark understood exactly where his place was.

In preparation for their guests and star patron, she had him run down to the cleaners for a last-minute pickup of a heavy stack of dresses (*can't they deliver . . . ?* Clark thought in protest). When he returned, Monica had him sweep up after the florist, who was busy refreshing the flowers all around the home (*what am I, housekeeping . . . ?*). After that, she sent him on a coffee run for her and the girls (*how am I supposed to carry eight large caramel frappes, extra whip cream, caramel on top?*) When he arrived back, she gave him the lay of the land.

The penthouse was so big they might as well have been walking the entire city block. "The 'basement' wing is for the cooks' kitchen, the entertainment center, the gym, and the employee entrance—that's you. The north wing on Main is for business—us. The south wing is for entertainment and Charisma's lavish parties; they really are quite extravagant. The one to plan them should be me, but that's the second's job . . ."

Is that jealousy I hear . . . ?

"On this floor are five balconies, a ballroom, and a garden and terrace to the east; the second, third, and fourth floors are Charisma's private residences. The guest rooms are on two and the children's wing is on three, while Charisma's master suite overlooks the park to the north on four. Both residences have their own private entrances.

"There's a sauna and pool below, and her dressing room above, all of which she lets *us*, her assistants, use. We get access to whatever fabulous dresses and clothes and gratis she has no need for, and we have major discounts on all of her collections." At this, Monica eye-shamed the hell out of Clark's clothes, slacks and a—thanks to Lorena—tieless pastel-blue button-down.

"What's not needed or doesn't fit here is relocated to storage not far away. Charisma is the owner of the world's largest collection of haute couture."

"I thought that was Celine," Clark said.

"Wrong. It's Charisma. Anyway, on the fifth floor is Charisma's private practice space, the tower. You can see all of Manhattan from it. Up there, one feels like a queen atop her castle, sitting at the top of the world. You can almost see the planets in the daytime. It's so magical it's almost surreal . . . but juniors never get to see that. The main floor and employee quarters are the most that most juniors ever really get to see, if they're lucky."

Clark tried not to let his frustration at her taunting him show or get the best of him, but she was proving that to be exceedingly difficult.

"Now, open this box," she said, pointing to a cardboard box in the basement-level pantry. It was full of merchandise, small white boxes containing *Charisma, "the new Eau de Parfum by Charisma Saintly,"* he could hear the marketing ads say in Charisma's lisping English accent that had plagued his phone since the day he interviewed.

The next abuse Monica doled out was so unexpectedly dastardly and yet so pleasant, Clark thought she might be kidding: she ordered him to spray the entire main floor, boardroom to elevator, drapes to cushions, ceilings to rugs, in the fragrance.

"It smells like cat piss," Monica smugly proclaimed. "No one on the team wears it but Charisma. No one likes it! Take one if you like, no one will miss it. Good luck!" She wore a look of smirking bemusement as she stepped away, like the evil stepsister that he never asked for.

Out of the box, the fragrance itself came in a heavy geometric glass in the shape of a diamond, "inspired by alchemists," the copy on her website had claimed. The juice inside was a sheer, lethal-looking chartreuse *(like her eyes . . .)*. He turned the box over and read the fragrance notes:

DARLINGS, I have created a one-of-a-kind white-floral chypre perfume that IGNITES the GODDESS WITHIN. Featuring a MIND-ACTIVATING BLEND of SEX pHERomones™, and an 8-HOUR SILLAGE that PROJECTS A MAGNETIC AURA of FEMINOSITY, LOVE, and POWER. Its ADDICTIVE TRAIL will BEGUILE the senses, and leave them wanting more.

My first signature fragrance MANIFESTS CHARISMA in the HEART AND MIND of every woman.

Made with love,
Charisma Saintly
xoxo

LIGHT top notes of mouth-watering Lady Apple and Côte d'Azur Citrus; night-blooming White Jasmine; and brave Borage, Bergamot, and Black Pepper;
HEART mid notes of English Gardenia and Tea Rose; feminine Lily of the Valley, Orange Flower, Geranium and Creamy Tuberose; sensual Frankincense and Violet; and charming New York Green Ivy and Magnolia;
SEX base notes of mesmeric Musk and Amber; earthy Oakmoss and Orris Root; Smoked Sage and Papyrus

Parchment with precious White Woods; and naughty
Tobacco, Iron, Leather, and Vanilla.
Always cruelty-free.

Clark stifled a laugh. *The buzzwords* . . . he thought. *She's either in on the joke or a total kook* . . .

To Clark, the fragrance was . . . creamy . . . earthy . . . and kinda dirty—in a good way. It reminded him of strolling past Astoria rose gardens in the summertime, and walking department store counters with his mother as a child, the way he'd imagine a chain-smoking rich-girl debutante might smell after a night at her boyfriend's. He actually sort of liked it and thought it kinda fun, so much so, in fact, that he snuck a spritz on his wrist. *Joke's on you, Monica* . . .

That day, he sprayed through no less than four large bottles around the main floor alone. The *ksk ksk ksk* of that old-fashioned tasseled atomizer echoed in his head long after he was done. The fifth bottle was put away in his backpack. He would forever remember that long, long day whenever he'd catch a whiff of gardenia and cigarettes.

On his next lap and the task that followed—candle lighting—Clark was paranoid, and for good reason, that he and the penthouse would go up in flames from all the fragrance sprayed. He carried a stepladder with him, lighting candles up and down the main floor. As he lit the last of them, a frantic maid almost ran into his ladder and knocked him off the top. She only cried "Sorry!" as she dashed away.

It was after six by the time that was done. The sun was lower on the horizon and streamed in through the open windows. He so wanted to take a break. Clark was well dehydrated from that vodka soda, careening quickly towards depleted and hungry once more, and his throat was dry with essence de Charisma. The event planner had him hang balloons and streamers: so many, in fact, that by the time he returned to the living room, the penthouse had transformed, and there was some sort of a celebration underway. A couple of employees from Charisma's namesake brand arranged goodie bags of her debut fragrance.

In the distance, he could distinctly hear Monica yelling at the maids, something about moving the trunks up to Charisma's room and laying out her dress. Alicia barked back at Monica, asking why this and that were not already done. "What were you doing these last few weeks?" he heard her criticize. *At least there's some justice . . .* he thought.

Afterward, Monica led him towards the front of the penthouse as he carried another large, rattling box. Her feet clacked away in the stilettos she never took off, despite all the walking. They stood in front of the coat closet: its doors lay flush with the mirrored wall in the foyer, gone unnoticed by Clark, who had sat on that velvet loveseat in front of it on his first day none the wiser.

"Leave it here for now," Monica instructed him, throwing the door open. "We'll return for it later."

Clark peered inside that dusty, crimson-colored hotbox . . . and then it happened, all too suddenly:

The elevator doors opened to chattering and clacking, stilettoed footsteps, one pair in front, and many pairs after. Monica turned and gasped. Hastily, she shoved Clark into the closet and closed the door behind him, sending him flying into a rack of coats. With a click, the door locked—and effectively locked him in.

"Darlings." He could hear an English accent in a lisping, mezzo alto, her voice somehow so resonant across the marble tile it seemed to travel from room to room. "I'm home."

Charisma had arrived.

CHAPTER V

VIP

$\mathcal{F}$rom inside the closet, Clark could hear the sound of chatter and footsteps—was it ten pairs passing? Twenty? Thirty, even? He couldn't be sure. Which one of them was Charisma?

Clark groped for a handle or some kind of discreet opening, but no luck. He turned on his phone's flashlight and found the light switch. Under the light of the single dim yellow bulb, he could see there was no window, no air vent, just racks of winter furs. "*Always cruelty-free,*" Clark parroted mentally. He pushed the door, but it would not budge; there was no service on his cell phone, and if there was, he wasn't sure whom he'd call. His knocks went unnoticed, and so there he remained.

He could almost swear he heard the scraping of chairs, and the clinking of stemware and utensils on plates. Dinner was underway. Before he knew it, an hour had gone by. He could make out more clacking footsteps and chatter as new guests entered from the elevator. However, Clark knew better than to draw attention to himself, lest he unintentionally upset someone, never mind incriminating Monica. He refused to risk the potential job loss. And give Monica the satisfaction? Never.

That's when the music started.

Now they definitely won't be able to hear me . . . Clark thought, kicking himself. Droplets of sweat formed on his furrowed brow and stuck to the back of his shirt as he sat against the wall in that stuffy, dusty closet.

An hour crawled into two. He tried not to panic—surely someone would remember him and let him out? But then, who would remember him?

As if his wish had been granted, the door clicked open, letting in fresh, fragrant, and air-conditioned air that billowed into the room. Clark stood up. It was Monica.

"There you are!" she exclaimed, throwing a couple of jackets at him. "Hang these." He was certain he could hear Charisma's boisterous voice over the music and banter.

"Come here, and quick! Before someone sees you," Monica growled, dragging him by the arm as fast as her high-heeled feet could carry her. "What you are still doing here is absolutely *beyond me.*"

"The door doesn't open from the—"

"Never mind your excuses. *Hurry up!*" The late afternoon had transitioned into evening, judging by the color of the sky outside the skylights as she dragged him through the kitchen and down the employee stairs.

"Best not to overstay one's welcome, wouldn't you say?" Monica flung him out the doors of Hell's Entrance and wiped her hands. The door clicked and beeped, and Clark was effectively locked out.

Indignation quickly welled up inside him. Was this what it would take to make it here? Being kept in the closet and jerked around? Clark did not have to wait long for a sign. At that same moment, from the other door behind him, Beard-o the Handsome Mystery Man appeared, the one from a few days prior, walking in from the freight elevator.

"Hey, bro!" he told Clark. "Here for the party?"

Clark had an idea. "Actually," he replied, "yeah, I am! Hey, what's the passcode to the door again? I forgot it. *Could this work . . . ?*

"You should write it down, man, so you don't forget it," Beard-o said. Clark reserved his eye-roll. Surprisingly, he showed Clark the passcode, who typed it into the keypad and committed it to memory, and then to his phone. The light flashed from red to green, and with a buzz and a click, Clark pushed it open.

"You're a lifesaver. Thanks . . . bro!" Clark said. The man gave him a wink and disappeared into the employee stairwell. Clark made his way through the doors and up the stairs himself. On the other side of the door, he almost bumped into none other than Miss Honey, who stood there with her hands on her hips in reproach.

"Oh, hi, Miss Honey!" Clark said.

"What are you still doing here, baby?" she asked. He could tell by the concern in those warm eyes that she was not pleased to see him. "I told you this is no place for someone like you. You better get on outta here. Git! Scram! Trust me, baby, nothing good to see here . . ."

Down the hall and around the corner, Clark could make out the shadow of guests and laughter coming from the living room. "Thanks, but I just wanna get a closer . . ." he said, but when he turned to look back, Miss Honey had already gone. Slowly, he continued down the hall.

He caught a glimpse of himself in a mirror: Clark looked damp and dehydrated. As a waitress ran a tray of champagne flutes back to the kitchen, Clark nabbed two. He tossed one back, set it down on a passing credenza, and with the other in hand, descended upon the party.

The scene was a sight to behold, fit for Gatsby. With all the streamers and balloons, and the light of the multiple chandeliers and candles, the entire space was aglow. The doors to the terrace steps below were ajar, to a backdrop of a glittering city framed by a summer sky splashing into the deep opal blues of a slow New York sundown. Standing in the center of the crowd, Clark could make her out in action, her flaming copper hair billowing around her: Charisma Saintly was the star of the pack, of course, in the middle of telling a story by the looks of it, talking candidly and waving a cigarette animatedly in one hand while holding a drink in the other. She wore a shimmering, short black dress that hugged her slim figure, sparkling diamond jewelry on her long arms and neck, and glittery, spiky stilettos fit for the pole. Charisma was larger than life in person, a glamazon, taller than he had imagined. Maybe it was her posture, how she seemed to tower over her guests, who laughed on cue and gasped when appropriate. Charisma was fabulous. Maybe it was just *her*, Clark thought.

He caught a bit of side-eye from a guest or two as he walked amongst them. They turned their noses up and looked away, or otherwise tried not to make eye contact. Clark was clearly underdressed in his baby blue button-down and not an ounce of black like the rest. He put them from his mind, and tried his hardest not to appear conspicuous. Clark posted up near a marble statue—Artemis the archer with her bow—and took a sip of champagne, attempting to melt into the background.

Overhead in the loft, Clark noticed assistants Alicia and Emily in intense conversation. On the main floor, a handful of attendants swirled around the guests with trays of hors d'oeuvres and every pastry and sweet one could ever desire; inside, a DJ stood mixing music; at the bar, two dapper bartenders mixed drinks of top-shelf alcohol; out on the terrace, and all around, the air was alive in gaiety, chatter, and excess. By the fountain and next to the velvet sectional were presents of all kinds, of boxes and bows of every color and size. The balloons he had hung had made sense (*duh, you nerd . . .*): this was Charisma's belated birthday party.

The guests were mostly women, a few men, many of them famous faces he might have known from TV or movies: a handsome A-list actor Clark definitely recognized, the infamous editor-in-chief of *The September Issue* wearing sunglasses indoors, someone he was positive was a '90s supermodel, and more. Almost all in attendance were dressed in black like Charisma. *Maybe they think they're witches too . . .* Clark took notice of the way they looked, the way they moved, how they hung on to her every word, how they all seemed to talk and act just like Charisma—especially Monica, who wore her hair in the same fringe, her makeup in the same style, who stood in Charisma's shadow so obsequiously and yet so ignored. She was a sycophant if he ever saw one. In a way, he realized, they all were.

As he watched, Charisma tossed her cigarette to the wind, leaving an attendant to chase it down and put it out into the ashtray only a few feet away. She turned on foot and her posse followed, moving like a swarm behind her. Offhandedly, Charisma almost set her empty drink down in midair—almost, because miraculously, luckily, just in time, a waitress dived and caught the glass on a tray, while another simultaneously handed her a fresh one. Charisma didn't miss a beat, and no one except Clark seemed to notice or care.

The music stopped, and the lights were lowered. A world-famous pop star entered from the north wing, microphone in hand, and sang "Happy Birthday." Clark watched as the guests sang along, parting the seas for her and for Charisma, while two attendants wheeled in a giant, glittering five-tiered birthday cake covered in sparklers. A spotlight descended, a photographer clicked away, and all eyes were on Charisma. Everyone and everything seemed to bend to her will, and Clark was captivated. He had never encountered a person so extraordinary, whom he seemed to know so much about and yet nothing about at all, whatsoever. As she blew on her candles, Clark knew one thing to be true, then and there: he wanted a piece of that magic. The guests clapped, the cake was wheeled away, and the festivities resumed.

What happened next, Clark wasn't sure how, but it happened all the same: somehow, as Clark began to slip away, as she stood there scanning the room in mid-laugh, of all the faces to notice, Charisma's eyes locked onto none other than Clark's. He froze in place. She paused too. Her smile faded, her head cocked to the side—and to his horror, the room's every occupant stopped to follow her gaze. In an instant, Clark had the attention of eighty, ninety, one hundred people, looking at him like he was a piece of dog's droppings under their nose.

Oh, shit . . . he thought.

From behind Charisma, Monica pushed aside a guest and spilled their drink onto their dress, ignoring them as they cried aloud in protest. Monica was leering at Clark through gritted, perfect teeth. He could think of only one word: *Run . . . !*

Clark darted in between guests, ducking under a tray of champagne and around a waitress. Another attendant almost crashed into him, but Clark bounded off her just in time. He ran until he was around the corner and far down the hall. One door next to the stairwell was ajar, and unsure of what he had glimpsed, Clark came to a halt, reversed, and did a double take: it was Melissa, bent over the powder room counter, snorting a line of cocaine through a hundred-dollar bill, and Charisma's niece, Alicia, standing next to her, sniffing and prodding at her own nostrils in the mirror. They both turned to look at him. Clark's eyes widened. He made a dash for the stairwell.

Down the stairs, he bounded through Hell's Entrance and landed in the freight elevator, panting. Clark did not dare stop, not until he landed on the noisy street below, onto the subway that came just in time, and up into the respite of his quiet Astoria apartment.

Exhausted, Clark showered, crawled into bed, and fell into an uneasy sleep to the sound of chirping crickets, the train nearby, and sirens in the distance.

There was a buzzing in his ears, which had not stopped burning red and angry since he had left Charisma's.

The birthday party was Friday. That Saturday, Clark brought his diary to the coffee shop: all that morning, he was eager to recount the oddest dream he'd had the night before. He had not forgotten it since:

> *I was standing in the center of a long stage under a single*
> *spotlight, in the middle of a kind of . . . event space. A meeting*
> *hall of sorts. Or was it a church? From all around and on the*
> *peripherals, I was being watched by hooded onlookers cloaked in*
> *shadow, whispering . . .*
> *Another spotlight flipped on, across from me, flooding the other*
> *end of the stage with light.*
> *Who appeared on that stage was none other than . . . me.*
> *Only, this me was older, or at least more mature, dressed in a*
> *sharp black suit and shoes, hair smoothed back. Rich. Smart.*
> *Successful. Powerful. Charismatic. A leader. Everything that I'm*

not. This Other Me, this Future Clark, I somehow understood,
was my ideal self.
The onlookers were whispering, so many whispers about me and
what I had become, what I had to do to get there, and what I
had yet to achieve . . .
I smiled at him. Other Me looked down on me—Current
Me— from atop his nose, sized me up and down for who I am,
and then he—I—actually rolled his eyes and looked at me with
contempt.
What a bitch . . . !
I have a long way to go before meeting him again . . .

As Clark filled an order ("One large *cawfee*, a splash of half-and-half, and two sugars"), he thought about how Charisma would be flying on her helicopter to her manor in Montauk for Labor Day weekend. That Monday, he would be totally off work for the first time in weeks. Clark planned on being in and out of intermittent naps, binging television and books and peanut butter with Oreos, all the while putting off from his mind the consequences he would face on Tuesday when the "Coven" reconvened . . .

Someone else was off from work that Labor Day too. Behind the coffee shop counter, he opened a text from an unknown number:

(9:30 a.m. Joey DiMuccio): Hey Clark from Queens, how
are you? This is Joey from Brooklyn lol. From yesterday.
What are you doing on Monday? Come out for a picnic
with me, if you're not up to anything.

A guy this cute wants to make plans with me . . . ? Clark thought.
On Labor Day . . . ?

(9:31 a.m. Joey DiMuccio): I know right? Making plans
with someone you just met for Labor Day . . .
You're probably busy. I could pick you up 🚗.
It'll be cute, promise =]

Part of Clark wanted to appear in-demand, busy, out with friends having a blast, or some other kind of nonsense he could think up, but another part thought, why play games when a guy this interested doesn't come around often?

(9:40 a.m. Clark Crane): Hey Joey, sure! I'd like that :]
What time?

Clark spent the rest of the weekend stressing over what to wear. Joey had requested him on social media, and looking through his photos almost made Clark's stomach flip. There were photos of Joey at work, Joey with his family at their Brooklyn pizza shop (DiMuccio's Pizza), Joey shirtless, his torso proudly on display, Joey at the beach in short swimming shorts . . . Clark was an excited-nervous he could not remember feeling in a long time.

That Monday, after practically trying on his entire closet, Clark settled on a comic-book tee and jean shorts, happy to be out of slacks and button-downs for once. He donned those well-worn high-tops.

As promised, Joey was double-parked outside Clark's building in a modest Honda Civic. He stood leaning on the passenger-side door, looking suave and debonair, with his dark hair slicked back and his Wayfarers on, dressed in shorts and a crisp, unbuttoned Henley. After hugging hello, Joey kissed him on the cheek before opening the door for Clark, who flushed a warm, conspicuous pink.

"What a gentleman," Clark mused. "I'm not used to it."

"Get used to it, baby," Joey said, looking over at him with his Mr. Big smile.

Clark had assumed when Joey said "the park" that he meant Central Park. Instead, he drove them east on the expressway towards Long Island, blasting pop music and singing along with the windows down. Joey was a fearless crooner, Clark learned.

"This is one of my favorites," Joey said, turning the volume up on an oldie covered by a young, modern jazz-pop star no longer living. He kept up with every note, even ad-libbed a riff or two. They pulled into the parking lot, in a park of sweeping green lawns and tall evergreens, where Clark took a deep breath of clean, non-city air.

"You're pretty good," Clark commented. "Where'd you learn to sing like that?"

"Oh, that? That's nothing. My grandma could out-sing the best," Joey said as he unpacked the trunk, producing a blanket and an heir-loom picnic basket. "She taught me about all the oldies and Old Hollywood. That's my hobby, I guess: I love watching movies. That's why I wanna be an actor." Clark carried the blanket and they started at a slow pace, walking through the grass.

"An actor? That's so cool," Clark said.

"Thanks! What about you, what do you do for fun?"

"Oh, me? Nothing exciting, I guess. I like to read. Maybe that's kinda boring . . ." Clark said. He didn't want to admit he couldn't afford to have many platform subscriptions.

"Not boring at all! That's great."

"Thanks, Joey," Clark said. "That's really beautiful, what you and your grandma share. Are you two close?"

"Oh yeah, very," Joey said. "She practically raised me and taught me everything I know: how to style myself, how to cook for myself, how to take care of myself. Nothing compares to how she used to cook though."

Clark asked, "'Used to'?" He regretted it almost instantly.

Joey looked at him with those large amber eyes and their long, straight, dark eyelashes: "Yeah. She passed, a couple or so years ago . . . Cancer. She toughed it out long and hard. I actually dropped out of college to care for her in the daytime when we couldn't afford hospice care. I started bartending to help with all the bills. She was so mad at me for that. I had grown up mixing her drinks for her. The rest of the family would get me to mix theirs, so I did what came naturally! I told her, 'You take care of me, I take care of you.'"

Clark wasn't sure what to say. After a moment, as they strolled, he said, "I'm sorry. I'm sure that meant a lot to her, and that she loved you very much."

"Oh yeah, for sure," he replied, looking up with a smile. "I loved her too. She was the matriarch of the family, no doubt. When she died, everyone was devastated. I was really beside myself. She left an inheritance for me, just a small sum of money to help with college, you know? It was the biggest of all of ours, everyone knew I was her favorite. I put it right back into taking care of us and our bills. I mean, my family and I, we lived pretty comfortably up until the stock market crash. We had a hard time after, and my parents almost lost the restaurant. They were getting behind on bills and they were about to lose the house, things were adding up, and with my little sister still in school, I had to help them out. I kinda had no choice."

They stopped to park under a shady tree and lay down Joey's large blanket. "Gosh," Clark said, furrowing his brow. "That's . . . wow. I'm sorry you had to put your goals aside. That must not have been the easy thing to do, but I'm sure it was the right thing."

"It was the only thing to do, you know what I mean?" Joey said. "'The things we do for love.' It's okay though, I've had a great life. I've got a great job. I've got a great family. All of us are really close. We got to keep the restaurant and the house, which is . . . where I live now." Joey averted his eyes. "I've got the basement all to myself! They pretty much let me do my own thing . . . How about you? Any siblings? Family?"

Were the tops of Clark's cheeks turning pink? He fidgeted in his seat as Joey opened the picnic basket and broke out the food, a collection of handmade sandwiches, chips, and dips.

"My family life is . . . kinda weird," Clark replied. "My parents divorced when I was little. I must have been four or five. I can almost remember life before then, when my grandmother was still alive. I remember things being so good back then. They always seem that way when you're little. Then came the stroke, followed by the aneurysm. After that, shared custody and child support were all I knew."

Clark unzipped the backpack he had brought and produced red Dixie cups, and a bottle of cheap white wine he had been saving, for what, he wasn't sure. Joey immediately took hold of it and the bottle opener, and uncorked it at lightning speed. *"Wartch,"* Clark said in an Australian accent. *"The cork whisperer at work."*

Joey looked up and winked. "Hey," he said, "I'm sorry about your grandma too."

"Aw, thanks," Clark said. "It's okay, I was so little anyway. She was the one to look after me mostly; both of my parents are workaholics. She loved me a lot. I was their golden child, after all, the favorite. I remember her reading to me, she was such a great storyteller, and the matriarch of the family, too. From what my parents say about that time, I don't think the three of them got along: Grandma Wanda didn't totally approve of my father, and he didn't really care for her either. She was a strong personality. I wish I could have grown up with her, to know her, and blah blah blah . . . Hey, you're not drinking?"

"Nah, I'm good. I have other vices," Joey said, producing a bottle of cola. He filled his Dixie cup, raised it to Clark, and said, "To grandmothers who cared."

"To grandmothers," Clark said, clinking plastic to plastic. They smiled and held eye contact as they sipped.

Joey pressed on. "Any siblings?"

"Nah, it's just me. But I wished I had one," Clark confessed. "Between the phone calls about late child support payments, the cold handoffs, the showdowns at the after-school pickup line, all to be left at home on my own, I always felt sorta . . . I dunno. Alone. They both deny ever triangulating me in any of it, saying they never wanted to make enemies of the other, but they did. It was only natural. They're only human, after all."

"Oh man. That's a tough spot to be in for a kid, for sure."

"Oh yeah, totally. It's no big deal now! Maybe my story isn't that unique," Clark said, taking another sip. "Why am I telling you all this? Haha . . . What about you and your family with coming out? How was that?"

"Oh, a breeze." Joey chortled.

Clark smiled too. "Are you being sarcastic?"

"No, not at all! I came out, well, sorta recently." Joey winced. "I think my Nonna Margaret knew before I did. That helped. I've dated girls, of course, but you know, it didn't take. Did you?"

"Date girls?" Clark hesitated when he said, "Um, well, yeah . . . Kinda sorta but not really . . ." Clark couldn't bring himself to confess he hadn't started seriously dating until recently too, at least not then and there.

"Cool," said Joey, unpressed. "Well, my parents took her lead and that was that. They didn't even bat an eye. I think the day I officially told them, they pretended nothing was any different. We all went out for dinner that night, and we had an expensive bottle of wine they were saving. They never admitted to celebrating exactly, although that's kinda what it was. I'm really lucky."

"Wow, that's refreshing," Clark said, wiping his lips between bites. He took a sip and shifted in his seat again. "A stable home life. Most of my friends come from some kind of abuse or estrangement or broken home."

"Well," Joey said, "I wouldn't say my home life was without its . . . peculiarities . . ." He topped off Clark's cup with another heavy pour. Clark wasn't sure what he meant.

"This BLT is delicious, by the way," Clark said. "Thanks for bringing the provisions! Did you make this all yourself?"

"Thanks for coming. Yeah, yes I did," Joey said, smiling from the rim of his cup. Clark thought he looked so handsome with his sweet smile and flirty eyes. Clark's own eyes landed on his broad shoulders, down his collarbone, to Joey's chest hair peeking out . . . He cleared his throat and quickly looked away.

"My coming out was, um, not as smooth," Clark said. "I think Maria and Ryan were in denial about it. I had kind of . . . grown up emotionally estranged from them? I didn't really know them, nor did they know me, so it's no surprise they took it as badly as they did. I actually regret coming out September of my freshman year; it turned into a bout of family counseling, pretending we were an actual functioning family—I mean, as if! As if we were an actual family all along. I called them out on it. My dad wasn't ever really in the picture and my mother was an emotional stranger to me; she doesn't even know who I am. They even courted conversion therapists. The first session was on my fifteenth birthday. I called them out on that, too. 'Happy birthday to me . . .'" Clark paused. "Aaand I'm rambling. Sorry for the overshare! If this is too much! You probably think something's wrong with me . . ."

"Hey," Joey said. "Nothing's wrong with you. It's not too much. I'm listening."

"Okay . . ." Clark said. "Thanks, Joey." His smile turned down a little at the corners. "Well, those therapists, they didn't take either, of course. They'd talk about me like I wasn't actually there, like I was some kinda object, something less than, just like everyone else growing up. I told them I was proud of who I am and the person I'm becoming, that there was nothing wrong with me. They said, 'There's no changing him if he doesn't want to change.' I think they were all kind of surprised to hear that come out of me at fifteen since I was kind of—well, I was super bullied—but I knew I had already done the brave thing in opening up. I knew that being brave was my only choice. It was survival.

"I came out to my mom first. I remember our family friend Patricia, her best friend growing up, told me, 'Just tell her! She has to know already. She's *your mothuh*! She loves you no matter what!' But my mom, she took it horribly! I think she felt somewhat betrayed, like I had broken some unspoken agreement. My dad followed suit. To think, I came out to grow closer to them. It just left me feeling like no matter what I did, I wasn't good enough for them."

Joey leaned in and said, "You did the right thing too, Clark, and the best you could do."

"Yeah, I guess so," he said. Clark looked down at his cup and threw back the last of its contents. Joey held the wine at the ready. "Thanks," Clark said, holding his refill. "Well, that was when I had just turned fifteen. I got a job working part-time at the coffee shop. I saved up all I could. The night after my last day of freshman year of high school, I packed up all I had and moved into my grandma's rent-controlled apartment, this cute little studio in Astoria that's basically a bedroom with amazing light, and walls coated an inch thick in paint. I dunno how my parents got to keep it after she passed. I think she must've been close with the owners of the building and they turned a blind eye or something. I never see them except to sign some papers every once in a while that say I've let them in for repairs. I've been living there ever since."

"That's amazing," Joey said, watching Clark with a caring eye. "That's so young to be on your own. I think you're amazing."

"Aw, thanks, Joey. I remember my first night, staring up at that ceiling. It's coated in paint so thick and dripping, I call it my papier-mâché apartment. I had never felt so scared and so free at the same time, you know what I mean . . . ?" Clark said, trailing off. "I think you're amazing, too."

"What about Charisma?" Joey asked.

Clark paused with his sandwich midway to his mouth. "What do you mean? What about her?"

"You're interning for one of the most famous women in the world. That's gotta be a big job with a lot of pressure."

"Oh, haha . . . Yeah, I'm just an errand boy. I'm the only guy. It's . . . kinda rough," Clark said, searching for words.

"Why are you doing it then?" Joey asked. By his lighthearted tone, the question seemed innocent enough.

"Hmm. I . . . guess I'm doing it because it could lead to other, better things," Clark said. "The opportunity kinda fell in my lap, and I'd be crazy not to take it, I think. A year there can open many doors, or so I'm told . . ."

"'*If you can make it there,*'" Joey mused.

"Yeah . . . What about you? Why Charisma? For that matter, why Northlight? You look like you could work at any gay bar in the city."

"I've done that already," Joey said matter-of-factly. "I've done the scene. I've dated those kinds of guys. Not for me. The money was . . . so good, but I work better hours at Northlight. The gay scene can be, I dunno. That lifestyle can kinda consume you: the parties, the people, the gratification, the alcohol . . . I'm better here—happier. I've already been promoted to assistant manager. I can audition in the mornings. I won't do it forever but right now it's all I know."

Here I am, telling a guy like Joey I want more, Clark mused, *when he's happier with less . . .* "I admire that," he said.

"Thanks! Yeah, it's made me reevaluate what I want, and what my goals are. Do you want to get married and have kids, Clark?" Joey asked.

Clark dropped his sandwich altogether. "What?"

Joey's eyes widened and he broke into a fit of giggles. "I meant someday, not with me! Hahaha! That wasn't a proposal, I swear . . . If I were proposing to you, I'd do it the right way."

"Oh! Hahaha," Clark got out nervously. His cheeks turned bright pink again. "With the right person, yeah. Someday. I think I'd be a great dad. I think anyone who's had a messy childhood wants that, to right the wrong their parents did, don't you? Do you? Want marriage and kids, I mean."

"Oh yeah," he said. "Definitely. I wanna put a down payment down, get a mortgage, and raise a family. I want the kids, the dog, the white picket fence: the whole nine yards."

"A traditionalist. I like that," Clark said.

Joey smiled. "A family man."

Clark smiled back. "I think you'd be a great dad." There was something about being around Joey that felt so easy and natural, that made Clark comfortable being his honest self. It made Joey even more intimidating, and at the same time even more attractive.

"I think you'd be a great dad, too," Joey said, slowly leaning into Clark.

"Sometimes," Clark said with a reluctant chortle, "I feel like I grew up so quickly that I just don't get any of it. Being an adult is so hard."

"So don't grow up," Joey said, leaning in even closer. "Stay a kid with me."

Joey was so close, Clark could smell his cologne. For a moment, Joey's head tilted to one side. They looked into one another's eyes, and then to one another's lips, and then to one another's eyes again, and then their lips once more. Joey smiled. They moved closer, and closer, as Clark's heart raced out of his chest, until . . .

"More soda?!" Clark blurted out.

Joey gave a knowing smile. "Sure! Thanks," he said. "Hey, I have an idea—to lighten the mood." Clark understood instantly where that telltale smell was coming from when Joey produced from his pocket a yellow lighter and a joint. "Want a hit?"

Clark looked at him, and with a hesitant smile said, "Okay. I have to confess something: I've never been high before . . ."

Joey paused and looked at him. "Never?"

"I mean, I've tried it once or twice. I'm from New York. It is the city's official flower, after all . . ."

"Baby's first high," Joey said. "I'm honored."

Joey toked the first puff and passed the joint to Clark, who took a drag, and coughed and coughed and coughed. He sputtered so hard for a minute straight that they both laughed. A couple nearby packed their belongings, stood up, and left in a huff.

While they finished eating, the two exchanged notes and giggles on the music they both loved, the TV shows they grew up on, and the movies they enjoyed. It turned out that Joey really did have a thing for witches too.

"Love them," he said. "Can't get enough of 'em. My grandma would always tell me to turn the sauce spoon clockwise for good luck. She and I would watch all the witch movies growing up. The one about the three Salem witches was our favorite."

"Get out!" Clark exclaimed excitedly. "Mine too! My birthday is a week before Halloween so I always wanted Halloween parties, even if I didn't have a lot of friends or family that would come. My mom would hunt through the TV guide when it was printed on paper— remember that?—and find all the witchy Halloween movies for me the week leading up. I always wanted to be a witch. To be special like that . . . What about you, when's your birthday?"

"April eighteenth."

"Oh, Aries . . . on the cusp of Taurus."

"You like astrology?"

"Yeah, I like it! My mom was big into it growing up. Okay, here's a corny question," Clark said. "What's your favorite color, and why?"

"Sage green," Joey said, "because it's peaceful. What's yours?"

"Mm . . . periwinkle," Clark said, "because it's the color of the sky at twilight, my favorite time of day."

Joey smiled. "What's your favorite ice cream?"

"Ohh, that's easy: pistachio with Nutella on top. What about yours?"

"Noice! Mine's mint chocolate chip," Joey said.

"Cookie dough and cookies and cream are a close second!"

"Definitely a close second. Can't turn down anything baked," he said wryly, passing the joint back.

Clark asked, "How about your . . . favorite smell?"

"Ohh, that's a tough one. Lemme see . . . amaretto and bitters, I think, because it's what my grandma used to drink, a glass a night. It kept her 'zippy,' she used to say. And cigarettes and roasting chestnuts, because they always remind me of Christmastime in the city. Oh! And the smell of cooking, like garlic and onions. That always feels like coming home. What about yours?"

"I love that! Okay, mine is, um, well, the smell of books! I love the smell of paper. Color me a nerd! And the smell of cookies baking—heaven. And coffee on the pot in the morning, like my mom used to do, although now it just makes me think about work . . . Ohh, and also that smoky smell of burnt-out candles, because it reminds me of birthdays when I was little, when I'd get to dress up as someone else and make a wish and blow out my candles and pretend that everybody actually loves me . . ." He trailed off and could feel the blood pooling in his cheeks and ears. "Hello, sob story, party of one!" *Stahp talking, Clark . . . !*

Joey leaned in and said in agreement, "This burnout loves that." Lightly, he gave Clark a knock on the shoulder.

Joey and Clark swapped the joint until it was an ember-less bud, sharing more and laughing more, and losing track of time. Eventually, they finished the food and snacks, and when their things were packed they headed for the restroom, and then back to the car. Joey offered Clark one more hit (Clark couldn't say no) and proposed another idea, if Clark was up for it ("of course," Clark said, not wanting the day to end, nor to admit as much). They left the parking lot and meandered down the opposite way, walking side by side, pinkies gently knocking into one another, until the path came to a stop: Joey had wryly led them to a grassy old playground, remarkably devoid of children. Clark raced him to the top of the jungle gym.

They laughed as they squeezed their big-boy bodies through its pint-sized openings. They dangled off the monkey bars, rode the slide to the bottom and back again, and took turns pushing one another on the swings, seeing how far the other could jump off. The whole day had felt so simple and so light, Clark could not remember the last time he smiled as much.

When they tired themselves out, Joey and Clark landed in the grass to watch the clouds. The first of the fireflies had come out to play, and the sun was setting low on the horizon. On that last day of summer, under that cotton-candy sky, Clark and Joey turned to look at one another, and as if like magnets, leaned in and kissed—gentle at first, then deeper kisses that gave Clark the butterflies.

The two held hands on their way back to the car and never let go.

Joey and Clark hit some traffic on their way home. Joey drove slow in the right lane, and Clark didn't mind. They talked about everything except work and their families, as the glittering skyline and the RFK Bridge approached on the horizon.

Before the roads grew narrow and they drove into the tight congestion of the city, Joey and Clark stopped for their favorite fast-food chain (the Other Red-Headed Girl, Clark mused, another taste they discovered they shared). They happened upon one of those miracle parking spots right in front of Clark's building, where they sat for quite a while, eating, listening to one another's music and stories, and then kissing some more. Joey knew exactly where to place his hands, and Clark knew exactly where to hold him. It was after ten on a school night before they finally did the adult thing they didn't want to do, and bid one another goodbye.

"*Arrivederci*, baby," Joey said with a smile. "Until next time."

"See you soon," Clark replied. They leaned in for a last kiss goodnight.

That night, Clark found himself in that dream space, meeting his Ideal Self again. The whispering crowd was rowdier this time, restless and moving about.

Clark's Ideal Self, who looked down on him with disdain, turned from Clark's face into Monica's, leering at him with her cold, gray eyes. "Never save the day, *Clark*, or you'll never be one of us," she sneered.

Her face erupted into sheets of fiery-copper hair, and Charisma's head stared down at him with those piercing yellow-green eyes. She laughed her boisterous laugh that shook him to his core. Clark practically jumped out of his skin as he startled himself awake, drenched in a cold sweat at three in the morning.

That was when the nightmares began.

CHAPTER VI

Bitchcraft

*C*lark knew there would be hell to pay at work that Tuesday.

Instead of addressing his misstep, however, having crashed the party just days before, Monica approached him with those high-arched eyebrows under her fringe, and that smile that didn't quite reach those icy blue eyes.

"After Labor Day comes Fashion Week, and it's zero to one *thousand* for us," she informed him with her nose turned up. "It's our busiest time of the year as we head into fall and the holidays. Charisma has her own collection to show, and it's the highlight of the season—obviously. Then, she attends a few select shows with friends, the who's who of the fashion world. It's a week of nonstop parties and events and house calls with some *very* important people."

"What's a house call?" Clark asked.

"A house call," Monica said with a roll of her eyes, "is not unlike a party, but more than a séance of yore. Charisma gathers the troops—us, that is, the assistants—and assembles at a client's home for a night of witchery: reading her clients, drawing the cards, sometimes a conjuring or two, maybe more. It's a chance to see Charisma at work. Nothing she does is ever cheap or tawdry. It's always a spectacle to behold—but she only books with *very* special clients anymore. She's a very busy woman."

"Ah, I see," Clark said, his curiosity piqued. "And when Charisma is unavailable, she sends you, right?"

"Correct."

Monica led him to "the Closet," which was where, she informed him, "we stock our resources." Monica told him this as they exited onto the third floor of the penthouse, and walked not far down the hall, stopping just short of an oak door.

She turned to him and the words emanating from her glossy pink lips dripped in sweet venom: "So, I heard you want to be more involved with the Coven. Is that right?"

"Oh, yeah, I'd like to be." Clark was a little embarrassed that he had been outed by Lorena. "Very much!"

"Well," Monica began, "if you finish all your tasks and help us prepare our kits—and you're on your *best* behavior—maybe you can come help on Charisma's next house call yourself . . ."

"Okay!" Clark said, bright-eyed. *Finally,* he thought, *this is my shot . . . I get to do something that actually matters here . . .* He couldn't help but entertain the prospect.

The Closet was less a closet and more a studio; without question, it was larger than his own apartment. All around were drawers radiating from the room's center like a sundial, with armchairs, a table, a mirrored wall opposite them, and even a small bar and refrigerator. But for Clark, there was something more that caught his attention.

Resting in the center of the Closet and elevated on a platform of three steps was a large terrarium atop a pedestal. It sat below a single, circular skylight, the Closet's only source of natural light. Planted in its center on a mossy base of smooth pebbles was a majestic miniature tree, whose many tiny leaves and branches radiated up to the edge of its domed glass house, as if rays of electricity in a plasma ball.

Or the veining of an eye . . .

To Clark's almost delighted surprise, and what he found to be the most peculiar about the tree inside, were the tiny, round, red apples it bore. The terrarium was a diorama. *An altar . . .* he thought to himself as he stepped up to approach, his eyes not daring to turn away. Clark's stomach twinged and his forehead tingled, and he wondered why he was feeling so *activated*.

Is it just me or is the tree moving . . . ? *Like a slight breeze blowing through its branches . . . ?*

"Ahem?" Monica said. Clark turned to look at her, and with a final glance at the terrarium, detached himself as told.

She put him to work for the foreseeable future, wiping down the contents of the drawers. Inside, he removed acrylic crate upon acrylic crate of crystals and candles of every color and size, next to bundles of sage and incense and dried herbs. Clark almost gagged handling candles labeled "human tallow."

"It is a privilege to be in the Closet," Monica announced, shooting him a look. "Most juniors never get to see it . . ." At this, Clark erased any trace of disgust from his face and put the tallow candles back.

There were a couple of jars of mandrake roots and "dead man's toe," finger-shaped fungi he thought were only in movies, and a giant selenite athame—*more like a sword*, bright white and translucent. Was his arm humming as if touching a current? He could swear it was electric with energy, as he picked it up and wiped it down.

Another drawer contained vials of oils and essences he had never heard of, sitting next to pickled remains of brains and hearts, even skulls. Next to those were heavy brass horse charms in varying symbols, and decks of hand-illustrated tarot cards housed in velvet pouches. There were blank, faceless plush dolls in the shape of humans, which Clark surmised were for cursing, scrying mirrors and crystal balls Clark imagined were for divination, and in one drawer— *of course*—teacup sets and tea leaves of every flavor for reading. Except, these were no typical teacups: these sets were hand-painted with runes and inscriptions.

All the while, Clark would steal a glance at the terrarium and its miniature tree, as if it were watching him back. There was no denying there was something extraordinary about it.

At the table, Monica broke away from her laptop to look at her phone. "Melissa needs you in the library," she said, "when you're finished."

Clark was not even aware there was a library. He had only made a dent in the Closet's cleaning list, to Monica's disdain. With an exasperated sigh, she escorted him downstairs to Main, to that first room he had explored on his first day, the one with the enormous portrait of Charisma.

"The library is where Charisma keeps her most valued possessions," Monica said, "so no touchy." She led him to a shelf on the northernmost wall, to a small statue of two hands intertwined. Monica grasped the highest of the hands at its middle finger and snapped it backward. With a crack, the bookshelf popped out of place in its mounting and swiveled open to reveal a hidden entrance to a softly lit study beyond. Inside, Melissa was already waiting.

"Oh good. I'll give him back to you quick, girl," Melissa said. "Promise."

"Yeah, right . . ." Monica flashed a terse half smile before turning on foot.

"Just kidding," Melissa said smugly once she left. She turned to Clark and sized him up and down. "I need you for a bit."

Clark gulped: this was their first time alone.

The library was filled floor-to-ceiling with shelving, containing many volumes of old books, most stored, dustless, behind windowpane cabinetry. The loft above contained more valuables illuminated under the soft glow of lamp light, including a bust of Medusa, an urn, a box, and a golden lamp, all of which said "Do not under any circumstances open." Propped in a glass container in the center of the room was an ancient-looking sword set in a laser-cut stone. All were stored away under lock and key. There were cameras everywhere, but the sword, Clark noticed, had its own. His imagination ran wild thinking about what knowledge awaited his discovery here.

"So," Melissa said suddenly to Clark, who was taken aback, "Gran died and I got the townhouse—finally! How about you? What's your story?"

"Oh, I, um . . . I'm sorry to hear about your Gran," Clark said, dumbfounded. "I'm from Astoria."

Melissa looked at him, perplexed, and then it dawned on her. "Ohhhh yeah, that's right."

Clark finished her sentence in his head: *"—you're poor!"*

Melissa returned to scanning the shelves, putting Clark to work doing the fetching and the heavy lifting. They spent about an hour loading up the table with a few volumes, some relics in foreign languages Clark couldn't read, which they handled with cotton gloves. "For my house calls," she said. Clark saw her snapping photos of some of the pages with her phone. What she was documenting and for what, he couldn't be sure. She definitely didn't let him open the books himself despite his deep, desperate longing to do so. All the while, Clark swore he could see Melissa staring at him out of the corner of his eye, but when he'd turn to catch her in the act, she would avert her gaze. That he almost preferred though: there was something about her emotionless, wild eyes when she looked at him that gave him great pause, a feeling both familiar and frightening. To Clark, it was as if she was ingesting, assimilating something about him . . . or from him.

The rest of the week, Clark was carted up and down the penthouse mansion, back and forth between Monica and Melissa. Helping them organize and restock the Coven's "kits"—black luggage bags of crystals, cards, candles, and other witchy paraphernalia—which really meant doing their work entirely while the two sat on their phones or laptops. Clark had been so determined to make it on the house call Monica had mentioned that he went above and beyond, hurrying from express train to crosstown bus to get his errands done as fast as possible, taking great care with every task.

"Extra whipped cream, please," he had requested to the baristas.

"Please send it back and replace it for my boss, *Charisma Saintly*," he had said at the department store shoe rack, striking fear into the snooty salespeople with his words alone.

Clark had completed his errands and his tasks so diligently, in fact, and without an ounce of recognition, and still he had yet to hear any word of when the house call would be and when he would be tagging along to see the Great Charisma at work. Then again, wasn't this all a ruse anyway? Parlor tricks, poppycock, and just a bunch of hocus pocus? He was beginning to think so. Clark couldn't help but smile to himself nonetheless.

Charisma herself was in and out on those days. Early to leave, late to arrive, often she returned to refresh her looks before making her way to the next show or party. Sometimes, he could hear her from afar like the Ghost of the Penthouse, catching flashes of the back of her copper hair and the trail of her *floral-fag fragránce*—a term he'd coined himself in a mocking English accent—dressed in fabulous outfits and shoes, with Alicia hurrying not far behind her. Often she was on the phone as she made her exit. *Sweetie darling sweetie . . .* he parroted in his head. *So silly . . .* Why did he love to hate her so much?

On the last day of Fashion Week, as Clark helped load up the elevator with the Coven's twelve luggage bags, he mustered up the courage to approach Monica.

"Hey, Monica?" *The closed mouth doesn't get fed*, he reminded himself.

She rolled her eyes, and turned around to look at him. "What?"

"Um . . . You mentioned being able to join the Coven on a house call with Charisma if I completed my tasks. I've cleaned up the entire Closet, done my runs around town, and restocked the kits as asked, and so . . . I was wondering if I could maybe come along with you all?"

Monica turned to look him dead in the face: "You? Come along on a house call? Are you insane? I promised you no such thing." She leaned within inches of his face and said, "I thought I already told you: a good junior never forgets one's place, and a good junior never asks for more. Now, get to that list of runs I've sent you by text, and *do your job*." And that was the end of that. With her back turned, he could have sworn he heard the word "psycho" uttered under her breath.

She walked into the elevator and disappeared, leaving Clark speechless, standing in that mirrored foyer, alone in that penthouse-mansion.

* * *

The whirlwind of Fashion Week had come and gone, and the following week, the momentum had not died down. Still, Clark could not
let go of the carrot Monica had dangled, nor the goalpost she had
moved. But what could he do, what could he say when he was just
the help himself? He thought it so cruel and so despondent that that
odd swelling of his tonsils had happened again. One day he came to
work so feverish that Monica had, disgusted, sent him on errands to
keep him out of the penthouse, "Lest you get us all sick."

"I remember once being so ill with food poisoning at a house
call with Charisma," she said, "that every few minutes I was in the
bathroom, absolutely retching." Clark thought it so shameless that
she even mentioned "house call" to him. "And still, I had to show up
and work. *That's* what being a professional is about. A junior once
called out sick on an event day and was never seen here again. Last I
heard she now works at the checkout of a grocery store—in Newark."

On that day and on his way out of Hell's Entrance, delirious
and discouraged, Carolina the cook surprised Clark by bringing
him to the downstairs kitchen. She sent him home with lentil soup
and an armful of Tupperware containing the kitchen's leftovers.
That was one thing to be grateful for: being able to eat lunch at
Lorena's behest could at least give him some sense of normality,
even if he was forced to work through it. It wasn't anywhere near
the extravagant meals prepared for the assistants. Usually, it was the
maid's meals or just the scraps, but still, it was something. It seemed
that the ladies of the kitchen had banded together to leave him
food to take home from there on out, of whatever leftovers would
otherwise go to waste, in a discreet corner of the fridge. It seemed
to Clark that this was their way of quietly letting him know he was
not as alone as he thought.

A few days later, one more surprise came unexpectedly.

Melissa was escorting Clark back up to the Closet where Monica
was when, in the elevator, she leaned in close.

"Hey, kid," she said in a lowered voice, "I'm getting the fuck out
of here. Why don't you come with me and make some real coin?"

Dare I ask why . . . ? Clark whispered back, "What do you mean? Where are you going?" He glanced up at the elevator's camera.

"I'm taking my clients and starting my own coven—and quick. I'm breaking out of this shit hole."

A "shit hole" . . . ? We're riding in one of this shit hole's three private elevators . . . "Aw, why is that?" he said, feigning interest.

"It's time I did my own thing. I've got my clients eating out of the palm of my hand; they'll come with me wherever I go. Life's too short to be working like this. Nobody becomes Charisma by working for Charisma!"

Clark squinted, skeptical at hearing all this.

"Besides, I'm tired of working with little *British bitch house sitters* like you-know-who. What are they paying you here, anyway? Nothing, I bet."

Why lie . . . ? he thought. "Juniors don't get paid."

Melissa stood up and back with a look of prideful contempt. "See what I mean?"

Clark almost wondered why she was confiding in him of all people, the junior, when he was just the help, but he figured that was likely the exact reason why. Under this roof, he was voiceless and powerless. When he paused to consider this, coming from a woman who had bragged about inheriting her deceased grandma's townhouse in their first moments alone, he was not surprised in the slightest.

Ding. The elevator door opened to the fourth floor and Melissa turned and looked at him, and in a flash, Clark had an idea. He was actually a little pleased with himself at how effortlessly the words had come, even through a throat that was still a little sore.

"Melissa . . ." Clark began slowly and quietly. "Who's that guy that's been coming up to the penthouse?"

"That's Charisma's financial advisor," she said dismissively.

"Nah, not him. This one isn't a delivery guy either. I mean, at least I don't think he is, I've never seen him with deliveries or anything like that. He's always sneaking out in the early mornings before I start."

"What's he look like?"

"He's youngish—older than me but not by much. Bearded, muscular, deep voice. Really hot. I just wanted to know if, you know, he's someone's husband, or someone's boyfriend . . ."

At that, as Clark made to step out onto the landing, Melissa blocked him with her arm. Hastily, she pressed Lower Level. The doors closed again, taking them back down for one more lap.

"No, none of our husbands look like that, they're old and dusty as shit! How many times have you seen this guy?"

"Oh, just a couple," he said. "He was at Charisma's birthday." Truthfully, Clark hadn't seen him since Charisma's return from holiday, but Clark couldn't get him out of his mind.

"Really . . ." Melissa said, racking her brain. She turned to face him. "You know you can tell me anything, right, kid? You can trust me." Her eyes were hungry with intrigue. "Promise."

"Oh, it's nothing, I swear," he demurred. "It's just that, I thought this was, you know, a mostly female-centric team, and that I was one of the only guys."

Melissa's eyes were searching, and Clark could see alarms going off in her head. The elevator opened and Melissa pressed the button for Four again.

"Yeah," Clark said. "He sneaks in—I mean, *he comes up* through the help's entrance. I'd seen him *all the time* when I started, before you came back from your vacation."

Spell it out for her, Clark.

"But then again, for those weeks, it was just me and Monica here, so . . ."

A bemused smirk crept onto Melissa's face. "Thanks for telling me, kid," she said with those wild eyes.

"No problem," he replied.

Ding. Clark and Melissa had arrived.

Melissa spoke briefly to Monica, something about a contract and "paying the paps at Witch's New Year," whatever that meant. No sooner had she left did he begin to sing like a canary.

"Monica?" Clark said.

She let out an exasperated sigh. "What? What is it now?"

"Just a question . . . I've been wondering: what's next for you after Charisma's?"

Monica eyed him suspiciously. "Think you're being funny? What are you getting on about?"

Clark's ears began to heat. "I mean, what happens when an assistant like you has done all she can here? Does she get promoted? Does she move on? Does she, say . . . take her clients with her?"

Monica looked at him through slanted, cutting eyes. After a pause, she answered: "A few witches have come through Charisma's and gone on to make a name for themselves. Take Queenie Mitchell, for example, whom Charisma once sent to the Carters when she was away. They loved Queen's work so much that they continued to book her, and the rest is history. Now she's practically American royalty in her own right."

Clark nodded in understanding, and in relief. "So, this Queenie Mitchell, when she left, Charisma knew?"

"Of *course* Charisma knew."

"And Charisma knew that Queenie was taking her clients?"

"Queenie didn't *take* her clients; Charisma had sent her blessings. She is like a fairy godmother that way. Nobody takes a client from Charisma and gets away with it, and I mean *nobody*. Why do you ask?"

"Oh, nothing," Clark said. "I'm still learning is all . . . It's just that, I overheard one of the assistants is planning to go out on her own soon, and taking her clients with her."

Monica turned away from her laptop and looked at him with narrowed eyes. "Who?" she asked. "Who's going out on their own?"

"Oh, I can't say . . ."

"Tell me," she ordered. "Now."

Bingo . . . Clark had struck a nerve.

"I don't want to get anyone in trouble," he said. "I thought you knew already . . . And Charisma," he thought to add.

Monica's ears perked. "Who? Is it Alicia?"

Clark shrugged.

"Emily?"

Clark shrugged again. "I haven't spent much time with either of them yet," Clark said carefully.

"I see . . ." A smile dawned on Monica's face and yet didn't quite reach those cold gray eyes. "Get back to work," she said. She stood up and, as quick as her stilettos could carry her, exited the room.

A few days later, it was one of those rare moments where Emily, Monica, Melissa, and Clark had the penthouse to themselves while Charisma and Alicia were out.

Monica led Clark to the main floor's north wing, where Lorena's office was, except she took him into a room adjacent with a long table and chairs. A meeting room. She had him lay out black folders at every seat. He slid one open: the contents were the financial forecast for the year ahead, of Charisma's various name brands. The numbers didn't add up to Clark. How else was Charisma making her billions? Monica appeared at his side suddenly and startled Clark, but she was luckily too enmeshed with her cell phone and emails to notice him snooping.

When the assistants entered, ahead of Charisma and Alicia's arrival, Lorena paused at the door.

"You," she said, beckoning that Clark *come here* with a crook of her index finger. Clark's stomach dropped. Would he be let go then for crashing the party? The two stepped outside into the hall of portraits, whose intent gazes seemed to be watching their every move.

"So," she said, "how has the 'experience' of working here been thus far?"

He wondered how to answer.

"You can tell me anything, sweetie," she said. "Trust me." Lorena looked at him with that all-too-familiar leer.

Clark wanted to tell her the truth—that Monica was a bully to him, how she had cruelly rescinded her offer to him at the eleventh hour, how Melissa had confessed to leaving and taking her clients with her. He knew, though, that nothing good would come of telling the truth, and so he did what he did best: he held his tongue. "Great.

I'm very appreciative of the opportunity of being here," he decided to say, and left it at that. He felt like a robot saying it.

"Good," she said. "I wanted to inform you that, after much . . . *deliberation*, we—that is to say, *I*—have decided to extend to you an invitation to join us for our Halloween party at So Below, Charisma's nightclub and event space—"

"Oh my GAWD!" Clark blurted. "Really?! I'd love to go, thank you!"

Lorena was visibly taken aback when he jumped up to hug her, and gingerly patted his back in return for his display of affection. She took a step back and smoothed her dress.

"You have Emily to thank this time, as she was the one who suggested you come. The theme is fairy tales, so dress accordingly."

"Thank you," Clark said again. "I'll be there."

Lorena replied solemnly, "Do not mistake my kindness for softness, boy. I haven't forgotten that you attended Charisma's birthday uninvited." At this, Clark erupted in a small sweat. "My word still stands. No funny business. No more stepping out of line."

"Yes, absolutely," Clark said. Despite what had happened the last time he got his hopes up, Clark couldn't help but feel elated, knowing he had something to look forward to. *Maybe good things happen after all . . .*

Clark was about to find out how wrong he could be.

CHAPTER VII

A Golden Opportunity

$\mathcal{S}$eptember rushed and bled into the sharp air of New York City fall.

The city was quick with transition and the crisping of caramel leaves. The sun went down sooner on those long October workdays: Clark would awake every day that month as it rose, and as the blue RFK Bridge disappeared into the morning sky. In the evenings, he would leave in time to catch the sunset outside the windows of his train rides home. Then, he would rise and do it all over again, his work grind seven to seven, seven days a week. Clark felt as if he was riding his body until the wheels fell off.

His only constant was his morning gardenia-tobacco spritz of *Charisma Eau de Parfum,* and the soreness in his throat that just wouldn't go—a consequence, perhaps, of biting his tongue and swallowing his pride as often as he did. Perhaps there was no helping it. Clark had gotten used to putting his needs and his very personhood from his mind when there was work to be done, dreams to chase, a life to upgrade. When he stopped to think for too long, however, he just couldn't be so sure what he was running towards, what he was leaving behind, or if his dreams were chasing him.

At Charisma's, pitting Monica and Melissa against each other had been a little too easy when they had already been looking for reasons to be hateful. Clark thought giving them a distraction in one another would lessen their abuse of him, but he was wrong. Nothing changed for the better. Not only were they working him, he was also answering to Melissa's personal errands on top of Charisma's, Monica's, and the rest.

Today at work, Clark had written in his diary, *after I ran her dry cleaning and walked in on her sneaking photos of books in the library again, Melissa gave me the rest of her box of cookies she raided from the pantry—only because she was too lazy to return it to the kitchen or throw it out herself. I'll take that as her way of being sweet. She seems to think I'm her little pet.*

I think she's gotten comfortable with me, to say the least . . .

Then, later in the day, Monica had an announcement for when the assistants were together.

"Girls," she said as she returned from the kitchen, "whoever keeps putting the empty fro-yo cartons back in the fridge, please refrain."

I watched a look of recognition flash across Melissa's face.

Monica said, "Some people are animals and were just not raised right . . ."

Monica cut Melissa a look as she sat down but it was too quick for Melissa to catch. Melissa mocked Monica behind her back, miming her words to no one but herself, and I almost laughed out loud.

Monica confronted her, of course. "Are you mocking me?"

Then they started to argue. Alicia had to step in and separate them.

Maybe this was a bad idea, telling Melissa that Monica, a married woman, is inviting a man to Charisma's during after-work hours, and Monica that Melissa is planning on leaving and taking Charisma's clients with her. All that means Monica and Melissa are at each other's necks more than ever. Maybe my pitting them against each other has worked a little too well.

I wonder what it will take to stop what I started . . .

Monica and Melissa had taken to shamelessly bickering so much that Clark was actually happy to be out of the penthouse and running errands—"Cici's Delivery Service," he and Joey had come to call it ("If only I could fly on a broom around town," Clark mused). Anything to experience the change of season in the city, and keep his mind off his birthday that was fast approaching . . .

Clark's only true reprieve in those days was his sleepovers with Joey, who had sorta kinda spent so much time at his that he had practically moved in. It started casually enough, when Joey met Clark the Tuesday after Labor Day to drive him home. Clark invited him up and he never really left. Clark was worried Joey would think his apartment juvenile and poor.

On the contrary: "I love it," Joey had said.

Slowly, Clark noticed Joey's work schedule transitioning to morning and afternoon shifts and not his coveted evening shifts, despite Clark's protests, just so they could spend time together. "Don't argue with your assistant manager," he said with a cheeky smile. "It's just weekdays. I'm keeping weekend nights at the bar. Besides, it's a chance to let somebody else move up."

Joey would arrive with "ganja and mangia," which he said to mean a lot of weed and a lot of food packed from Northlight's Michelin-star kitchen, or his mother's home-cooked leftovers, or pizza from around the corner, or takeout, or fast food, whatever they could manage. Joey understood Clark's limited means. He didn't even judge the dollar-store taquitos.

Sometimes Joey would even cook for them: chicken parmigiana, salmon with asparagus, tortellini with red sauce, Nonna Margaret's famous meatballs (the way Joey would talk with his shoulders, bumping them up and down and mocking a Brooklyn accent, was enough to catch a giggle out of Clark).

First, the cabinets were filled with seasonings, then the drawers with changes of clothes, and then, well . . . Clark didn't mind any of it though. He loved the company. He loved watching Joey cook. He loved to be with Joey. They'd eat in bed and put on a movie just to kiss to, any excuse to spend their nights in together. Anything to not sleep alone during Clark's recurring, almost nightly nightmares of the assistants and Charisma and their wicked laughter, waking him at three in the morning every time.

To Clark's fond delight and appreciation, Joey even let him vent about work.

"The other day, all the assistants and I were together when Monica goes, *'Whoever smells like garlic and onions should really consider* bathing *before showing up to work'*—looking right at me, of course." Clark delivered this in Monica's affected way of speaking as he washed the dishes after Joey's cooking.

"And was she mistaken?" Joey teased.

"She isn't wrong!" Clark said. He stepped away to put a saucepan under a leak from the nighttime rain.

"You smell like roses to me, baby!" Joey said. He hugged Clark from behind and kissed him on the neck. "No, really. Like flowers and something woodsy-smoky. I like it!"

Clark didn't tell Joey that he'd started wearing copious amounts of *Charisma the Eau de Parfum*, hoping to mitigate any criticism and throw her off his tail, or at least avert Monica's attention. In the way Joey couldn't keep his hands off of him, however, the perfume seemed to work as advertised.

"Oh—and I finally got to assisting Charisma's niece, Alicia."

"The one who was powdering her nose at the party you crashed?" Joey asked. He wiggled his nose and took a seat at Clark's little drop-leaf table.

"Ha! Yeah, that one. She's actually a really cool girl! She made a comment about my high-tops. She said, 'That's so brave of you,' that she used to wear the same in middle school. *'Brave of you.'* Can you believe?"

"I guess with this group, that's a compliment," Joey said.

"Yeah, tell me about it! Progress. She's closer in age to us than to Monica and Melissa. Monica caught her and me chatting and tried to steal me away, and Alicia put her in her place. 'Leave him alone and do it yourself. He's mine.' I mean, who would mess with the boss's niece, you know what I mean? When Monica left in a huff, Alicia told me about how she knew Monica growing up, as if she was dying to gossip. She said her family is super well known in the wi—*their* community, and that they *'quite wrongfully'* think they're better than everyone else."

"*Whaaat?*" Joey remarked sarcastically. "I don't believe that for a minute." They both giggled.

Clark couldn't bring himself to explain everything to Joey—not the part about them thinking that they were witches and running some kind of occult operation. *At least not yet anyway . . .* He couldn't risk losing Joey's respect or interest. He cared a lot about him . . . *a lot* a lot. "I know, right?! Alicia even mentioned something about how growing up, there was an I Hate Monica club. The superintendent practically asked her to switch schools, and not because *she* was the one being bullied."

"Wow, that's crazy," Joey said. "But how do you know that's true?"

Clark paused. "I'm not sure. Why would Alicia lie?"

"Why wouldn't she?" Joey asked. "That's just petty gossip between bored, catty, rich mean girls."

"Yeah, maybe . . ." Clark said. *You're losing him, Clark . . .* he thought. "Still, maybe it's truer than not. I feel kinda . . . bad for her."

"You do?" Joey asked in surprise, crossing his arms.

"Yeah."

"Why?"

Clark shrugged. "Because maybe if she had been loved the right way, she wouldn't have turned out to be so vicious."

Joey shifted in his seat. "I dunno, Clark. Some people are just rotten to the core, no matter how much love you give them. You can't out-love someone's shitty personality."

"Hmm, you're probably right . . . Oh! I almost forgot to tell you! The other day, I accidentally forgot to give Monica's credit card back after a run to some boutique or other, and you should have seen the bitchfit she threw."

"No . . . !"

"Yep. Words like 'incompetent' and 'useless' were thrown around."

Joey put his glass down. "Clark! She can't say that to you!"

"Yeah, well, she did. No matter how much I tried to reason with her that it wasn't my fault she never asked for it back and sent me on the next errand super quick, the blame still landed on me. I had to turn right around when I got back home. And then she made me chase her all around the city because by then, she had already left Charisma's and gone out to some apartment on the West Side High-way. That woman is *impossible*. By the time I got home, I was totally *exhaustles*. Ugh! You should see the way they look at me like I'm some poor little bug from Queens! Like some kind of second-class citizen." Clark looked around his shoebox apartment with an expression he was sure said, *Well, maybe they're not wrong . . .*

Joey stood up. He wrapped his arms around Clark and playfully gave him a tight squeeze. "Hey, baby, I'm sorry. You shouldn't be treated like that," he said. Joey always had the best reactions. He always knew the right things to say or what not to say, or when to gasp, or when to laugh. Their high-time sleepovers were Clark's little adventures, a sooty respite from his workdays, innocent and carefree.

The first night Joey slept over after their date on Labor Day, Joey said, "I have a surprise for you." He held out a small confection for Clark. "*Wouldst thou like to live deliciously?*" he asked.

Clark gasped in feigned shock. "You devil, you! Is that, a treat? For me?"

"Just for you, baby," he said. "You know I wouldn't show up empty-handed." They each downed a single mini edible brownie. Clark and Joey gorged themselves on pizza and soda that night and laughed until they were unable to stay vertical. They fell back into hand-me-down pillows in an embrace of sweet, deep kisses as the sun set, while swallows flew low and gave chase outside, and butterflies tapped on the windows. That night, they didn't let go. That night, Joey traced the constellations of Clark's beauty marks. That night, Clark and Joey flew.

In his dreams, Clark lifted up off his bed as if hooked by the navel, where the butterflies lived. First, he looked down at his body and saw himself sound asleep. Then, he looked to the opened win-dow and flew out of his apartment, over the watchful tower eyes of the RFK Bridge, and into that uninterrupted Astoria night sky.

Friday the 24th of October arrived. It was Clark's birthday, and he was twenty-four years old.

At Charisma's, the girls were preparing for something.

"Remind me, babes," Melissa asked Alicia, "what time is the eclipse at its greatest again?"

"11:42," Alicia answered.

"She's crazy," Melissa said. "What is she thinking, doing this during an eclipse? She knows better than anyone that that kind of chaos magic is unpredictable."

Alicia shrugged.

"There's an eclipse tonight?" Clark asked. Neither Alicia nor Melissa answered. Clark pulled his phone up to confirm.

"Um, excuse me," Monica snapped, "what do you think you're doing?" She looked down at the phone in Clark's hand and back at him, and so did Melissa and Alicia. "Don't you have something better to do besides be on your phone? Your job, perhaps?"

"I was looking up . . . Never mind." *It's not worth it, Clark . . . Play nice and don't let her win on your birthday . . .* he thought. Besides, the sun was out. Clark was wearing his favorite, baby-blue button-down. There was nothing that could ruin his day.

When he was done helping Monica and Melissa pack their kits of crystals and sage and other trinkets, seeing them off to their respective house calls, Emily handed an ancient tome to Clark and let him into the Closet. In front of the almost wall-length, gold-framed mirror opposite the door, they stopped. Emily held her open left hand towards her, flipped it out towards her reflection, and then pushed her palm up into the air. The mirror clicked, and it swung open to reveal yet another secret door. Clark's body erupted into a sweat. Surely it was a high-tech mirror? Facial recognition technology?

It revealed a landing of an iron and glass staircase, containing hanging broomsticks like a billiards hall. She sent him up that winding staircase to a circular room. It was lined with floor-to-ceiling windows, their shades shuttered down to diffuse the sunlight outside. There was a decal under the floor's glass surface, of a large, faint white ring that paralleled its perimeter. Enclosed within that circle was an opening in the floor, under the glassy surface. Clark drew nearer to it and looked down onto the top of the terrarium in the Closet. Clark felt as if it was staring back up at him.

"She calls this the Tower," Emily said. "It's Charisma's own private practice space. Witches have been relegated to practicing underground and in hiding for so long; here we work out in the open. The Coven will be meeting tonight for a ritual ceremony—and you are going to help prepare our circle." She held up a piece of chalk.

Clark asked, "I am . . . ?"

"You want to be more involved with the Coven, right?" She gave him a teasing nudge and plopped the chalk into his hand. "Don't be scared."

"But I'm not a, you know . . . one of you," he said. "I wouldn't know how."

"Oh, please," Emily said. "It's all about intention. All you have to do is focus on us having a successful ceremony, and draw steady lines. Easy."

Clark looked at the floor and then at the chalk, rolling it over in his hands, and then at her.

"I'll show you," she said with a glint in her eyes.

First, Emily had him trace the circle already inlaid under the translucent floor. Then, she held a roll of twine and extended it at different angles, which Clark used to trace straight lines. While they squatted and drew, they chatted excitedly about Halloween and what they would wear, and what parties from previous years were like.

"This was before I worked for her, but one year, they had a Halloween party so big it didn't stop until the second of November."

"Oh, wow," Clark said. "Thank you for suggesting I come," he added.

"Of course. You've made it this long, and that's an accomplishment on its own. You're one of us now."

Clark couldn't be so sure about that.

"So," Emily continued, "how are you liking it here so far?"

There it was . . . that question again . . .

Then, in a lowered voice, she added, "We're all so full of shit, aren't we? At dinner with the Coven once, I heard Alicia say, 'This steak is absolutely *gorgeous.*'" Emily said this in a most mocking English accent. "I mean—'gorgeous'? Really? It's a steak. Like, shut the fuck up."

Clark unwittingly laughed.

"And Monica—man, can she be a real mean girl, huh . . . ?"

Clark looked at her, not wanting to say a thing. Where was all of this going and what was she asking of him? Was it appropriate? Was it a setup? This was his first time alone with Emily, and she was, after all, another one in Charisma's ranks. Clark couldn't help but look around for cameras or eavesdropping ears in that furniture-less, resonant room, and down where the floor dipped into the opening to the Closet, and the terrarium below them.

"No cameras here, babe," she said. "No one can hear you, don't worry. But, it's cool, it means you're a good person for not wanting to talk shit. I understand . . ."

Clark surprised them both when he replied anyway. "Yeah, she's a total frigid bitch."

Emily gasped at what he had just said aloud, and Clark felt like a kid cursing for the first time. They laughed. Maybe he had been waiting to say that.

"No one really likes her here. Her family is well-connected, and she *is* good at what she does, but I mean, none of us are actually friends. Just coworkers. Two witches don't make a right, I guess. Maybe it's for the best, boundaries being healthy and stuff." A sad smile registered on Emily's face. Clark nodded and met her eyes, which were a twinkling blue-green. "Welcome to Girl World!"

"I, uh," he said, "kinda get the feeling I'm always being watched and listened to when I'm here . . ."

"That's because you are," she said. Clark's stomach did a flip, and he instantly thought about his chance encounter with Miss Honey, and his lean-in in the elevator with Melissa just a couple of weeks prior. "But not here. Not by Monica, not by Lorena, and not by Charisma." She mocked, "*It's* so *good to see you, sweetie darling.*" To Clark's delight, he and Emily stood up and feigned an air kiss cheek to cheek, first on the left, and then on the right. They smiled.

Emily showed him how to draw sigils and runes around the circle from the book they took up, and when completed, they both stepped back to admire their handiwork. Within the pentacle were smaller circles and crescents: they had drawn phases of the moon.

"Good job, babe," Emily said, holding out her hand for the chalk.

"Thanks!" Clark said. He couldn't remember receiving praise or recognition for a single thing he had done there, not a one, and he couldn't help but smile up at her. It was her birthday gift to him if there ever was one. Somehow, Clark's sore throat felt a little bit better that day. He plopped the chalk into her open palm.

The moment their hands touched, Emily inhaled a sharp breath and looked at him with wide eyes. Clark didn't make anything of it.

It was half past seven and the sun had already set by the time Clark raced out of Charisma's building, already late for his birthday dinner. Monica had kept him longer than usual, having him unpack her kit while she and the others headed to the kitchen for a "family meal." It was almost as if she knew she would be keeping him from plans. At the coffee shop, there was always a tray of cupcakes with a candle and a card.

Clark so wondered what it would be like to sit with the Coven, what they talked about over food, what it would be like to have a seat at that table . . .

Clark's social media was decidedly quiet that day, and there had been almost no birthday messages. He checked his texts on the walk up, pausing at stoplights:

(11:11 a.m. Patricia Hartford): Happy birthday, Clarkykins! I'm sorry I can't make it tonight, Ma's sick and I'm taking care of the doc's cat while he's out of town for work. I send my love with Nancy and Paul. Come over soon, I'll cook you something! Love you! It's 11:11 make a wish!

(1:10 p.m. Maria): Happy birthday, pumpkin! It's officially your birth time . . . I'm sending you some money. Buy yourself something nice. Love you— Mom

(4:42 p.m. Katie Bredford): Happy birthday to my beautiful friend with an even more beautiful soul <3 I can't make it out tonight, I'm sorry. I'll make it up to you. Love you xo

(5:30 p.m. Krystal Johnson): Happy birthday, boo! I'm headed into a dance class and then I'll be right there! <3

(5:59 p.m. Justin Trinh): Hey ghourl, I can't make it tonight. Let's meet for drinks this week or after Halloween. First round's on me. Happy birthday!

(6:45 p.m. Alexander Watkins): Hey cutie, happy bday! I can't make it for din after all but lmk if you're out and about tn.

Clark made a mental note to take Patricia up on her delicious cooking. She had been suspiciously absent since that summer when she last spoke with him about the interview. His mother, on the other hand—while he was grateful for the text and the money that would go straight to bills—he would get back to . . .

Clark's friend Krystal, whom he had known since middle school, was always out to a party, on a date or two, or out to dance class, so he expected nothing less of her. Justin, Clark would catch later. They'd met at a gay bar and would go out now and again, Clark's ventures being infrequent. Their nights would always end in Justin leaving him for a guy, a pattern Clark had come to accept. Alex, he'd met on a dating app, and after the first kiss asked to be friends (although Clark could see the dismay register on his face, Alex agreed, better to have him than to not). While Clark was a little sad but understanding to hear Justin and Alex wouldn't be joining, he was the most disappointed to hear about his college friend Katie. She was the closest thing he had to a best friend, one who was always down for a walk, a movie night, a pedicure (and a picture), and one whom he rarely saw, so Clark was used to this from her too.

By the time Clark arrived, the rooftop restaurant of Northlight was electric and alive with patrons dressed in their Friday night best—the nouveau riche and old money, young and old alike, on their pregame before hitting the town. Northlight was loud and raucous with the sound of feverish conversations and stemware clinking on tabletops and the drone of waitstaff and bussers darting in between tables. It was most certainly the night of a full moon, he thought. Clark gave his name at the stand, and the hostess gave him a knowing smile.

"Happy birthday!" she told him. "Right this way."

As they walked past the bar, Joey flashed him a smirk and a wink, mouthing, *"Hey!"* The hostess informed him that—surprise—he was booked at the best section of the restaurant, at a table with the best view. Clark knew he had Joey to thank for it; he had admitted as much to Clark, having surprised him with a reservation made over a month prior. The gesture was so thoughtful that Clark could not recall another one quite like it.

Already seated and awaiting his arrival was Patricia's daughter Nancy, her husband, Paul, and their four-year-old, Eva. "There he is!" they chimed in unison.

Clark gave them each a hug and a kiss on the cheek. "I'm sorry I'm late! I got caught up at work."

"It's okay, *Mistuh Big Shot*," Nancy ragged in her thick, nasal Queens accent. "It's all good. Happy birthday! How's work going?"

Clark smiled and sighed. "I'll tell ya about it."

Joey came up to the table. "Happy birthday, Clark!"

"Thank you, Joey!" They shared a hug, chest to chest, much to the envy of a few of the women sitting at the bar, judging by the looks on their faces over Joey's shoulder. There were a few other looks from the neighboring tables, particularly at Nancy and Paul and their bridge-and-tunnel, sneakers-jeans-and-jerseys manner, out of place in a restaurant like Northlight. Clark admired that Joey didn't seem to care either way.

He introduced himself with his overeager and firm handshake, and with a slap on the back, asked Clark, "What can I get you to drink? First round's on me, anything you like!"

"Anything?" Clark asked coyly. "Why don't you surprise me?"

Joey smiled. "One birthday surprise for the cutest boy around, coming right up!" After taking Nancy and Paul's orders, he took his leave—and both of them watched the back of him as he walked away. They turned to look at one another, and then at Clark, whose face was deepening into a blush. Paul whistled.

"Oh, so now we know why you wanted to meet here," Paul teased, smoothing his goatee and nodding. "Who's the guy, Clark?"

Clark explained how they met on the job about a month prior, and how Joey was the one to suggest hosting his birthday there.

"Not too shabby," Paul replied, holding up his thumb and index finger to sign "nice."

"I'm just happy you guys could make it. Thanks for being here," Clark said. "A couple of my friends aren't coming after all."

"That's okay! We're happy to be out," Nancy said. "We don't get out to many fancy places with Eva—isn't that right, sweetie," she said, tickling Eva. Eva didn't flinch, too deep in her coloring on her children's menu to acknowledge her mother. She drew a princess in a tall tower being struck by lightning. "Besides, we're better than friends, aren't we, Clarky? We're family. You and I, we've known each other our entire lives. Remember when I used to babysit you? Wasn't that fun?!"

Clark grinned. His phone buzzed; Krystal had texted him back:

(8:05 p.m. Krystal Johnson): My love! I'm finishing up a drink real quick with the crew. I'll leave for you right after, promise!

Joey returned soon after with their drinks. "Bartender's special: a midnight margarita for the birthday boy." Clark's margarita was a dark periwinkle over vaporous, smoking dry ice, with red chili-pepper salt and a star-shaped flower tucked in. "A circle of salt for protection, a lime for purification, a blue-borage flower for courage, joy, and a spicy rim—salty and sweet with a bite. Cheers!" Joey gave a wink to Clark and smiled as he left them. Clark blushed even harder.

* * *

When the pleasantries were over and the meal underway, Nancy and Paul reached for his gift: a black button-down one size too big, from one of those department stores that resold clothing at heavily discounted prices.

"You didn't have to get me anything! Thanks, guys!" Clark said. "I can wear it to work. They like wearing black. *A lot.*"

Nancy asked, "How are you liking this new job? It's an internship with Charisma Saintly's personal team, right? Ma told us."

"Yeah, it's great," Clark began. "Except, well . . . it kinda sucks!"

Clark unloaded it all on them, speaking fervently with his hands, how he had quickly become the errand-boy-lackey he had never imagined being, working from seven to seven, sometimes out in the city all day. He explained how juggling his time there with weekends at the coffee shop to get by meant he was not only exhausted but depleted in every way; how Monica had been bullying him, reprimanding him, and had even gone as far as to "accidentally" lock him in a closet. "Not even the doorwomen will look me in the eyes," he confessed. The note he ended on was that through everything, he hadn't even personally met Charisma yet.

At first, Nancy looked at him and then Paul with crinkled eyebrows in disbelief, and then, her face softened with understanding. "Aw, I'm sorry, Clark. But, you know what you gotta do, right . . . ?" she asked. "Suck it up and stick it out, or quit."

Clark was taken aback. "What? What do you mean?"

Paul leaned in. "How old are you, today, twenty-three?"

"Twenty-four." Clark pulled his hands under the table.

"That's right. Twenty-four . . ." Paul said. "Listen, this is the problem with your generation: entitlement—"

"Paul, lemme do this," Nancy said, putting her hand up. "You twenty-somethings put in the bare minimum and fail to develop the work ethic necessary to get the job done. Then you call it a 'toxic' workplace, and you quit! I've seen it firsthand: you learn it in movies and on TV, see it on social media, how to get rich quick without putting any real work in, but you can't get something from nothing."

Clark had to remind himself that Nancy was only older than him by seven or eight years, and Paul a little over ten.

"You are lucky to be in a workplace like that, let alone employed, especially without a college degree."

At this, his ears blushed red.

"You're *lucky* to be in their presence, Clark. You could learn a thing or two from them. You know, your generation is so impatient, jumping from one job to the next, that if I see a résumé like that at the doctor's office, I throw it out! I don't even waste my time! No sense in entertaining someone lazy who can't stick it out. Ma's been at the doc for over thirty years. How long have you been there? A month? Maybe two?"

"Yeah, but . . ." Clark began, "this feels, like, weirdly exploitive and—"

"Clark," she said. "It's a competitive internship. You gotta get your head in the game. The common denominator is *you.* Change it up. Do something different. If they don't respect you, make 'em! Take this golden opportunity for what it is, make the best of it, and if you feel any differently, then leave. Honestly though, if it were me, I would march right up to that Charisma and introduce myself to her personally. Show her who I am and what I'm made of. Otherwise, if you can't run with the big dogs, you better stay on the porch. Sorry, but it's the truth . . ."

Make them respect me, and march right up to her . . . he mused. Clark had not forgotten about how Charisma had looked at him at her birthday party. He wasn't so convinced Nancy's old-school, working-class approach applied, but something about her words remained. Still, Clark wondered: could he resign himself to the fact that maybe this was the price he would have to pay for success? For his dreams to come true?

Is this as good as it gets . . . ?

As the plates were taken and the table was cleared, Clark couldn't help but notice how many times he had looked to the door, half expecting a friend to surprise him and show up. He reached for his phone to text Krystal.

(9:19 p.m. Clark Crane): Hey boo, you coming?

He didn't have to wait long for the reply:

(9:24 p.m. Krystal Johnson): Hey my love, I'm sorry, I'm
super tired. I'm gonna head home. Lemme catch up with
you another night this week <3

Clark put his phone away, and when he looked up, a small chocolate cake was floating from the kitchen to the table, held aloft by a
crooning Joey DiMuccio, with a single birthday candle alight in its
center. As Clark looked across the table at the busy restaurant, where
Friday-night guests corralled around friends and plates looking so
unburdened and carefree, Clark couldn't help but feel a little disappointed, even a little envious. That Ideal Self from his dreams, so
actualized, so tangible, and yet so out of reach, frowned in disdain
and disappointment across his mind's eye. But then, as he looked up
at Nancy, Paul, and Eva, Joey, and the neighboring tables smilingly
watching, he thought, so what if he was young and poor and figuring it all out? So what if none of his friends showed up? He was just
happy to be surrounded by people who gave a damn, at a table he'd
probably never have gotten on his own, drinking something other
than tap water.

"Make a wish, Clark!" Joey said. As he looked into that candle,
he wondered what it was that he really wanted. He thought, *I wish
. . . that something amazing would happen . . . That this year will be
magical, my best yet . . . That this is the year all my dreams finally come
true . . . Security, purpose, and love . . . I'm gonna have it all . . .* He
blew the candle out to the congratulatory clapping of those around
him.

The plates were dispensed, the stations returned, and life resumed,
all so fast: Nancy and Paul to entertain Eva and her slice of cake, Joey
the handsome spectacle shaking drinks behind the bar, and the guests
in neighboring tables back to their lives.

Hard part's over . . . Clark thought to himself.

When the waiter arrived with the check, Paul snatched the bill from Clark's hands before he could even read it. "We got this," Paul said sternly. "Put your money away. Our treat."

"Yeah, don't get *goofy*," Nancy said. "You deserve it, Clarky. Happy birthday."

By eleven o'clock, Nancy, Paul, and Eva had long since bid Clark farewell. Dinner was ending, the night was underway, and Clark had found a single seat at the end of the bar. The DJ looked oddly similar to the one at Charisma's birthday . . .

"Birthday shots!" Joey said over the music, sliding up to him. The smell of the tequila alone was enough to send Clark reeling. "Cheers, baby!"

"Cheers!" They shot it back. Was this his Fifth? Sixth? Joey kept refilling his midnight margaritas and Clark had lost count.

"I'm here for another couple more hours," Joey told him. Clark knew that when a native New Yorker told you they were a "couple" of anything away, not to believe them. "Please stay! You're more than welcome to hang!"

But Clark could barely get a word in between all of Joey's orders and the hubbub. "It's been a long day," he said. "I think I'm gonna go home." Despite Joey's protests—"*It's a full moon. The weirdos are out,*" he said with a wink. "Don't go home alone without this weirdo"—Clark told Joey not to worry about him; that he would be fine. Clark even refused a cab ride, stating that Joey had done enough for him and he couldn't accept. Then Joey's manager, Louis, called him over, and Clark didn't even get a chance to get a goodbye kiss before departing.

Maybe it was instinct leading the way, or maybe it was just the tequila (*definitely the tequila,* Clark thought): as he exited Northlight, he walked the electric streets of NYC, not in the direction of the train, but retraced his steps instead, and found himself in no time standing outside of the employee entrance of Charisma's building. If he could just catch a glimpse of their ritual, he thought, he could see what kind of witches they were and what they were up to. Clark was just taking Nancy's advice and being an opportunist, after all, and this opportunity had come to Clark a-knockin'.

"Hello?" he said up to the camera, ringing the doorbell and giving a dithering wave. "It's me, Clark, the new junior." The red security camera light stared back, unmoved.

"Remember me? From . . . every morning at seven?" A thought occurred to him: *What if it's a different security guard this late at night . . . ? How will you be let up now, Clark . . . ?*

"They're expecting my help upstairs at Charisma's—something about a, uh, meeting. A small party, but—please don't ring them. That would be very bad."

Clark looked up at the camera. *Please let me up, please let me up . . .* he thought.

"Yep! Very bad!" he said to the camera. "Oh, you know them! They wouldn't want to be interrupted by anyone, not around this time of night, let alone because of silly ol' me."

The camera blinked back at him.

"Nah, you wouldn't want to make Monica angry. Or worse: Charisma. You know what happens when they get angry . . ."

A second later, and the light flashed from red to green and the door clicked open with a sustained buzz, granting him entry to the elevator up to Hell's Entrance. "Thank you!" he said. He withheld his surprise.

Clark had never seen the penthouse like it was that night: a home once abuzz with servants and assistants was now deserted and still, the help seemingly having been dismissed long before. Clark crept slowly through, around shadowed corners and statues that had taken on a new life of their own, cast in subdued relief by the city out the windows and the trail of candles that guided the way. All was quiet save for his deft footsteps, controlled breaths, and the thin, shrill ringing in his ears. In the dark of night, the penthouse had a completely different feeling: a large home with too much dead air.

With nimble, tiptoeing steps, Clark deftly crept up the stairs so as not to be heard, up to the fourth floor and to the Closet. He crouched low in that dark room, peering up through the window in the ceiling to the floor above. Sure enough, there was movement in the shadows of the Tower.

Clark approached the secret door from earlier that day, and in the mirror, held his hand as Emily did, first palm open and towards him, then away, then up.

The door opened with a small click.

He checked his watch: 11:33 p.m. He was just in time.

Without a sound, and slowly, Clark crept up the iron banister, step by step, and at the top, raised himself up ever so carefully, and peeked over the Tower's glass floor.

"Open the shutters," Charisma instructed.

The hushed voices of the Coven came to a sudden silence, storing their phones away and taking their places about two feet apart atop the circle he and Emily had drawn earlier that day. Except, it wasn't just Lorena, Alicia, Monica, Melissa, and Emily. There were six more women, twelve in total, of a mix of ages, all dressed in black. Some he did not recognize, a couple that he did from his errands. All had the same hollow eyes. He had a clear view of Charisma, who stood on the circle's northernmost edge, and the tip of the pentacle's star. As he crouched low at the lip of the floor, Clark prayed with all his being that he would go by undetected.

Monica was the only one to produce her phone, and with the push of a button, the shutters on the windows retreated into the floor to reveal a three-sixty-degree view of the city all around. Opening, too, to the night above them was a skylight that Clark had missed earlier. The October air nipped at their heels. The flickering candles around the room's floor were the only source of illumination—that and the streets and buildings far below them, a gentle nightlight. All was eerily quiet as high as they were. The coven stood reflected in that glassy floor that fell away at its perimeter to an edgeless infinity. Clark thought how they might as well be suspended in midair.

How not one of the Coven could see Clark hiding was beyond him. Maybe it was because he had practically stopped breathing. Clark did not dare move a muscle or make a sound, lest he be discovered.

"Alicia, what time is it?"

"Eleven thirty-eight."

"The eclipse is at its peak. It's time." The Coven watched Charisma with their undivided attention. She said, "Let us begin the Drawing Down of the Blood Moon."

She spoke evenly, without raising her voice. The Coven repeated after her. It was if even the walls and every building of New York City were leaning in, listening intently to her every word:

> "On this, the Night of the Divine Feminine, under your
> Eclipsed Glory, we stand. Mother Moon, by the Maiden,
> Maid, and Crone, we invoke thee, Harbinger of Fruitfulness,
> by seed and by root. We invoke thee, by stem and by bud.
> We invoke thee, by life and by love. We call upon thee to
> descend upon us, thy Body, of this thy Priestess, of this thy
> Coven, of these thy Assistants, and of this thy circle, to ask
> that you may bless us with your light . . ."

Clark became aware of two realities happening simultaneously before him, without seeing either of them clearly or at all, and yet all the while knowing both to be true:

In the first reality was the spectacle he bore witness to. The ladies stood encircled, with Charisma leading the ritual under a glass ceiling and clear night sky above. In the second, he only caught flickering glimpses until he was certain, until he understood it to be so true he knew it in his bones, in the knowing of his being, until it was as if it was happening before his very eyes: a bright red light descended from the sky above, like a stream of sunlight through a parting of clouds or a canopy of trees, through the windowed ceiling and into the middle of the witches' circle, imbuing its chalk drawings with its energy.

That red light traveled down to the in-between of the Tower and the glass window in the room's center, into the floor below, and Clark understood too, knew without evidence, that there was yet another member present of Charisma's circle: her terrarium was alive with the moon's light, feeling, responding, answering back and reaching skywards.

"Mother Moon, Great Illuminator of Truth, Energy of the
Feminine, attend our rite. By Love and by Light, enlighten
what is dark, strengthen what is weak, mend what is broken,
lift up what is fallen. Guide us tonight. We beseech thee . . ."

Quiet at first, from a few inches beyond their bodies, to a roaring
fortissimo reaching to the windows and beyond, the witches were
bathed in shimmering, waving halos of celestial light, of earthy ever-
green, cold navy, sisterly rose, blood-red crimson, and royal night-
shade. The auras undulated and danced bright and big to every word
of Charisma's voice, soaring into the open air and night sky above,
and merged into one vibrating, humming chorus of fiery light. The
ringing in Clark's ears crescendoed to a shrill pitch, and the middle
of his forehead prickled so intensely, he winced, and reached up to
scratch it. All was aglow in the Tower.

Charisma raised her arms skywards, and so too did the Coven.

"No longer is it the Time of Man, the Time of Penumbra,
the Time of Great Tempering. No longer is it the time of
War, of Loss, of Chaos.
"Tonight, we beckon the new. Tonight, we call forth the
Era of Woman. No longer will we hide in the shadows. No
longer will we be silenced. As the eclipse wanes, our power
reveals, grows, and strengthens, casting all into the Light of
Our Love.
May our power reign supreme . . ."

Clark looked down and could See too, both in that double vision
of his eyes and the eyes within his mind, that the aura of his own
hands, arms, and body was also aglow as theirs was, his a lilac-indigo
and periwinkle blue. A serene sense of calmness descended upon him,
of peace and of safety, as if he were a child again in the presence of a
guardian that had always been there just beside him, or always within
him, one filled with unconditional love and joy. It filled him with a
connectedness to everything, one he had never felt before. So, too,

were the dark corners of his being called upwards, forwards, all of the pain in his heart, all the shadowed parts of himself unknown to him and buried deep inside him, illuminated and made clear, and then made light. He felt like everything would be okay.

His aura radiated outwards and upwards, lifting up and taking flight, until it merged with the Coven's, powerful like theirs—stronger even, brighter, dancing with childlike wonder. Clark was an unwitting part of the ceremony.

Charisma lowered her arms and smiled. Gazing at her handiwork, however, she caught something out of the corner of her eye and raised an eyebrow. Still, she brought the ceremony to a close:

"We honor thee, O Glorious Oneness. We thank thee . . .
"As we will it, so mote it be . . ."

The twelve women looked at one another's auras, and the giant light surrounding them, with soft satisfaction. After some time, the light waned and returned to whence it came, though its intensity remained, humming, hanging thick in the air of the Tower. The terrarium below hummed too, like a cat purring after being fed.

The Connectedness remained, along with a self-assuredness, a feeling he couldn't quite remember the last he had known; not since he was little. Clark felt like he could do anything. For the first time in a long time, Clark had hope.

"Darlings . . ." Charisma began carefully with venomous ease. "There is one *other* part of tonight. Something in need of your attention. Something of principle, of great importance. Something . . . or *someone* . . ."

The Coven looked at one another, confused. Their auras flickered and hid away, out of sight, and Charisma spoke with a venomous ease that was as soft as it was menacing. "There is a spoiled, rotten apple in our bunch."

The Coven held onto her every word with bated breath.

"We have a traitor in our midst."

Behind the banister, Clark broke into a cold sweat and shrank. All good feelings had exited the room, including his own, dissipating like the moonlit auras.

Charisma spoke quieter still. "In this life, you are my inner circle. I consider myself to be a patient leader—a *generous* leader—wouldst thou not agree? I hold my life's work to the utmost importance, to the utmost respect, and I demand absolutely *nothing* less in return . . .

"For Emily, I had allowed grievance leave on her beloved mother's passing, for months. For Monica, I had introduced her *beloved* husband, who gave you the wedding of the century and two beautiful daughters as I had predicted. Melissa, I had allowed connection to the very best of my clientele, did I not? The presidents, the politicians, the lawyers, the financial officers, the capitalists . . . For the rest of you, Claudia, Beatrice, Lara, Victoria, Corrina, Gabrielle: I share my many Gifts, and bestow upon you opportunity. Connections. Riches. Worship. Babies."

Slowly, the Coven followed her forbidding gaze, until all came to rest upon a single member: "Melissa."

Her face fell from smug satisfaction to sheer and utter terror.

"No . . . !" she cried out, her eyes wide with fear. "I—I didn't do it! I swear! It wasn't me!"

"One of our own, ladies," Charisma said slowly, "has been courting and collecting *my* clients. This *pathetic* witch has planned to take my clients and go rogue, to start a coven of her own and usurp my throne, seemingly right from under my nose . . .

"This witch," she continued, "is a traitor to us all. Wouldn't you agree, my darlings?"

No one dared speak a word.

"It's not me!" Melissa cried. *"I swear!"*

With that double vision in his mind's eye, that ringing in his ears, a prickling of his forehead, and the uncanny feeling of déjà vu, Clark watched in awe and in terror as Charisma's charged aura surged and radiated outwards. Her lip curled as she uttered that single merciless word: "Liar."

"No! I would never! I love you! I've always loved you!" Melissa exclaimed. "You've got it all wrong!"

"When one bad apple spoils and rots, the others will surely follow," Charisma said without raising her voice. Her words were even, steeped in menace and finality. "That apple must be disposed of."

"No! I'll do anything! Anything you want! I promise! Please!" She began to tremble uncontrollably, as mascaraed tears lined her cheeks in black.

Charisma only stared down at her from atop her nose. Unmoved, she said, "One does not suffer a traitor witch to live."

"No, please!" cried Melissa. "I didn't mean to! I'm sorry! Please don't! *Please!*" Her desperation echoed, hanging in the air in that dark, round glass tower. The women of the circle merely watched, for they all knew what was to come, what none of them could stop.

"And what does a witch do to her traitor sister, my darlings?"

Sparks like lightning discharged from her pulsating aura, a glowing crimson halo that grew black and tall around her, electric with rage. Step by step, shaking her tear-streaked face, an overwrought Melissa broke the circle and carefully backed away, shaking her hands.

"Please, leave me alone! *Leave me alone!*"

At this, Charisma's face broke into that peculiar and dangerous smile, stopping just short of the apples of her cheeks, failing to reach her cunning green eyes that burned with danger. Her answer was simple: "She fires her."

"No! Stop! Leave me alone! LEAVE ME ALONE! PLEASE! NO! NO! *NOOO!*"

First came the smoke billowing from her nose, ears, and quivering mouth. In a flashing instant, Melissa erupted into screaming flames, a human bonfire from head to toe. Her shrill cries filled the air, reverberating against the curved Tower windows and licking the tall, open glass ceiling. Clark understood, without a doubt, then and there, that Charisma was a real, actual witch, with real, actual power, and she didn't just "fire" Melissa: she set her on fire. The women flinched back, their cold eyes illuminated by the light of that great golden blaze.

"Do not break the circle," Charisma demanded of them.

Wailing, Melissa hobbled away on high heels. After only a few steps, she came down hard to her knees. Melissa fell forward onto the glass floor, and crawled towards the iron banister staircase. Smoking, smoldering, and hairless, the fire died to embers as suddenly as it had started. Gasping for air with shaking, rasping, heaving breaths, her blackened arm outstretched, she opened her encrusted eyes—and stared right at Clark, hiding behind the banister.

"You," Melissa seemed to be mouthing.

Then, her head slumped over, her whimpers subsided, and a single bloodstained tear escaped her eyes, menacingly affixed to his. The smoke escaped the opening in the ceiling, and Melissa lay silent and still.

CHAPTER VIII

Impractical Magic

Clark's hair stood on end. The coven stood breathless.

"Ladies . . . we have one more rotten apple to tend to," Charisma said, this time even calmer and more forbidding than before. "Ladies, please, open the circle for our little *guest.*" She turned, her circle followed, and suddenly, to his complete and utter horror, all the hollow eyes in that glass tower were aimed at none other than him. He had been discovered.

"Come here, boy," Charisma said.

Clark's foot slipped as he ducked, and he fell back onto the stairs. His stomach might as well have fallen through his pants.

Oh my GAWD . . . ! he thought in a panic. *I'm gonna be next . . . ! She's gonna kill me like Melissa . . . !*

"Now," Charisma said with finality. Slowly, he raised himself up. Melissa's eyes were still staring blankly at him. The Coven looked at him blankly too at first—except for Monica. Those cold gray eyes and arched eyebrows cut him a look of sharp menace, that eased into one of smirking dark delight. And then, he locked eyes with Charisma, whose acidic green eyes seemed to bore right into his soul, causing him to avert his gaze and look down. He dared not meet those menacing eyes again.

Clark joined their ranks atop the circle, right where Melissa had stood in between Emily and Alicia. Both were expressionless and neither dared risk a look at him, not once. He was unable to stop himself from shaking.

"And you," Charisma said with a whip of her neck and a single look. "Wipe that smug, *disgusting* look off your sorry face." Abruptly, Monica came crashing down to her knees on the cold hard floor, as if against her will.

"Yes, you, Monica, who outed Melissa. For that, you shall be rewarded. But not tonight. No, not now . . . Conspiring against a sister witch, *and* fornicating with a man under my own roof, no less . . ."

Monica gasped. Clark might have felt some smug sense of justice himself under more normal circumstances, had Monica not looked up at Charisma with pure terror. He did not wish it on his worst enemy.

"You thought I would not find out . . . but you thought wrong. Under my roof, I. See. All. In my house, in my Coven, nobody suffers a rat." There was no magic wand, no finger pointed, simply a single, demeaning gaze from down her long, straight nose. Monica uttered a guttural, piercing, bloodcurdling scream that made Clark's hair stand up on end, and didn't let up. She floundered and writhed on the glass floor, wailing and seizing as if by electrocution. Could it be, was Clark seeing Charisma's aura burst into bolts like black-hot electricity, coursing from her being, and striking down on her?

After many long moments, when it was finally over, Monica lay there crumpled on the floor and pulled her knees into her chest, unable to hold in her sobs, or her tears. Not one of the Coven came to her aid. All was still, save for the charged air and whimpers, and the smell of Melissa's body on the floor not far, smoldering and smoking.

Charisma spoke again: "You only have one thing to fear in this wide, miserable world. And that thing is *me*. Let this be a reminder. *Get up!*" she spat at Monica. "And clean up this mess." She said to the rest, "The ritual is complete. You may break the circle." With a turn on her heel, Charisma walked to the banister and down the stairs, one *clack* at a time. One by one the Coven queued behind her, and descended the stairs in a single-file line of black dresses and numb, listless faces. Clark remained frozen in place.

After what felt like a lifetime, Clark watched as Monica propped herself up by one arm, then by two, and with a stumble, stood and straightened herself. The mascara had run ugly and black down her cheeks, and she sniffled, wiping the tears away . . . until she noticed him lingering.

"What in the FUCK are you looking at?" she spat darkly at him. He flinched. Monica pulled out her phone from her pocket, scrolled through it, and brought it to her ear.

"Yeah, hi, it's me," she said with a sniff. "I need another fucking cleanup . . . Now, at the Tower . . . YES, I BLOODY WELL SAID NOW!" She hung up the phone abruptly, and slowly descended the stairs. The tower's shutters drew to a close behind her.

On that commute in the early morning hours, there was no get-away yellow cab, no Joey to drive him home, just the quiet train ride on the Astoria-bound amongst the after-midnight passengers. Looking back, Clark could not remember the journey, let alone arriving at his door or even getting into bed. As he stared up at the ceiling, he could not forget Melissa's screams, her burnt body, and those blood-shot eyes affixed to his . . . wondering if he was the reason that she had been murdered.

That night Clark dreamt of a hollow sky, so outside his other dreams, so outside of himself.

There were screams, hellish screams. In the darkness, a pair of yellow-green eyes stared at him. Charisma's terrarium ascended from the shadows, its tree rustling in the wind and turning sky; the sun set and the moon rose in continuous succession through its leaves. The dirt amongst its roots squirmed with worms, wiggling up like fingers. Roaches and flies and crawling bugs broke the surface too. Then the tree burst into a magnificent fire and all at once disappeared into smoke.

The face of Emily burst out of the haze, maniacally laughing, hovering over him. She turned into Alicia, then into Monica, laughing more gravely still, and then to Melissa, who erupted into flame.

Her blackened face was screaming into his, her deadened body strad-dling him, riding him—shaking him, scaring him in his own bed—but Clark could not scream, could not move, could not stop her, only watch in horror.

In Melissa's red, menacing gaze, Clark saw the Great Eye that had always been just there, in his mind and in his present, awake again, blinking open. He had been Seen.

Then he awoke. The smell of smoke hung in the air of his apart-ment; so too did the feeling of being watched. His sweat-drenched forehead prickled. He reached to scratch it.

Clark turned to his bedside table: it was three o'clock in the morn-ing. The witching hour, or so he remembered from his fairy tales.

He slept with one eye open the rest of the night until the sun came up and his alarm went off. It was time to go to work.

The funeral was held first thing that Monday morning.

Clark had seen the headlines; he didn't have to do much digging. *A woman was found dead early Saturday morning in Upper East Side fire,* said the news. While the city slept, an entire townhouse and its contents had gone up in flame, a freak accident, the coverup at play.

It was all happening so fast, Clark had just been going through the motions, his body being carted wordlessly through the experience of it all. The Coven arrived with Clark in tow in their black town cars and SUVs, veiled and dressed in their funeral best and blackest. So too was Clark—he wore the black birthday button-down that Nancy, Paul, and Eva had given him. If he were being honest, he had not felt altogether conscious since his dinner the Friday night prior, unable to tell a soul about what he had borne witness to. Not to anyone at the coffee shop that weekend, nor to Joey, who was a text message away, nor to Patricia, whom he hadn't seen in months. Clark was so numb that the inconsolable weeping of a swarthy, dark-haired woman had barely registered a blip to him. She must've been Melissa's mother, he figured.

He was surprised to see Ms. Charisma Saintly roll up—naturally, in her own car and with a bodyguard. She approached the Coven at a leisurely stroll, cloaked in sunglasses, a wide-brimmed hat, and a parasol. She stood watching the services under a gray city sky as a storm was rolling in. Charisma seemed to bring the storm with her.

As the hearse pulled in, and the pallbearers slowly walked the casket to rest over the grave, Clark understood without a doubt, then and there, that he had seen too much; there was no leaving now. As the rain began to trickle, Clark understood that if he so much as stepped a toe out of line, he would be next to be lowered into the ground. That he himself was in deep, deep shit.

He imagined himself stepping forward as a single drop of rain would mask a tear. He would make a prayer for the fallen. *I'm sorry,* he would say, tossing down the rose he held in his hand, and—

"How DARE you . . . !"

Clark's eyes widened and he erupted in a cold sweat. Everyone turned to look at who had spoken, even the priest. It was Melissa's mother—she looked his way and shouted words that would never leave him: "How DARE you show your face here?!"

But Mrs. Silvestri was not speaking to him. He turned and saw, to his surprise, that she was speaking to Charisma behind him. Everyone did: they stopped to watch as Charisma stood unflinchingly, unable to be read through her big, dark sunglasses. Mr. Silvestri and her sister held the woman back by the arms.

"What is *she* doing here?!" Melissa's mother croaked. Spit and snot flew from her face, as she screamed, "YOU did this! You did this, *and now she's gone!* My baby is gone . . . ! How dare you show your face here, you . . . you *BITCH!* Get out! GET OUT! *GET OUT!*"

The clouds darkened and shifted in the gray city sky. There was a tingling in the middle of Clark's forehead, and the hairs on his arms suddenly stood on end. Within a split second, a bolt of lightning struck the coffin with a crack and a flash of fire and thunder. The mourners screamed and fled and chaos ensued, as Mrs. Silvestri and her family were knocked onto the ground. But that was not the worst that happened.

The pallbearers were knocked back too, and dropped the casket in the shock of being struck. Two of the straps snapped, and the coffin slid into the open grave. The lid flew undone and off as it hit the bottom, and Melissa herself made an appearance at her own funeral, flung headfirst out of her coffin. She hung there, arms askew, and her body half out. There were shrill screams at the sight of her hairless, crisp corpse.

Mrs. Silvestri fainted.

That morning, when they entered the main kitchen of Charisma's penthouse, Emily bounded up to Clark first thing, shaking him out of his stupor (he could hardly stop thinking).

She grabbed him by the arm, swiveled him around, and said, "Let's get a coffee and get out of here."

There was no protest from Clark, and none from the Coven, as she dragged him back to the elevator, through the lobby, and into the parked town car outside. She told the driver, "To the café, Oksana, thank you. Have you met Clark? He's the new junior. He's been with us since August."

Clark replied, "Hi, it's nice to meet you." Oksana only looked at him in the rearview mirror and wordlessly nodded.

As they drove, Emily asked about Oksana's family off Brighton Beach in Brooklyn. Clark only watched and listened. Emily looked so beautiful with her long blonde hair that she let out of its ponytail, cascading like water over her funeral black. What did she want to talk to him about? Was he in trouble? Clark was a kind of nervous-excited to be playing hooky with someone like Emily—a flushed hyperaware he only knew around the Coven, unsure of what would happen next, of what they could do to him—but with Emily he felt different. Curious. Captivated even. Clark wondered if there was something more than met the eye to her.

Pay attention and don't fuck this up, loser . . . he thought. Was that a blush of his cheeks he was feeling?

They drove a few blocks north to—*should've guessed it . . .* —the café where he had interviewed just a couple of months prior, attached to what he identified this time as *C Hotel.* This time there were other patrons inside, and, just like last time, that morose waiter was on the clock. Clark noticed he was a little happier to see Emily, or rather, less disgruntled by the way he attentively took her order. Clark thought this was a good sign. The waiter still did not acknowledge his presence, but Clark knew not to take that personally.

No sooner had he sat their coffees down ("iced with oat milk—make that two, please, thank you") and left, the dial on the volume of the world around them turned all the way down to mute, until they could hear not a single sound outside their table except for one another, not even the sound of the soft rain that had started outside.

"How is that happening?" Clark asked. "Are you doing that?"

"Doing what?" Emily asked.

"That thing with . . . the volume?" Clark said, waving his hands around. "It's so quiet, my ears are ringing."

"I'm not sure what you mean," she said, looking at him curiously.

"Oh, um," he began. "I can't hear a thing past the table and . . . Never mind . . ."

Emily took a sip before speaking. "Sometimes," she said, "magic happens to all of us, in the most unlikely of ways, at the most unlikely of times. One just has to be willing to see it."

Clark crinkled his nose. "I thought only witches can do magic."

"I mean, in a way, yeah," she said. "Lorena and I, we've talked about that. She and the Coven think a witch is born, not made, but I wonder if that's Lorena being Lorena and not the full truth."

"That's so cool," Clark said. "I wish I could do . . . *that.*" His words felt hollow, all things considered, and he stopped himself.

Emily asked, "You ever practice, babe?" This time, Clark knew what she meant by "practice." He thought about the rooftop the night of the interview and the eyelash wish he made, and how he had awoken to the text from Monica.

"Nah," he replied. "But I am totally into witches. Always have been. I'm a Halloween baby."

Emily smiled and put down her coffee. "When's your birthday?"

"I just turned twenty-four on the twenty-fourth . . ."

Emily looked at him with knowing eyes and nodded as if to say she understood what had come to pass. "Twenty-four on the twenty-fourth. Happy belated birthday, Clark."

"Thanks, Emily," he said weakly.

Cheerfully this time, she asked, "What's your birth time?"

"Um, one ten in the afternoon, I think."

"Ah," she said. "Your moon is in Taurus."

"Yeah, it is," Clark said. "How'd you know?"

"Oh, I just do. Like how you were born on a Thursday under a full moon. Witch things. Your Tenth House is in Scorpio at zero degrees, which means you're either very rare and special, or you're going to . . ."

"Or going to what?" he asked, raising an eyebrow. *Why did she stop herself . . . ?*

"Oh, nothing! Your birth chart is shaped like a diamond. Did you know? That means you're a gem, Clark." She smiled.

"Oh, thanks! I should've known . . ." he said somewhat wryly, a little uncomfortable at being read. "How old are you? How was twenty-four?"

"I'm twenty-six on the twenty-first of February, so I've got a couple more years on you. Yeah, twenty-four was . . . Oh, I dunno. I guess I was just getting to know myself better. I mean, we're always getting to know ourselves better, aren't we? Are you from the city, Clark?"

Clark replied with facetiousness: "Just over the bridge in ye ol' working-class Astoria." Clark told Emily about moving out of his mother's the day after he graduated freshman year of high school.

"I see," she said, with that knowing twinkle in her eyes. "They're not always easy, those parents!"

Clark appreciated her levity. "Haha, yeah, tell me about it," Clark said. He began to bite his straw.

Emily said, "My fam, they're Greek. We venture out to Astoria for dinner sometimes, but these are no Astoria Greeks. I never knew my real father, he left before I was born. My stepfather left a lot to be desired, and my mother passed away, um, just a bit over a year ago, when I was twenty-four . . ."

"Oh, gosh," Clark said. "I'm sorry to hear that." He reached out across the table and touched the top of her hand. Instantly, a thought flickered across his mind, gone as fast as it had come, something about a kind woman with a deep sadness, and the discovery of a body. Clark drew in his breath, and Emily drew back her hand. The way she looked at Clark, something registered on her face.

What was that . . . ? he wondered.

"Thank you," she said, rubbing her hand. "It's funny, all this power and sometimes you still can't do a thing to help another person."

Clark wasn't sure what to say. "What do you mean?"

Emily looked at him for a moment. She took a sip before speaking. "My mother was very well-respected and loved in our community—maybe a little aloof sometimes as a mom, but I could trust that she loved me. She just kept the leash long, and left me to my own devices—"

"Mine too!" Clark said.

"Yeah. But when we were together, we were best friends. To be fair, the way my parents lived, all the traveling and the partying and the expensive things . . . that lifestyle can really get to your head. At least, that's what I was told about my mother's relationship to my stepfather. It was . . . complicated; tumultuous, even. I think she felt obligated a lot, and she couldn't be everything all at once. When it came to my stepfather, he was a . . . not a nice man. A popular and astute man, a political man, but not a warm man, and not a warm father. Not to me, anyway. I was always the runt of the family, the youngest. *The Blonde Sheep.* I don't have dark features like my family. My mother always said I took 'the best' of my father and her. My sisters were daddy's girls—stepdaddy—but I was my mother's through and through."

Emily gave her coffee a stir with its metal straw and watched the ice revolve around the glass. "Well, that was growing up. Both my sisters married off early and I left home to travel after college. I just needed to get out."

"Did you grow up here?" Clark asked.

"Yeah, here in Manhattan. Oh, you know, they shipped me off to boarding school and to Greece in the summer growing up, all the things rich parents do. I left home because it was something I chose for myself. That, and I put off assisting Charisma like my sisters had for as long as I could because I knew it would . . . consume my life. I just wanted to be free for a little. To get away. To breathe."

Clark nodded. "I know that feeling."

"Right. The thing is, I didn't realize how my mother was feeling, how she needed us here. How she needed *me*. I think the way she was living, without us, it was a lot for her. That day I came back, I wanted to surprise her. I remember it was a sunny day, and the windows were open, there was a soft breeze in the house, and her favorite flowers were in the vases. Sunflowers. She used to whisper in my ear that they reminded her of me, and that they were her favorite, like I was. Everything seemed normal up to then . . . Well, no, not normal— something seemed off when I came home but I couldn't place it. The doctors said she had taken all of her pills and passed in her sleep, maybe an hour or so before I arrived."

Clark took a sip of coffee, in hopes it would suck back the tears that were coming up.

"There was no way I could have been any earlier," Emily said.

Clark spoke slowly when he said, "There was nothing you could have done, Emily, I hope you know. It wasn't your fault."

Emily looked at him with her sad smile. "I know. You're right. Well, I was the one to call 911, and tell the family, and I was the one to make the arrangements. The services were beautiful, of course, like her. I did everything that she would've liked. You wouldn't believe how many sunflowers we purchased. She was wonderful. I miss her! Every day. I wish I had spent more time with her instead of running away . . . Eleni was her name. 'Helen.' I was named after her but it never felt like me, so I adopted an American name. Clients think Emily's easier. Now I'd do anything to be reminded of her. She taught me that in life, helping others is the most important thing a witch can do with one's Gift."

Clark crinkled his nose. "'Gift'?"

She answered after some thought, moving her long blonde hair out of her face. "Every witch has a specialty, a Gift that aligns with her calling. As a witch, you are supposed to use your Gift 'in the service of others, for the highest good of all,' *blah blah blah*, whatever that means! That's our 'purpose,' just like anyone else's in life, I suppose. Like, if you're good at writing, then you might go into journalism. See what I'm saying?"

"I think so," Clark said. "What's yours? Your 'Gift,' I mean."

"Well, my 'Gift' is the Gift of Prophecy, like my two sisters. We are the descendants of the oracles from Ancient Greece, maybe earlier even, civilizations that predate Ancient Greece—or so I've gathered," she said. Her face fell a little, and she continued: "For my sister Delphi, it's the Prophecy of Fortune. She can foretell how someone will make their money, and how their business will be navigated. My other sister, Alexandria: she has the Prophecy of My Big Fat Greek Love. You can guess what that means. She can see who someone will shack up with, how many babies they'll have, yada yada. Both have assisted under Charisma, like so many great witches before who've gone on to do big, big things."

"What's yours?" Clark asked, too curious not to.

"Me, well," she said, "I have the Prophecy of Death."

Clark looked around the café. The other patrons were none the wiser. "The Prophecy of Death?"

"It means that I can see how a person is going to die."

Clark couldn't help but press on. "What's that like?"

"Well, unlike my sisters, my Gift came early—too early—before I could really understand it let alone what death is, maybe before anyone else could understand what was happening with me. Except for my *yiayiá*—my grandma. *Yia-yia*, I would call her. She understood right away. When I was little I predicted her husband passing. I said something was wrong about "his bones," and it turned out to be bone cancer. I was only four years old. They say growing up in witch households does that to a person, that there's something about proximity that makes the witch in us reveal ourselves. At least, *proximity* is sorta how it happens for me . . . My predictions come in visions, or in understanding, or sometimes in dreams even, but the how notwithstanding, it usually starts with physical touch."

Clark thought there was something beautiful and macabre about Emily and her sad smile, as she spoke to him so matter-of-fact.

"While my sisters predict futures for fortunes, I garner a different kind of clientele. The biggest of us, actually. Almost everyone is interested in knowing how they're going to die because everybody wants to live forever—unless they're smart. See, when you know how you're going to die, you become obsessed with it. Pretty soon, you're avoiding other people, people you once trusted. You're avoiding leaving home. You're avoiding *being* home. You avoid life altogether. When you see death in everything and everywhere, at some point, you're gonna stop living. But death, she comes for us all, no matter how we try to avoid her. If it's your time then it's your time. And it's just . . . hard to see something you can't stop, no matter how much you might love someone . . . With *Yia-yia,* I knew when and where, and how it would happen, and she never let me tell her. She was wise. But with my mother, I could never see it. Maybe I didn't want to. A block. Kinda ironic, huh . . ."

Clark didn't know what to say. The implication of knowing the way someone would come to pass, even the ones closest to you. What could he say? "But that's so cool," Clark finally remarked. "I mean, you're so *special.* I've always wished I could be half as special, with a Gift . . . like yours." He regretted saying that almost immediately. "I'm sorry," he added. "That feels selfish to say. But then I could really help people and make a difference."

"No, you wouldn't want a superpower like this one, trust me . . ." Emily said gravely. He could tell—she spoke in a sweet, low-affect mezzo-soprano, but her blue-green eyes betrayed her. "Besides," Emily continued, her face softening, "you're already special. I can tell you're a really nice guy. That's your superpower."

"I'm not that nice," Clark admitted with a small sigh. After a moment, he said, "I feel bad for Melissa."

"Please, don't waste your breath pitying her, Clark. It's wonderful you're so empathetic, but sometimes in life we dig our own graves." She sipped the last of her coffee and set the glass down on the table. Clark found something about her words to be unsettling, even dissatisfactory.

"Did you know?" Clark asked. "About Melissa, how it was going to happen for her?" He couldn't help himself.

"Well, yeah," she said. "I knew it would be by fire and while she was young, but I couldn't tell what the context would be. See, with prophecy, it isn't always specific, and the future changes all the time. Sometimes, it's so clear it screams, but other times it's all subjective, relative to choice even. But mostly, things like that are already written, already affixed. I remember the first time we met and I 'read' her. I saw her engulfed in flames, but not really sure of what I had just seen." She chortled at this. "It definitely scared the shit out of me to take transportation with her, like cars or airplanes."

Clark asked, "Can you see how you're going to die?"

"Hmm," she said. "No one's ever asked me that . . . Some things are outside of my jurisdiction, but I've had a hunch, and usually, my hunches are correct. The thing is," she continued, "it's funny, but— I'm not afraid to die. No point in worrying, in being afraid of what happens to all of us in the end. If I die, I die."

"I get that," Clark said. Though did he really? "Are you ever able to save people?" This he regretted immediately too. *Clark, what is wrong with you . . . ?* "I'm sorry, I didn't mean to . . ."

"It's okay," Emily began slowly. "I mean, that's the goal, isn't it? Yeah, I've helped a few souls. Kept a couple of backstabbers away, foiled a few plots, kept a murder from happening. That job bought me my loft in Tribeca and I'm still seeing the spoils. For the most part, though, no. Those clients were only prolonging things, putting off the inevitable. Like I said, death is always on her own time."

Then, Emily went even graver still. "There's only one client on record who's been able to successfully stave off death, and rewrite her destiny . . ."

"Who? Who is it?" He was almost afraid that he knew the answer.

"You know whom I'm talking about . . . She can be very convincing, that Ms. Saintly."

Clark couldn't think of any other person he was both so tired of talking about and at the same time completely enthralled with the idea of talking about. "But, how? How can she . . . escape death?"

"Oh, lots of ways. But I mean, she can't escape death completely. Not exactly. We're all mortal, even her. There's just more to her than meets the eye," Emily said.

Clark had a funny feeling in the pit of his stomach and that tell-tale tingling in the middle of his forehead. He thought of that great big eye from his nightmare, that had somehow both opened above him and *in* him, staring straight at him, and that had scared him sleepless.

"There are some things too complicated to explain. At least right now."

Clark furrowed his brow. "Okay . . . How about this: What happens when you see a particularly gruesome ending? Like, so gruesome, so grizzly, there's not a chance in hell at stopping it. What do you tell your client?"

Something flashed across Emily's eyes. "Sometimes, I just have to tell them, 'A long time from now, when you've grown old and gray, you're going to pass from this life painlessly to the next, in your sleep, with a successful life behind you, surrounded by safety, comfort, grandchildren, and the people you love.'"

They both giggled, Emily stifling hers behind a manicured hand.

"That's awful!" Clark said.

"Yeah, but it works! Better they come upon it unawares, lest the blame fall on me. You should see my contract. It's easier for all involved, trust me."

"I can only imagine," Clark said. What a contract for a witch like Emily could contain, he wasn't sure, but he hoped to know one day. She had a glint in her eyes as she smiled at him that put him at ease. There was something special about Emily, something different from the others that he had not quite noticed before but that he could feel all the same. Maybe it was her sad blue-green eyes under a fringe of impossibly long lashes, eyes that looked back at him without pretense or judgment. It was as if Emily had been carrying the weight of the world on her shoulders seemingly all her life, and that the truth of that weight had been resigned to the deepest depths of her inner oceans. Maybe that glint was a determination to hope in spite of all of it, Clark surmised.

But Clark couldn't resist going one step further: "Can you see how I'm going to die?"

Can she judge . . . ? It's only natural I ask . . . At least, he hoped it was.

"You?" Emily looked into his eyes and took his hand in hers. "Clark: a long time from now, when you've grown old and gray"—a smile broke across her face and they giggled again—"you're going to part painlessly in your sleep, with a successful life behind you, surrounded by safety, comfort, grandchildren, and the people you love."

Clark feigned a gasp. "Daaang, that bad, huh? Why you gotta do me like that now!"

"You'll be all right," she said. "Don't you worry, babes. Everything's gonna work out just fine for you." Clark wanted to believe her, but something about her words gave him pause . . . He tried his luck and pressed her just one more time, looking up at the cameras before speaking.

"What about Charisma?"

"What about her . . . ?"

"How will it happen? Or how will she 'stave it off'?"

Emily took a deep breath: "That one I've been asked before. Many, many times before. What I can say is this: eventually, the fall of Charisma is going to come at the hands of someone very close to her, someone in her inner circle, a betrayer whom she doesn't know is right under her nose the entire time. How, though, I can't see—but she's paranoid as fuck about it. She doesn't trust a soul, not even her own mother. To her, everyone's a suspect, and rightfully so. Everyone's after her and her throne. That's why she keeps her circle tight, and her coven small. Under no circumstances are you to tell anyone I told you any of this, okay? Promise?"

"I promise," Clark said. "I swear. But what she did to Melissa . . . Emily, she has to be stopped."

"She can't be stopped," Emily said. "She's done it before and she will do it again. Charisma isn't what she seems, Clark. She's more powerful than you know."

"Then, she has to be exposed! Other people have to be warned about her!"

Emily shook her head. "And who would believe you? What you saw, what happened to Melissa, that's just the tip of the iceberg. Now, you've seen too much and you can't just quit. How do you think she'd react knowing she's down an assistant and a junior? Can't you see? Nobody just 'quits' Charisma. Nobody just walks away, nobody is just let go. She's a monster behind closed doors, sure, and she also has a queendom of flying monkeys, and lots and lots of money at her disposal, with lots and lots of power and influence at her command. You'll only get yourself killed in the end, and I don't need a premonition to know that."

Clark's throat had gone dry. A sip of the last of his coffee didn't help. "But . . ." Clark started to say. "Ugh! I just wish there was something I could do. Anything."

"There's nothing you or I or anyone can do. The sooner you learn that, the better your chances are of staying alive. Otherwise, in the end, you'll end up just like Melissa . . . or worse. What Charisma would do to you, she'd make you wish you went as easily as Melissa, and she'd make it look like an accident too. At least right now, you're on her side of the fence. Stay on her good side. *Stay alive, Clark.* Do that for me."

Clark put on a dissatisfied half smile but nevertheless nodded. Emily reached out for his hand across the cold table, and he reached out with his to hold. From that moment on, for the first time at Charisma's, Clark found a friend in Emily. He figured there was just something about watching your coworker die that could bring two unlikely strangers together.

Outside their table's sound bubble, the soft rain had subsided. Emily paid, and they made their way back to the penthouse.

On their return that gray, rainy Monday morning, the interviews started right away and lasted until the evening; not in the café across the street like Clark had been relegated to, but in the penthouse.

Beautiful, affluent women arrived to meet with Lorena, in their designer best, all in black. As Clark stole a look at their purses, their dresses, their shoes, he realized he was beginning to feel a little envious of the women around him. How was he helping others afford their wealth when he himself could not afford such luxuries, not a chance in hell?

As he chauffeured the ladies one by one to Lorena's office, Clark wondered what made these candidates so special, so deserving. He wondered if one of them would be the one to undo Charisma. If he were being honest, Clark wished on every black leather stiletto that strolled in that day that he could be a witch too, so he could be the one to do it. Maybe he understood why no one had accomplished it yet: no chance to dethrone the queen if you're kept so busy working under her thumb that you can't.

Some of the women looked around the penthouse like it was Narnia. Clark knew they weren't the ones who would make it. The candidates hardly looked at Clark, let alone spoke to him. He had come to expect it. He was less than *dogs' droppings* under a witch's nose, he parroted to himself in an English accent. Most took one look at his black thrift-store shirt and worn-out oxfords and no more. It was as if he didn't exist. But as one woman seemed to lead *him* toward the first-floor offices, as if she knew where they were going, he was caught in a state of surprise.

"Hey, kid," she said in a hushed voice. "My agent wouldn't say but word on the street is that Melissa got herself fired, and that she ended up dead. Do you know what happened to her?"

Clark looked at the woman: she was ice blonde, impossibly tall and rail thin, and unnervingly beautiful. Her face was pallid and stone-cold. *Should I warn her . . . ? Tell her the truth . . . ? Spare her the same fate . . . ?* Looking into those pale blue eyes reminded him of looking into Monica's cold steel-grays. *It would only be a matter of time before she came for me too . . .*

"Not a clue," Clark lied. They reached Lorena's office. He knocked three times.

"Come in," said Lorena from inside. "Both of you." The woman turned to look at him.

"Stella, darling! Lovely to see you, dear," Lorena said, reaching her with an air-kiss on Stella's left cheek, then her right. "You," she said turning to Clark. "Leave Monica to greet our guests and go clean upstairs." She eyed him with the read-between-the-lines face she wore, and left no room for misunderstanding: Lorena meant the Tower.

This must be my punishment . . . At least I'm not getting "fired" . . .

Without emotion, Clark said, "Yes, ma'am."

"*Don't call me that!*" she snarled back. Stella flinched. Lorena turned to her and broke into an exasperated, sheepish smile. "Please, have a seat, darling." Clark held the door open for Carolina the cook, who'd appeared with a tea tray, and then shut the office doors behind him.

In the Closet, Clark took a deep breath and stepped into the mirror opposite. *Mirror, mirror on the wall,* he thought, *will I amount to anything after all . . . ?* He did the hand gesture: the secret door clicked open, and up that iron and glass staircase he went.

The space looked almost exactly as they had left it on Friday night, with burnt-out candles and wax on the Tower's perimeter. The chalk circle remained smudged and broken, and only ashen remains were left where Melissa's body had lain on that glass floor. Clark looked up at the ceiling licked by her flames. There was not a mark in sight.

Fireproof . . . he thought to himself.

A draft shot through the room and down his spine. He could almost imagine how she had been zipped up and taken away, could almost follow the smudged footsteps that led back down the way he had come. Melissa's pleading, and her screams, echoed in his mind's ear like it was happening all over again. He even swore there was still a hint of singed flesh in the air. He was feeling dizzy. Desperate for fresh air and circulation.

On the northern side of the room, he fumbled with the lock on one of the wall-length windows. Without warning, the window whipped open with a burst of howling wind. It almost sucked Clark into the open air and to a thousand-foot drop. The window rotated on its hinge and slammed against its neighboring window with a loud, low *thud*, once, then twice, and again and again.

A familiar voice came from behind him. "Grab one of those hooks, baby, they're for the windows." Clark turned to discover it was Miss Honey. "Careful now!"

Sure enough, there was a long hook in the grating, which Clark grasped. He hung on for his life as he hooked the handle, and pulled the window in towards him, fighting the October breeze. He was so precariously perched on that ledge that he could see a couple of the gray stone gargoyles flanking the floor below, and the long, long way down . . .

"Geez," he said, "what's a window like that for?"

"You know what it's for . . ."

Clark paused. *The broomsticks on the landing below . . . It couldn't be* . . . "For flying?!" he exclaimed. He was afraid to think of what other purpose it might serve.

"Why are you still here, baby?" That warm smile of hers had vanished, replaced by a look of sad concern.

"I . . . don't have any other choice right now."

"Sure you do, baby. You always have a choice. Choose *you*. Choose better. Leave and never look back. Put this all behind you before they put you six feet under like they did that girl. What's it going to take to convince you?"

"I can't," Clark said. He almost felt ashamed. "I'm scared. And I feel like . . . there's something more I need to do here."

Miss Honey gave a slow shake of her head. "No, sweetie. You play their game, and you'll see how wrong you'll be. You think you're ahead of the game, then the rules change," she said, words laced with melancholy. "The rules always change because it's *her* game, her rules. Playing with her is a losing game, one you will always lose. You're in deep, baby. You're in deep . . ."

Clark trusted there were no cameras there but he spoke in a low voice regardless. "You're right," he said. "I should've listened. What do I do?"

"There's nothing you can do if you won't leave, baby," she said. "Except for one thing." At this, she turned to the middle of the room, to the window in the floor to the Closet below . . .

"What? What is it? She can't keep doing—"

"Hello . . . ?" One of the maids was coming up the stairs carrying a bucket and a mop.

"Hi, Marcia," Clark said. "Me and Miss Honey were just—"

But Miss Honey was nowhere to be found. He looked around in shock.

"I'm sorry, *cariño*, who?" she asked, confused.

"The maid, Miss Honey: thin, small woman, short hair. Sounds like Eartha Kitt? I swear she was just here a second ago but . . ."

"Oh no, *mi amor*," she said, setting the bucket down. "There's no one working here by that name."

CHAPTER IX

Halloween

$\mathcal{I}$t was nine o'clock by the time Clark finished scraping the last of the wax off the Tower's floor and returned home. Punishment indeed. He would never forget mopping Melissa's ashy remains from the Tower's glass floor. There was so much he could not stop thinking about.

Since the night of his birthday, Clark had become hyper-vigilant and on guard, and with more sore throats to show for it. Who was Miss Honey, and what did she know? What was the one thing she was going to mention before she disappeared into thin air?

Mostly, Clark wondered about how to stop Charisma.

Even as Joey showed him one of his favorite cult witch movies—the one about the Italian dance company—Clark could barely stop himself from ruminating.

"If you get past the corny dubbing, it's a classic! I can't believe you haven't seen it yet. You'll love it! *Witch witch witch!*" Joey echoed the narration and giggled, squeezing Clark into his side with his arm over Clark's shoulder.

That night Clark dreamt himself as the film's female protagonist, the intuitive uncovering the witches' murderous plot. One of the instructors with villainous eyes easily became Monica, another

Stella, the woman who'd interviewed with Lorena. In the movie's secret room, Clark discovered the blue-flower mural door. However, instead of delving deeper into the depths of the conservatory to where the queen bee lay, the Mater Witch, the door opened to reveal the Tower's stairwell—and to Melissa's piercing screams, rushing down in a mighty wind that rocked him back as if a train blowing past.

He awoke at three in the morning, as per usual.

Clark wrote in his diary by the light of his lava lamp every night while Joey loudly snored, none the wiser:

In every fairy tale, in every story, the witch always has a
weakness. The hero always finds the witch's Achilles' Heel hiding
in plain sight.
The overconfident blind witch is tricked into the oven by Gretel.
Rumpelstiltskin gloatingly reveals his name and the queen gets
to keep her baby.
The Wicked Witch melts into a puddle.
But what is Charisma's weakness . . . ?

Clark spent his commutes and his evenings combing through interviews and articles and videos—anything he could to dig up information on Charisma, in hopes of finding some kind of weak spot.

There was the face of her luxurious life, for one. Her travels, her fashion. For another, she seemed to have a persuasive way of speaking and a lot of "friends," this and that celebrity and politician; a Potemkin village. A web search showed Charisma was a generous donator to many a charity, and interestingly, an investor in Big Pharma. Another search of the church her gargoyles were supposedly imported from came up empty, until he dug a little more. A single headline emerged, one he had to run through a translator, of a beautiful stained-glass cathedral that had mysteriously burnt down in a village over.

But what would any of this show? Who was this woman and her glamorous web he had become entangled in?

His preoccupation did not help the nightmares either. There were the screams and the terrarium, and the faces hovering over him, maniacally laughing—of Monica, Lorena, Alicia, and then Melissa, charred, bloodied, and staring into him with those menacing wild eyes—shaking him and riding him while Clark could only lie there, powerless and mute. Her voice in the wind shouted, "Witch! Traitor!"

In every dream, he saw that giant eye opening above him, yellow-green and venomous, watching him; every time, he would wake up at three in the morning in a cold sweat; and after every dream, he would wake up with the oddest feeling that he was being watched . . .

Joey told him he was croaking and moaning in his sleep, and on a couple of occasions, even having to shake Clark awake, Clark coming to in a sweat-drenched shock to the comfort of Joey's big, teddy-bear-brown eyes.

Clark was barely sleeping, having considered staying awake until three in the morning lest the night terrors come, but he knew that would not do him any good. He was growing apprehensive nonetheless for the hours of the early morning, without much to look forward to in the day let alone at night. His throat was in a perpetual hurt.

Clark was worried he was starting to obsess.

As for work and what had become of Melissa's position, Monica had gotten her just reward and the promotion she had always wanted: "Now, Monica is fourth assistant with Melissa's—that is to say, Charisma's—accounts on *top of her own*," Emily had confided. Alicia had told her it was part of Monica's punishment. They had paused their hushed conversation as Monica hurriedly walked past: her hair looked unbrushed and her eyeliner was smudged ever so slightly out of place. She had been on her way to her second house call of the day.

Allegedly, Emily whispered, Melissa had been Charisma's top producer after Emily, and Monica was oh so jealous of Melissa. "Now, Charisma is holding Monica to both workloads until they find someone new, which could be tomorrow, or months from now, or even years . . . but I don't imagine it will be long. Some of the clients just don't like Monica. Some have heard about Melissa's passing and are even threatening to revoke their contracts unless Charisma comes in her stead. When they're yours, they're yours, you know what I mean . . . ? Never mind. The point is, it's *insane*."

Despite all this, Clark's plan had backfired: Monica had been even more vicious than before, full of resentment, and not attempting to hide it.

The previous day, she had sent Clark for a coffee order, and when he returned, told him, "Did you smack your big, fat head? I didn't order this."

Clark was confused and beside himself. He had always double-checked the orders, triple-checked them even. Coffee was his second language, and he knew that what she had relayed, he had delivered. But no: Monica said this with that dangerous smirk of hers, another smiling assassination. She told him, "A typical man you are. *Lazy.* Go back and do it the right way, or go back to your shoebox in Queens where you belong."

After the longest week yet, the Friday of Halloween—and the party of the year—had arrived.

By the time Clark headed out from home, the city was brimming with New Yorkers in costume, parade-goers en route, and kids finishing their trick-or-treating. Clark adjusted his tights his entire commute to the venue in Chelsea, to discover there was a mob swarming the entrance, and a line around the block to get in that was equally as stressful.

Clark had never been to So Below. He had heard of the space in Charisma's orbit of course, well-read by that point. At its grand opening, in a red carpet interview, Charisma had said something about not wanting to mingle with just one person at a party but "all types" of people. That So Below would be the egalitarian party of days gone by, harkening back to the New York City of the '70s. It seemed to hold up to its reputation.

The glitterati A-list of New York were all in attendance that night. Clark had overheard some of the guest list, having hand-delivered most of the invitations like the flying monkey he was: famous actors and musicians, designers, athletes, entertainers, and drag queens alike, stepping out of their limos and cars and onto the red carpet, dressed in their designer Halloween looks. While Clark reminded himself of the old adage, *A friend to all is a friend to none,* the guest list was diverse and the kind of cosmopolitan he had come to expect of an NYC event, a feat Clark was somewhat impressed by, owing to Charisma's monochromatic inner circle and clientele.

Meanwhile, Clark entered at the velvet rope of the VIP line, pulling at his collar, and standing behind someone he was pretty certain was a pop star. He was dressed as a polyester Frog Prince, complete with lily-pad shoulder pads.

"Name?"

"Clark Crane," he told the promoter. "I'm with Charisma's team." Both the bouncer and the promoter sized him and his dime-store costume up and down and up again, but checked the list still, seeing that he was serious. Clark bit his tongue, twiddled his thumbs, and looked around: since the invite, Clark had spent the last few weeks stressing about what to wear until the last possible second. Despite it being his favorite holiday, picking a costume left him frozen in place every time.

I'm nowhere near beefy enough to be something hunky, like a superhero or a gladiator . . . Nowhere near out of touch enough to be something goofy like a slice of pizza . . . Nowhere near bold enough to bare my midriff or wear anything skimpier, like a sexy cat or pirate . . . Nowhere near committed enough to be something dead or grotesque, like a zombie, not after Melissa . . . What is a boy to do . . . ?

The promoter turned to the security guard and said, "Remember the old days? 'You're not getting in tonight, honey, not with those shoes!'" They both laughed riotously. Clark's ears turned a shade of pink.

"Go ahead, sweetie," the promoter said to him. "You'll see her table."

Reflexively, Clark replied, "Thank you."

Without warning, the crowd erupted in raucous screams and chaos: Charisma had stepped onto the VIP red carpet with the

Queen of Pop herself back from tour, pausing for photos. To the crowd's delight, Charisma had arrived dressed as Snow White's Evil Stepmother, complete with the heaving-est of bosoms, and holding a skull-shaped, poison-apple purse, dripping in red glitter. The irony was not lost on him whatsoever.

There she is, lining up for a photo when she just murdered her own assistant . . . Fooling the world . . . 'Duper's delight' . . . I wonder what they'd think of her if they knew she's an actual witch and not just playing pretend . . .

Clark looked up at the sign above the marquee: So Below's name was reflected upside down. The doors opened to the bass of the music below, and he took to descending the stairs.

Inside, the party was well underway, with dancers in cages and bottle girls with sparklers. After a quick look-see, he saw Charisma's cadre of girls up in the VIP section across from the DJ. The bouncer didn't believe him when he said he was part of Charisma's table, and Clark was about to be escorted away when Emily came up and gave Clark admittance. The Coven and Charisma's management and handlers sized Clark up too, from his shoes to his little frog crown, and then went back to pretending he didn't exist. He did not hold his breath for a warm welcome, but somebody took notice of him.

"How *cute*!" Emily shouted over the music, tossing back her long blonde hair. "The Frog Prince? Loves it."

"Thank you!" he exclaimed. "Fairy? Seriously, so gorgeous!"

She waved him an "oh stop!" They air-kissed once on the left and then on their right, their new inside joke, her cheeks shimmering in the light.

"Why the Frog Prince?" she asked over the music.

He felt a small smile break onto his face, amazed that someone like Emily would take interest in him. "Because a princess finally gives a frog a chance, when he's the only one that knows he's special all along!"

Emily smiled back. She produced a small locket from her birdcage purse. "Want one?" She unclasped it: inside, there were small crystalline rocks like candy.

"I dunno . . ." he said, looking at the others. They pretended not to notice or care. Could he, the junior, partake? While at a work function?

"Suit yourself!" She placed one on her tongue, winked, and took a sip of her champagne.

"Wait!" he said. "Okay okay okay!" Clark was not the proudest of this side of his personality, how much he wanted Emily to like him, fully aware of how quick he was to give in to influence, but he gave himself a pass, if just this once. *When else will I have a chance to party like this . . . ?* Emily dropped the crystal in his hand, a waitress handed him a glass of champagne ("Thank you!"), and he tossed it back. One flute turned into two, and then three, dancing and talking with Emily.

He overheard Alicia talking to Monica, deep in a confab over cosmos in their English accents: "At least this year I had enough time to get ready! Last year, after her house calls, you girls had left and she left me all alone with the junior and our kits—just so she could go off partying!" Monica shook her head.

As the night progressed, Clark noticed something he was not used to: how the raucous crowd on the dance floor watched his every move. Usually, Clark was used to going unnoticed or unwanted and didn't really enjoy going out. He'd sneak a peek out and see them, staring back with ravenous eyes every time.

"Don't forget: this is Charisma's world, and here, everybody wants to be us," Emily said in his ear over the music. Maybe she was right. Everybody, except the belle of the ball herself. The VIP was MIA. Clark watched her light up cigarette after cigarette (security not blinking an eye, of course) as she was busy entertaining guests at other private sections. Eventually, she slipped away, not to be seen again.

Clark didn't mind Charisma's absence though: Clark was in and that's all that mattered. He was sitting with the in-crowd, hanging with the cool kids for once, and here, his glass never ran empty. To Clark, this was the lap of luxury. He was living high and large.

"Let's dance!" Emily shouted. "Our princes await!"

"Okay!"

She held Clark by the hand as they deep-dived through the crowd of those covetous onlookers, which was as nerve-racking of an undertaking as he thought it might be. Every pair of eyes was ogling at him. Some people moved out of his way; some touched him; some shoved him; to Clark's astonishment some even said, "Hi." Some didn't even pay him a single glance as he caught a glimpse of a group of handsome, fashionable men. They danced intoxicatedly in their sweat-drenched harnesses, their under-clothed, sculpted bodies catching the light and his envious gaze.

"Don't worry about them," she shouted. "Look at me instead." Clark didn't notice the tingling in his forehead growing more intense, nor the club spinning around them. He could smell the perfume of her blonde hair as it tossed around her, cotton-candy sweet. Clark felt like a kid again. She laughed, and he laughed back. The world and his worries, everything else melted away in the oceans of her blue-green eyes . . .

The next thing he knew, Clark came to in the bathroom, hovering over an empty toilet, mouth agape. He groped at his side: his phone and his wallet were still in his pockets *(no one's gonna pickpocket this polyester prince . . .)*. The time was two fifty-five in the morning and his forehead tingled so much it itched. He was out way later than he'd planned on being. Where was Emily? Where had the time gone?

Clark stumbled to the sink, bypassing a heavy-petting couple. Clark looked at his dilated pupils in the mirror. *I must've blacked out . . .* he thought in a haze, having only experienced as much in the movies. *It's okay . . . Breathe . . . Just retrace your steps . . .*

I'm at So Below . . .

There was drinking and dancing . . . and a pill . . .

People were pulling at me, trying to touch me, kiss me . . .

Just find Emily and the Coven . . .

Clark stepped out of the bathroom. So Below was a different world; the music was harder and darker, and he realized he was in a different part of the club. Somewhere adjacent or below the main floor, drowned in red light—*a dungeon,* he thought.

He walked along the walls, past groping couples and throuples who paid him no mind, until he came upon a lounge. The woman in the middle chair stopped her conversation at the sight of him, dressed as the Big Bad Wolf wearing Little Red Riding Hood's cloak. She was so impossibly beautiful she made Clark stop short, too. Clustered at her feet, an eclectic posse watched him with curiosity. The red party lights reflected off her high cheekbones and into her honey-colored, almond-shaped eyes, which bored into his. She looked somehow so familiar, like he had seen those eyes before.

"Hello, Clark," she said.

"Hi! Sorry, do I know you?!" he asked over the music. Guests on the walls nearby peeked their heads up, talking into one another's ears.

"No," she said, "but I know you."

Have I met this woman before . . . ? Clark's gut was turning but he wrote it off.

"Oh, okay!" he said. "Well—hi!" If the assistants were famous, who was to say the juniors couldn't be too, he decided. She smiled with a glint in her eyes.

"You can call me Mother," she said. "I think you could be the answer we've all been waiting for."

One of the group dressed as an ax murderer with a swine mask walked over with a single, small purse in the shape of a picnic basket, and issued him a single business card. Clark took it in hand, and turned it over: it was blank, save for a single phone number.

When you're ready to join a real Coven, call me . . .

At this, a sudden foreign thought unbelonging to him, Clark's eyes widened and his stomach flipped. *Did she just . . . ?* Clark thought. He could have sworn Mother's lips were pressed together in a smile and yet he had distinctly heard her all the same.

There was a high-pitched scream and laugh, and Clark turned: the partiers and their hungry eyes looked different, an orgy of sweaty, pulsing bodies, undulating and groping. His eyes came to rest upon a group of people who were what he could only refer to as pasty, licking the arms and the necks of those sweaty, harness-clad handsome men. One pulled away, raising his devilish eyebrows and red eyes up at him. He began to laugh at Clark's shocked face, while a red, dark, and syrupy substance dripped from his mouth.

That's when Clark made a run for it.

That Saturday, Clark didn't have the luxury of calling out. He was thankful at least to have scheduled a shift switch with Gloria. He woke up a zombie, still intoxicated and hungover, which no amount of coffee could cure, no sticks of gum or extra spritz of Charisma could cover.

At home he lit a white seven-day candle for the Day of the Dead. He placed it next to the photo by his bed, and whispered, "Miss you, Grandma." That night, Clark passed out for a long and dreamless sleep. He didn't feel mostly like himself again until the following morning.

On Monday, Emily was out for a house call and Monica had put him back on the grind, sending out thank-you notes and running party favors to the millions of addresses of attendees. Clark found no answers until days later when he caught her privately.

"What happened?" he asked.

Emily said they were dancing and drinking and he insisted on staying. That Emily had tried to put him into a car but Clark hugged her goodbye. Clark of course did not remember any of this. Emily didn't have his phone number, but since they were having a good time, she'd assumed that all was well and Clark had gone home. She apologized profusely, "for being a bad friend." The two exchanged numbers.

It was around that day that Clark noticed one thing that had started to change for the better: the doorpeople, the delivery workers, the mail carriers, all the bees on the fringes of Charisma's orbit and her well-oiled machine, started to take notice of him.

"Maybe they didn't think you'd last this long," Joey had suggested.

"Maybe they're impressed that I did," Clark replied. Either way, he ran with it: he had made it a point to introduce himself and get on a first-name basis with everyone possible, or to at least make sure that they knew his. The following week, Clark even brought the coffee shop's leftover pastries to the front desk of Charisma's, to the door-woman with the strong lip liner who had kept him at arm's length. Miranda was her name, Miranda *from the Bronx*, she had said in her thick accent. He left more confections with the deliverers, the dry cleaners, and the maids.

Slowly, they started to look him in the eyes. Some even returned his hellos, even remembered his name. None of them, however, would talk business, let alone about Charisma.

A couple of days into November, as Clark dropped by the front to pick up another rattling package, Miranda made a point of thanking him for the treats.

"No problem! Um, hey," he said in a whisper, "can I ask you something?"

Miranda raised her eyebrows.

"Do you know what's in *these*?" Clark said, motioning to the boxes. "What goes on—"

"Shh!" Miranda snapped. Her little five-foot-two self grabbed him by the arm with a vise grip and dragged him out to the front.

Outside, she looked around before speaking barely above a whisper. "Are you crazy? Yeah, I got some idea, probably like you. I got some stories. I know the guy who does her . . . *cleanups*. He's got some stories too, even more than me, but I can't talk about it here. Or at all. Whatever it is you want to know, I can't say. Sorry, man, hope you find what you're looking for, and hey, take my advice: don't go talk-ing about her, or any of this for that matter, *to no one, ever*. You trust nobody around here. Got it?"

Clark nodded. He was almost grateful she told him that much. *Clark like Kent saves the day again . . .* he thought.

With Halloween out of the way, Joey had made a date with Clark for a surprise outing that Thursday, and it was all that he looked forward to for days. After work, Joey had picked him up in front of Charisma's, his car small and old amongst the black SUVs. He drove them down to Brooklyn, to a place Clark had not been to since he was little: Coney Island.

Clark gave him the update on the hour-long car ride, including his errand-hopping tour of Manhattan's rich and elite, his *cawfee* runs, and Monica's ever-changing orders, which had become abusively ridiculous, and always went untouched.

"Ugh, why's that *gabaghoul* Monica like that?" Joey said to Clark's amusement as they walked down the arcade. "I wish she'd just leave you alone."

"Be careful what you wish for," Clark said.

"Hey," Joey said. "Why do you say that?" he asked curiously.

"Nothing," Clark began, "it's just that . . . that coworker who died, Melissa—"

"Yeah, I remember . . ." Joey began.

"Yeah, her. I sort of made a wish and . . . I had hoped to take the heat off me but, well . . ." He looked at Joey, praying that he wouldn't think any less of him.

"Wait, what's this about?" Joey furrowed his eyebrows. "You're not seriously blaming yourself for Melissa's death, are you?"

Clark sighed. "You're right," he said, exasperatedly sweeping his hand through his hair. "Let's drop it. Sorry I brought it up, I'm being silly."

"Hey," Joey said, pulling him in close, "I got you. No need to explain." He glanced at a blushing Clark, who in turn looked down at their held hands and the ogling passersby as they came up onto the pier. Clark blushed harder, knowing what he was thinking could be read all over his face. It only made Joey hold his hands even tighter. Clark didn't mind: there was something about his presence that made Clark feel protected.

That November day was unseasonably warm even by the beach, and as the day drew to a close, the chill picked up. After chili dogs and funnel cake, arcade games and funhouses, and a goofy session in the photo booth ending in a kiss they held extra long, Clark and Joey finished the night on the Ferris wheel, looking out at the Atlantic and the sparkling skyline in the distance. Joey leaned in for a love bite and an inhale of Clark's neck . . .

"Hey, Clark, I've really enjoyed spending time with you and getting to know you," he said.

"Me too, Joey."

"I'm falling for you real hard, Clark," he said. "I think . . . I mean, what I wanna say is . . . Well, that I think I . . . I love you . . ."

Clark froze and stared back at him.

"I know it's early! You don't have to say it back! I just . . ." he said, searching for the words, "wanted to tell you. Life's too short, you know what I mean?"

"Thank you . . ." Clark said. "I'm not sure what to say." *What can I say . . . ?* Finally, here was someone he was really into, someone real and right in front of him, baring his heart, and even if it all felt too fast, Clark was elated. Joey was like a gift from the universe. *A wish granted . . .* The way Joey's smile dropped slightly at the corners tugged at Clark's heartstrings.

Clark said, "I think I love you, too."

Joey turned to look at Clark, and that smile . . .

The breeze was stiff and the cold penetrated their jackets, and the two huddled together for warmth. They looked into one another's eyes and kissed, so aglow in the carnival-colored lights that he could fly up out of their little cabin. It was fireworks.

As they held hands on their way to the car and talked about plans for the week—of more kisses to steal on Clark's drive-bys to Northlight when the manager wasn't looking—Joey did have one thing to ask.

"Clark, why are you so cagey about work?"

Uh oh . . .

"Cagey? What do you mean?"

"What I mean is that you've told me about some of the things in your day-to-day at work, but you've never really given me the specifics of what you do. I feel like you're keeping me in the dark about it. You can trust me, you know that, right?"

Clark flushed. "Um, well . . . I've sorta told you as much as I know. I have no idea what's in the envelopes or the boxes or who a lot of these people are. 'Fraid that's above my pay grade! Mostly I just do as I'm told." He felt bad for lying.

"Maybe you'd better stop doing as you're told and find out about who and what you're working for," Joey said, unlocking the car.

"Yeah, you're totally right, and I hope to do just that. Monica is meaner than ever and stressed now that she's picking up Melissa's slack and I'm just . . . really confused about what to do about all of it," Clark confessed.

"Is any of this worth it?" Joey asked. "I know it's cool to work for her and her name will take you places, but is it worth all this? All this stress? They're not even paying you!"

Clark replied with a sigh. "A year here and I can go . . . anywhere." His eyes trailed away at his words, which sounded empty.

As they sat in the car, Joey paused and looked at Clark. He said, "You know what's odd, Clark, is one day, I was downstairs handling one of those mystery-box deliveries from some mean intern when the bottom gave out completely. It spilled all over the sidewalk: pills and blank orange pill bottles, *everywhere*. We spent a long time cleaning it all up before opening, but there must've been a hundred or so nine-to-fivers passing by who saw. Crazy, right?"

Joey turned on the ignition and said, "I think Northlight is a total drug front." Clark's eyes doubled in size as they pulled out of the parking lot and drove away.

"Clarky!" Patricia chirped in her nasal Queens accent. "Hi, sweetie!"

"I've missed you!" Clark said to her, giving her a kiss on the cheek and a hug.

"Oh my goodness, I've missed you too!"

It was Thanksgiving and Patricia had invited Clark to dinner, along with—for the first time ever—a plus-one.

"Come in, come in . . . And this must be the handsome Joey you've told me all about—except, you didn't tell me he's even more handsome in person!"

Joey gave her a hug. "Thank you for having us," he said, his hand creeping up to hold the small of Clark's back.

Patricia squealed, "Oh my gawd, what a gentleman!" When Joey was out of earshot, she mouthed to Clark, *"Such a hottie, too!"*

When Patricia had originally invited them, Clark had jumped at the opportunity: he had been dying to get some answers from her, like what she knew about the Coven. Maybe she hadn't known completely herself. Whatever the reason, Clark was on a mission.

"Patricia, can I talk to you about something?" he asked quietly when Joey disappeared to the kitchen to drop off the bottles of wine they had brought.

"To me? Sure . . . what about?" she said. Was that reluctance he sensed?

"It's about—"

"Hi, Clark!" Nancy said, coming up for a hug. "It's nice to see you, hun."

Nancy, Paul, and Eva were all there, as well as Patricia's ninety-nine-year-old mother. Even Patricia's new boyfriend, Neil, deep in conversation about football with Paul. The next thing he knew, Clark was exchanging pleasantries and hugs and introducing Joey to his adopted family, the business of the holiday taking over. His question would have to wait.

Soon they were all settled in at the table around Patricia's many "Live, Laugh, Love" plaques and trinkets, in her comforting home that smelled like apples and cinnamon, for buckets of red wine and Patricia's delicious cooking, of honey-roasted turkey and ham, holiday stuffing with cranberry sauce, candied yams and mashed potatoes, corn and casseroles, and salads and biscuits. Clark engorged himself, of course, as much as was politely possible.

Round and short, unlike her mother, Nancy insisted she load up his plate to second and third helpings. "Don't be shy," Nancy said. Clark caught out of the corner of his eye a crayon drawing of Eva's hanging on Patricia's wall: it was of Hansel and Gretel, chomping into the side of the witch's candy home.

"I'd like to make an announcement," Patricia said. "I am happy to say that for the fifteenth year in a row I am being recognized as Employee of the Year at work—with a bonus! It took many an overtime, and many a sacrifice, but I did it!"

Nancy gasped. "Of course you are! That's my ma!" Nancy said, raising her glass. "Not only did she provide us with this beautiful meal and her lovely home this evening, she raised this family single-handedly when Pa died, she has kicked ass at her job, and she has gotten yet another accolade for all her hard work. Incredible! We know how hard you work. Congratulations, Ma! We're all so proud of you. Love you!"

"Aww, I love you too, sweetie! Thank you," Patricia croaked through teary eyes.

That's when the conversation came around.

"How's the job been since we last talked?" Nancy asked Clark. Conversations around the table paused as everyone turned quiet to listen.

What do I tell them . . . ? That my boss is a murderous witch who owns the city . . . ?

"Things have been, um . . . Well, my . . . manager, one of the assistants, likes to move the goalposts." Then he was off, telling the table about how Monica had tricked him into an empty promise of going along on a house call, how she had been jerking him around with coffee orders and errands and deliveries since his first day. The stories came up like word vomit. "Her behavior is so cruel it's like she hates me, and I have no idea why," he relayed.

He revealed how Melissa had confided in him that she was going to steal clients, how she "mysteriously turned up dead" the night of his birthday, and how the "company" had commenced interviews for her replacement the Monday morning right after the funeral. Patricia and her family looked at one another, shifting uncomfortably in their seats. *Reel it back, Clark, you're losing them . . .*

"And our booker—our HR—she's so neurotic, there's no reporting anything to her because nothing good will come of it, and . . . Ugh! Yeah. I can't even call out when I'm sick or I'll lose my job for sure. I'm just the lackey intern at the bottom of the food chain. You guys won't even believe what happened to the intern before me . . ."

Nancy sighed and wiped her mouth before speaking. "That's right, Clark: nothing good will come of it because *no one likes a complainer.*"

Joey cleared his throat and opened his mouth to speak. Instead, he took a sip of wine.

"Clark," Nancy began, "you gotta change your perspective. Not everyone thinks like you. Change your attitude and your life will follow," Nancy said, tapping the side of her head with her finger.

"Yeah, sure, okay, but—"

"It's not that your manager is jerking you around, it's that things change in business."

"I know that, but—"

"It's not that your manager hates you, it's that you are there to serve a role and do your job."

"Of course, but Nancy—"

"Toughen up, Clark. If you want to grow up, you'll have to put in the work and learn. Stop being so entitled and don't take things so personally."

Joey furrowed his brow.

Clark looked around the table, at their wide-eyed stares and Nancy's face of smirked satisfaction. He wished that someone would come to his rescue. But who would believe him, when he hadn't even told them the full truth? "Maybe you're right. I dunno . . ."

"Joey," Patricia squeaked as she lifted her glass to her lips, "this wine is delicious!"

"Thank you," he politely replied. "We serve it at Northlight. One of Charisma's favorites." He shot a glance at Clark like he wanted to say something. Clark was just grateful that somebody had changed the subject.

"Well, thank *you* for bringing it and for coming," she said. "I think we're all ready for something sweet! Who wants dessert?"

She and Paul passed out Patricia's infamous homemade baking that Clark grew up on, of pumpkin, pecan, and apple pies, peach cobbler, and an assortment of Italian cookies with coffee. When the table was cleared and everybody had all but unbuttoned, Patricia disappeared into the kitchen with a handful of plates, and as Nancy began to follow her, Clark insisted on taking the task off her hands. He wasn't about to let Patricia get off that easily.

He helped Patricia load the dishwasher while she rinsed the

plates. Clark made sure he and Patricia were alone before breaking the unusual silence.

"Hey, um, Patricia?" He double-checked: Joey and Paul were chatting away in the living room while Neil was passed out, snoring on the recliner. Nancy and Eva were watching the television.

"Ye-es?"

Clark spoke in a low voice. "I've been meaning to talk to you about something . . ."

"Oh, haha, what about, sweetie?" she croaked, extra nasal and squeaky.

"Nothing, it's just that . . . I don't even know where to begin. Patricia, why didn't you tell me?"

"Tell you what, Clarky?"

"That Charisma and her assistants . . . are a coven."

She almost dropped a plate in the sink ("Oopsies!"). For a split second, Patricia stole a look at him. "Clarky, what are you talking about?"

"You knew what she is all along, didn't you? Why didn't you warn me about what I was getting into?" Clark asked. "That Charisma and her assistants are witches?"

Patricia stopped mid-rinse.

"Witches? What? Sweetie, I'm not sure what you're going on about." But Clark didn't buy it.

"C'mon, Patricia. Did you know they only hire women? Monica sure was shocked as hell when I turned up for the interview."

"Oh, this is about your first name, isn't it?" she asked with a smile and a nod. "Hey, you know what, Clarky, I know it's your father's, and your father's father's. Say what you want, but it landed you a meet—"

"No, it's not about that," Clark said hastily. "C'mon, Patricia!"

"Charisma Saintly? Don't be silly . . ." Patricia walked around him to load the last plate. "I'm not sure what you're talking about." Clark could tell, she was definitely avoiding looking him in the eyes.

"You know what I'm talking about. She's the witch-queen of the world and you didn't tell me? That her assistants are part of her coven, that she's running an empire from her home, right here in New York. Only I didn't think she was serious about it, not at first. You have to have had some idea. Please tell me the truth."

She turned to face him.

"Please," Clark said. Patricia saw the despondency in his eyes, and broke.

"Oh, Clarky . . . I'm sorry! Really I am," she said. "I didn't think it would be this hard on you. I feel so bad! I thought this would be a good opportunity. The coffee shop is great and all, but I thought it would be good for you to, you know, spread your wings a little. To be in a real work environment. To see how someone important like Charisma does business."

So she has *been avoiding me . . . That's why I haven't seen her since this summer, before she suggested I meet Monica . . .* "Patricia, you don't have to apologize, I'm grateful for the opportunity, seriously, I am! It's just that, you know, could you have prepared a guy? Just a little?!"

Patricia paused, placing her pressed hands to her lips and taking a deep breath before speaking softly above a whisper. "I was worried that if I had told you what you were getting into, you would never have gone through with it."

"Yeah," Clark said, "maybe you're right. Maybe I should have taken out a few student loans. Stayed at the coffee shop. Gone back to college part-time. Maybe I'm not cut out for this. I've never been an assistant before. What do I know? Now I'm failing at it with nowhere else to go, and no way to leave . . ."

Patricia grabbed him by the shoulders. "Hey, sweetie, look at me. What's meant for you won't pass you by." Clark was immediately reminded of C Café where he first met Monica, and walking past it two or three times before finally landing on it.

"That's only the fear talking," Patricia said. "But what you fear isn't failing at the job—which you're not—nor is it the fear of not being enough—which you are! Do you get what I'm saying?"

"Not really," Clark said skeptically, looking up at her.

She grabbed his hands and held them in hers. "The only real failure is what might have come if you hadn't taken the job, and who you'd face when you'd look in the mirror. The real failure would have been *not trying*. That's all, Clarky! What you fear is you! Meeting yourself at the finish line on the other side of your dreams, the *you* you haven't even met yet." She petted his hands, and said, "You know I love you like family, Clarky, don't you?"

Her eyes were glassy and so were Clark's. Here she was, the woman he had known all of his life, now a few inches shorter than him, admitting her failure and asking for his grace. Clark decided he could give her that. He'd be ridiculous not to. She had given him so much, after all. He thought about that Dream Him he met, that Perfect Him that seemed so tangible and yet so out of reach. What would that Clark do in his shoes?

They leaned in for a warm hug. She smelled like Charisma's perfume.

As they broke away and chuckled at their own glistening eyes, one deep, dark, ugly thing nagged at Clark, something brewing in him that he hadn't been able to voice until then and there. "Patricia . . . ?" he began slowly. "Can I ask you something?"

"Don't get goofy!" she said, wiping her eyes. "Of course, Clarky, you can ask me anything."

Clark searched for the words: "What do you do if . . . when . . . you know someone is hurting other people?"

Patricia's smile fell instantly. "Who's hurting other people? What's going on, Clark? Are you okay? Is someone hurting you?!" The concern in her voice made Clark almost regret asking.

"No, it's nothing! I mean, no one. It's not me—yes, I'm fine," he said. She gave him the side-eye. "Actually, alright: I don't know. It's just that . . . someone . . . told me—*showed* me, rather—that they're hurting other people. And I'm not sure what to do about it."

"Who is hurting people, Clark?"

He said, "You know who I'm talking about."

At this, Patricia did something that took Clark by surprise: swiftly, she closed her kitchen curtains and peered over the kitchen counter to make sure they were not being overheard. Then, in a hushed voice, she leaned in, and spoke very slowly, just above a whisper.

"Sometimes, Clark, in life, it's best to mind our own business."

"But," Clark began, taken aback, "if you know better, shouldn't you do better?"

Patricia shook her head. "I know you want to be a good person, but sometimes, doing the right thing isn't the right thing to do. Remember that, Clark. Take it from me, it'll keep you out of trouble. Just drop it and do your job. Keep your nose down, and ask no questions. Do you hear me?"

"But—" he began.

"No, Clark. There's nothing you can do," she said. "Drop it."

By the time Clark and Joey got back to the car, a few pounds heavier and carrying Tupperware of leftovers, Clark was bursting to relay what Patricia had disclosed.

"Did you have a good time?" he asked of Joey first. "What did you think of them? They're great, right?"

Joey was quiet. "Yeah they're great, Clark, I had a great time . . . except . . ."

"Except . . . ?" They paused outside the doors. With the press of his keychain, the doors unlocked.

"Except," Joey began again as they sat inside. He put his key into the ignition and then removed it. "I dunno how to explain it. It's like they all seem to keep you under their thumb? They're denying your experience and answering for you like they have all the answers, and you totally let them!"

"What . . . ?" Clark said, flabbergasted. "I don't let them do anything."

"Look at how Nancy reacts to you being jerked around at work."

Clark furrowed his brow. "No way, they're not like that. They care, they just . . . have a funny way of showing it. They just—they just see things differently. It's the Queens in them, they're old school. They just don't get it . . . Right?"

"I'm not sure," Joey said with a sigh. "Maybe. Yeah, they care . . . But Clark, why didn't you stand up for yourself?"

"Stand up for myself?" Clark wasn't sure how to answer. "I didn't want to come across as ungrateful for the opportunity. I am, I really am grateful to be at Charisma's. I have Patricia to thank for it."

"Clark," Joey said, "Patricia got you the interview but you got the job. And just because you stand up for yourself doesn't mean you're ungrateful. You don't have to be grateful for everything: not for the abuse, and not for the way Nancy talked to you tonight. After the conversation you told me about at your birthday dinner, you're only making it okay for her to keep doing it."

"You're right . . ." Clark said, looking at his hands. "Thank you," he added. He started to pick at his nails.

"I just want what's best for you," Joey said, grabbing Clark's hand with his free one. They looked at one another. "To see you happy. You know that, right?"

Abuse . . . Is that what's happening . . . ?

Joey put the key in the ignition and started the car.

Clark bit his lip in thought as they drove on those quiet suburban streets back to Astoria, the New York City skyline looming into view.

When it came to Charisma and the others, Clark knew one thing to be true:

He was going to have to stop playing by their rules.

Charisma and her coven had to be stopped—and he would have to be the one to do it.

CHAPTER X

Errant Boy

"Come here, loser," Monica said to Clark first thing Monday morning, December the first. "You're coming on a house call."

Clark was shocked. "I am?!"

"Yeah," she said. "'All hands on deck' or whatever." She rolled her eyes.

That day was chaos as the coven prepared. Clark loaded up a few deliveries into the Closet, and then redistributed those supplies into the coven's many black designer luggage bags. After lunch, Clark helped load all the luggage into the SUVs, except, owing to Oksana the driver and Miranda the door-lady's hands-off approach, "helped" became "did it all himself."

Then the moment had come to ship off, and there she was, the subject of every conversation, looking calm and cool as ever: Charisma sauntered out of the elevator and out the lobby doors. A couple of passersby stopped to gawk at seeing her appear, pulling out their phones for photos. Charisma had a way of making everything look so easy, when behind the scenes Clark knew it was a facade, one that took an empire of little helpers to maintain.

Clark rode in the backseat of one of the blacked-out SUVs all the way down to Tribeca in rush hour traffic. It was after six as they rolled up to another lofty penthouse. She greeted this group of "darling" clients like they were girlfriends, with air kisses and hugs.

Inside, Monica ordered Clark to carry heavy bag after heavy bag up two flights of stairs, until a maid asked, to her bemusement, why he was doing such a thing when the elevator was but feet away. Monica disappeared behind a corner with a smirking grin and a flash of her cold gray eyes. Clark's sore throat had become so irritated and himself so mad, he could scream.

The guests filed one by one into a parlor room of a few chairs and tables under candlelight and drawn curtains. When Charisma and the coven had entered, Monica stopped short at the door. Just before Clark could enter the threshold, she said, "Not you," and closed the door firmly in his face.

A maid entered the space with a tray of food, and Clark could overhear Charisma telling a story: "So there we were, sitting on the beach in the Riviera at Cannes, and I was like, 'Darling, really? You can have any man you want, are you sure this is the one? And she said, 'With all of my heart.'"

The ladies *aww*ed.

"So we MAN-ifested it," Charisma said, to resounding giggles. "The two are now happily married and the It Couple of Hollywood, she with her hit TV show and three beautiful children, and he his—" The door closed. Clark hurried to press his ear up to it. He could just make out the murmuring fervor of Charisma's quick, passionate, emphatic voice, and the responding laughs and gasps of her audience, but was hardly able to make out the words at all. He sighed as he slid onto the floor, unnerved and dejected, twirling the strap of his backpack, trying his hardest to hear what was happening inside, to no avail. The indignation welled up inside of him.

Why does *Monica hate me so much . . . ?* he wondered.

When it opened next, Monica appeared. She snapped at him to get up. "Quick, make yourself useful and fetch the selenite wands," she ordered. In seconds, Clark located their trunk and produced them for her. Monica snatched them right from his hands and disappeared back into the room.

Minutes passed and felt like hours when he heard gasps and screams. "How did you know?!" one woman shouted. A few seconds later there were a few raucous laughs. That's when it happened.

"Where is it?" Clark could hear Charisma demand. The room fell silent. He could hear steps hurry to the door as Monica burst into the hall seconds later, this time in a panic.

"Oh my GAWD, where is it?!" she said in a manic frenzy, digging through kit after kit.

"Where is what?" Clark asked.

"I know I packed it," she said. "Shit shit SHIT!" Monica was tossing bags upon bags out of the kits all willy-nilly.

"What are you looking for? Let me help you," Clark said.

"AS IF you could help me," she spat. "Where is her fragrance?"

"We didn't pack it," Clark said.

"WHAT?!"

"It wasn't on the list."

"Who CARES if it wasn't on the list, it's supposed to be here! What good are you if you can't even do your job properly?! UGH!"

"But . . . you wrote the list! I'm just following orders!"

"Oh, *piss off*!" she spat. "Move!" Monica pushed him out of her way. His foot was caught on the strap of his backpack, and Clark fell to the floor, knocking something hard and glassy loose . . . And then he smiled: peeking out of his backpack was the tasseled atomizer of his one-ounce bottle of *Charisma*.

Monica looked at his face, which had broken into bemused splendor at what he had come to realize, and then at the bag at his feet. They looked at each other. She made a dive for it but Clark pulled it close with his shoe, too quick for her to grab.

Here's to "never saving the day" . . . he thought. He dashed around her, crumpled on the floor, and ran that little bottle of perfume into the room. The ladies stopped what they were doing, and the coven watched in astonishment as, with her back to the door, her hand held out, Clark dropped the bottle into Charisma's waiting hand.

"As I was saying, I knew the ingredients I wanted for my first fragrance. I wanted a *sillage*, a trail, something with presence and a magic coat tail. I wanted something commercial but unique. I had the best nose in the industry—a true alchemist, really, she's a miracle worker—to help produce the juice. We patented this mix that bypasses the olfactory senses into the part of the brain that stimulates intuition and confidence, and acts like a love potion to—"

Monica had returned to her place in the lineup, and the hatred was radiating off of her. Clark could hear the *ksk ksk* of the fragrance's tasseled atomizer and the "mmm" of the ladies before he closed the door behind him with pride. At the words "love potion" and the thought of Joey always kissing his neck, however, well, Clark decided to worry about that another time . . .

After nine in the evening, as the ladies filed out, they were clutching their chests, murmuring such thoughts as, "That was the best reading I've ever had," and "I've never told a *soul* that happened! How did she know?"

The Coven appeared after, and then Charisma, holding in the palm of her hand the used and well-loved bottle from the bottom of Clark's neoprene backpack. Charisma did not once raise her voice, only spoke dangerously low, slow, and quiet. "Which one of you bitches forgot to pack my fragrance?"

No one answered.

"Let me ask again: I know none of you packed this, this filthy, sad excuse of a bottle," she said, shaking Clark's tatty bottle about. "How in the bloody hell am I supposed to run an empire if my own team is unprepared? Huh?! *We just launched this!*" She was wearing a black leather corset under a tight jacket, a skirt, and heels. Clark thought she looked like a ringleader.

There was, again, no answer.

"Right. Which one of you saved the day? I know it wasn't Monica. Whom does *this* belong to?"

Monica hesitated before starting to speak, but then Clark did one more bad thing, the only thing he could do: he spoke up. "I did," Clark said.

It was as if one of the trunks had suddenly spoken. Slowly, they all turned to look at Clark, a room full of witches staring right at him.

"Good job, Clark!" Emily said.

With a look of bemusement, Charisma turned back to the Coven, and said, "Well, I'm glad fucking one of you was doing their job." She shot Monica the darkest of looks. The bottle was dropped into her hands, and Charisma walked away. *Clack clack clack.*

"Way to go, genius," Alicia said to Monica, once Charisma was out of earshot.

"You didn't think to pack them? An oversight, don't you think?" Lorena turned to address the group, landing with finality on Clark. "Here, you are all replaceable. One must never forget your job, nor your place." She followed Charisma out.

When the assistants were alone, Monica was absolutely fuming. The steam whistled higher and higher like a radiator in winter, until the very air around her grew malevolent and red, and she snapped.

"You don't *actually* wear this, do you?" she asked, turning on Clark and advancing on him. "This, a *women's perfume* . . . ?"

Clark didn't answer.

"Here," she said, hovering over him, "we are of the opinion"—she stepped into his face—"that men should look"—she punctuated—"and act"—with a jab of her finger in his chest—"like men!"

"Leave him alone, M—" Emily began, but Alicia put her finger to her mouth with a "shh," and Emily's lips snapped shut, tight and fast, as if out of her control, rendering her speechless.

Clark thought he was going to be sick. He let Monica talk to him like that, touch him even? What would become of him? He wanted to crawl into a ball and disappear . . . but another part of him had something else to say.

"You can't talk to me like that," Clark snapped back.

"What did you say to me?" Monica asked, low and deadly.

"You heard me," he continued, enunciating every word and taking a step toward her: "You. Can't. Talk. To. Me. *Like. That!*"

Alicia let out a gasp and a laugh.

"Excuse me? You're just the help! You're just some poor cretin I picked up off a dollar store bargain rack in Queens!"

Emily and Alicia gasped.

"Do you forget who you are talking to? We are beauty and grace," she continued, "and you will never be a woman, you will never be a witch, you will never be anything like us, no matter how much you might wish to be." She looked to the others for support, but they did not budge. "You will never amount to *anything.*"

"And what will *you* amount to, Monica?" Clark asked, red with anger. "A mean girl? A bully? A cheater? What did I do to you, huh? Where do you get off, being so bitchy?!"

"A cheater? What did you do to m . . ." Then, Monica gasped.

Emily and Alicia looked at one another as Monica's face fell from furrowed disdain into absolute astonishment and rage.

"It was you . . . ! YOU ratted me out!"

The girls gasped too.

"Prove it!" he said to her.

"I knew it," Monica said, right up in his face. Her eyes were full of fire and menace. "I'll make sure you regret that . . ."

"What is going on here?" Lorena asked, clacking back.

Monica stood back and pointed at Clark. She exclaimed, "He's scaring me!" Suddenly, she was smaller looking, hurt even. Monica reverted, a little girl again.

"You," Lorena said, turning on Clark and aiming a finger. "What did I say to you about causing drama, ay? I thought I told you no funny business, boy. I should have fired you at the Blood Moon, but I won't make that mistake again!"

The blood rushed into Clark's face. *Fired . . . ? For this . . . ?!*

"Oh, please, Mother, he did nothing wrong," Alicia said. "It was her. And besides, she deserved it. We're down an assistant; how do you think Charisma will take it that we're down another junior too?

Besides, don't fire him just for putting her in her place. It was bound to happen, the way she treats him."

Lorena looked at her, and then at Clark, and then at her again. She grunted. "Fine." Turning to Clark, she said, "Pack this all up and take it downstairs to Oksana. *Now.* And you," she said, pointing at Monica, "come with me."

Emily and Alicia filed away, following in Charisma's steps, high heels clacking behind them. Monica shot him the darkest and most venomous of looks before disappearing after them.

As Clark was breaking down the setup inside, alone, packing Charisma's designer trunks and luggage bags, he thought, *So Alicia sees it too . . . ? Do all of them . . . ? Why hasn't anyone said anything . . . ? Maybe they just don't care . . .*

Or maybe they were just waiting for me to say something . . . for me to take up for myself . . .

Oksana and the driver helped him load the luggage into the cars ("Let's get the fuck home," she said in her thick Russian accent) and then back up to Charisma's and the Closet.

By the time he left hers, it was close to midnight. He couldn't wait to tell Joey about what happened.

Monica was nowhere to be seen the next day, seemingly avoidant of Clark. Even if he had scared her away, he knew she'd be back. Charisma was out for the day too, Lorena had informed him. Playing hooky. She handed him a stack of envelopes.

"Deliver one fragrance each to these addresses," she said, with a stack of notes. "And this one," she said, giving him a single envelope, "is Charisma's. Guard it with your life."

The look in her eyes seemed to spell the end of him.

Before he left, he was to clean out the coat closet in the foyer, and sure enough, that box Monica had thrown in along with him from months before was still there, long forgotten. He ripped it open: it was full of blank orange pill bottles, just as Joey had said. But Clark wasn't surprised. Nothing surprised him anymore.

Clark made a plan of attack to accomplish his deliveries quickly on that brisk December day: first to the two addresses on the Upper East Side, then on a crosstown bus to the Upper West, then a giant building on Columbus Circle, then to Flatiron, West Broadway, and SoHo, and then back uptown towards Charisma's. How he missed the grittier, realer parts of the city: St. Mark's Place from his youth, the East Village, Canal Street, and the Lower East Side. He would end the tour with her final envelope, delivering it to an address not far from the penthouse.

The entire time, he looked down at that last envelope in his hand, flipping it over, practically crawling out of his skin to know the contents inside.

At the end of that afternoon, the setting sun had bounced off of low gray clouds and cast New York into a heavenly, yellow-gold light, before descending into an early evening.

Clark entered a ritzy building with gold doors on Fifth Avenue. Upstairs at this client's, a woman told him, "Wait here," before retreating down the hall from which she came. Clark didn't have to wait long, maybe a minute or two, before she was back. She handed the envelope to him wordlessly, and Clark, meeting her eyes and knowing his manners, said, "Thank you, ma'am, have a nice day."

As he maneuvered around the corner downstairs and outside, Clark paused to examine it. Clark's imagination went a little mad imagining what could be inside, and he did the unimaginable: he slid it into his backpack.

At home that night, Clark carefully held the envelope aloft, examining every angle of it. The paper was textured and rich, with a red wax seal like they all were. The eye with twelve eyelashes stared back at him, stamped in its center. Slowly, steadily, he knifed the wax seal open—and accidentally jabbed into the webbing of his hand. A couple of droplets of blood fell on the envelope and a bead of sweat formed on his brow. Surely Charisma would see that it had been tampered with now. Clark kept on.

He opened the envelope and removed the notecard inside, to reveal: nothing.

The notecard was blank.

He wrapped his hand in toilet paper to stanch the blood and squeezed. Curiously, he watched the red soaking through the veining of the toilet paper.

Maybe it needs a sacrifice . . .

Clark lifted the paper and let a single droplet fall onto the card. Nothing.

Clark slammed his fist on the table, the notecard now ripped and stained, the eye a taunting reminder of his doom. *Fuck . . . ! Breathe, Clark . . . Now what . . . ?* Clark racked his brain and paced his floor, biting his nails.

Think, Clark, think . . .

He remembered Miss Honey telling him about the notes on his first day months ago—but what was it that she said? He closed his eyes.

Feudal Europe . . . He remembered something about Feudal Europe . . . And candlelight, something about reading the letters by candlelight. "Sometimes they're just invitations and little 'thank yous,'" he remembered her saying, "but other times . . ."

"They just need a little light." The memory of her words echoed in his mind. A little light? But what did she mean? Clark held the card up to his lamp, but could make out no etchings of a pen, no signs of use.

Miss Honey wasn't implying that . . . No, it couldn't be . . . Clark had watched one too many movies. If he was wrong, it would destroy the letter completely.

His back dripping in a nervous sweat, Clark produced one of Joey's lighters from his kitchenette and held it under the letter. Over the flame, nothing happened . . . until he moved it lower to the middle. Jaunty scribblings appeared, which Clark surmised could not possibly have belonged to Charisma on account of having seen her flowery handwriting, which decorated the visuals of her branding from her websites for her fashion line.

Yes, the Powers have much in store. I look forward to discussing with you and the Order tomorrow night.

The handwriting faded as the letter cooled. Clark held the flame under the card once more, only to discover that the writing would not return.

Clark had a headache, his head spinning with disappearing ink and "the Powers." Who were "the Powers"? And "the Order"? Who would be collecting, and why?

"Witch secrets," Miss Honey had said.

That night, Clark dreamt again:

He was standing in an In-Between, a limbo that had always been there just under the veneer of the everyday, the daydream place he'd often slip into and out of. A single spotlight appeared, just like in the dream in September, in that shadowed hall of onlookers.

Who stepped into view this time was none other than the ever-elusive Miss Honey. "Look, baby," she said. She tapped on her forehead three times.

"I'm trying, but what did you mean?" he asked.

Her chest heaved up, and with a giant sigh and high-pitched ringing in his ears, Miss Honey went up in smoke. Standing in her haze was someone who smiled warmly at Clark.

"Grandma Wanda?" She smelled of gardenia and soap, a fragrance he could fondly recollect, and at the same time, was sad to have almost forgotten.

"Look," his grandmother said encouragingly, tapping on her forehead.

"I'm trying to, but I'm confused," he said.

Her smile of deep affection made his eyes cloudy and his lids heavy. "You have all the answers within you, pumpkin," she said. "I love you always." She blew him a kiss. In a flash of bright, white light, she morphed into his Ideal Self, looking down at him with a furrowed brow.

"Look," he said to Clark, this time more gravely than the women before. No sooner had Ideal Clark pressed his finger to the middle of his forehead than Present Clark was bombarded with images of lightning and thunder over mountains and rivers in a hot primordial planet, of mists descending on a valley—or was it an island? He couldn't be sure. He had visions of worms wriggling up out of the earth, of snakes, beetles and roaches surfacing up from mossy rocks and dirt and skyways, and suddenly, Clark was looking at a giant, wide, ancient tree atop a steep hill, its leaves and his hair rustling in the wind, dropping the fruit that it bore at his feet: shiny, red apples.

The howling wind of many whispered voices and ringing in his ears deafened his senses, and his perception shifted as the middle of his forehead prickled. It was all too familiar: Clark realized he was on the inside of Charisma's terrarium.

The rustling leaves on the wind whispered a single word to Clark as he watched the tree go up in flames, a great, giant bonfire that turned the world around them red and yellow. In a flash, it stopped just as suddenly as it had started: a vision. It was the word "Fire."

The whispers stopped. He looked up at the primeval sky. Then he turned around: a cloud from the misty perimeter was slowly ascending up that hill, and coming upon him. He had the distinct feeling that he was being watched, and he had an idea by who . . .

The whispers turned into screams as the mist came lapping at his feet. Kicking and stomping, Clark shouted, "No! *No!*" He fell backwards and, in an instant, he was right side up again, standing in none other than the quiet stillness of his sleepy Astoria apartment.

It was nighttime and the lights were off, as he stood by the rightmost window looking out at that uninterrupted northern sky. There were no crickets chirping. Something was off. The atmosphere was different. Hollow.

"Where are you going?" Joey asked from just behind him. He was sitting up in bed. Clark looked to Froggie on his shelf, the picture of his grandma on his bedside table, and an empty blue-and-white coffee cup next to it that read, *We are happy to serve you.*

"I'm not sure . . ." Clark said. He turned to the window, searching for something he didn't understand, something he couldn't see.

Joey asked, "You know you don't have to, right?" He folded down the covers next to him, and smoothed it with his bare skin on sheets. "You can forget all about them. You can choose to stay right here with me." To Clark, he looked so beautiful, naked in bed, illuminated by the glow of the ominous black-blue sky outside.

Clark checked his watch: it was three a.m., the witching hour again.

He looked down, and the next thing he knew, he was wearing his coat and his hat. In his right hand was a broomstick from the Closet. Was it writing he was seeing, runes that appeared etched into the broomstick and glowed like invisible ink in the dark?

"There's something I have to do," Clark said again determinedly, turning back to the window. It slid open seemingly on its own, beckoning his flight. Clark mounted the broomstick and a gust of wind seemed to sweep in and all around him. With a hook of his navel and the feeling of butterflies, he launched into the air and out the window, flying into the night. The broomstick seemed to guide him, knowing where to go.

Astoria, usually so full of life, was silent. There was not a soul alive to be found underneath him, not on the empty streets below lined in dead-branched trees, not in the drawn-dark windowed homes, not a pedestrian or a moving car in sight. The eyes of RFK Bridge, too, were dark: the only light came from a sun eclipsed by a full moon and the glowing, low, gray clouds above. In the distance and shooting up into those clouds was a red beam of light. It called out to him, murmured his name in the dry rustling leaves on the onyx roads below, in the sharp December breeze whipping his face and whistling through those buildings and in his ear. He looked down at his reflection in the East River he crossed. Was it real? Was this really happening? It certainly felt like it. With one hand, Clark wiped a wind-streaked tear from his cheek. The broom was positioned like a missile straight for Charisma's building as he sailed into the dark city, an Other New York.

He came upon the Tower and encircled the building. There was that telltale tingling in his forehead again: that light he had followed beamed like a beacon up into the clouds, and the whispering was coming from the terrarium as if it knew he was near, calling him closer.

Instantly, Clark's mind's eye was flooded with imagery: the giant apple tree was set ablaze in a powerful, mighty fire, blue and bright. And then, he saw the eyes of Charisma's portrait boring into him, saw its frame engulfed in flame—but not caught in it, repelling it all around, impervious to fire. Clark understood then, as if he had always known, that the terrarium was the very same, great, imposing Eye that had opened on him months ago, ever-present and ever-watching—and it was staring back at him too. It knew he was there.

Suddenly, the clouds shifted and the air turned, as the middle of Clark's forehead prickled fiercer than ever. In unison, the stone gargoyles on the building's four corners sprang to life, their bodies animated, the size of lions, looking up at him with menacing red eyes of hellfire. It was a trap, and Clark had been lured right into its hands.

He watched in horror as they spread their wings. With a synchronized dismount, they swan-dived into the air. At first, they encircled the Tower, beating their wide, mighty wings in synchronization—and then, in single file, they flew upwards, straight for him.

Clark soared up and dropped into a nosedive, missing the snapping jaws of the first gargoyle by inches. They dove behind him. There was whistling in his ears and his eyes streamed against the wind as he plummeted headfirst into the darkness of the deserted street below, urging the broomstick faster. He could hear the howling of the gargoyles giving chase, closing in on him. As they caught up to him, clawing at the broomstick's bristles and then his body, he swerved, and the shadowed ground that he could barely see approached, nearer and nearer—one hundred feet, then fifty, then twenty—as he careened towards it, a gargoyle snapping and growling just behind.

At the last possible millisecond, Clark pulled up hard and fast. The bottom of his shoes skidded dangerously on the pavement, and he kicked up off the empty street, wobbling unsteadily. *Bang!* Clark turned to look: the first gargoyle had crashed and shattered into the pavement, shattering into a million pieces of glittering rock and cracking Sixth Avenue beneath it. The dust and debris, however, billowed and blew into the air, revealing the other three gargoyles searching, following close behind. Their red eyes locked on him, and they uttered a murderous roar. Clark felt frightened in ways he hadn't imagined in his wildest nightmares.

Clark zoomed over and under traffic lights as fast as he could muster, hoping, praying for a diversion, to lose them—but they were faster. A sharp right almost hurled him into a lamppost, another into the swinging claws of the nearest gargoyle, and then he heard a shatter: the second had smashed through a building's windows, spraying glass-like shrapnel all around, cutting into his jacket. Clark yelped and shielded his head.

He recognized, by the glint of the river, the empty street ending, and the mass looming up at him, that he was flying east on 59th Street: he was approaching the Queensboro Bridge, dark and eerily traffic-less. As fast as his broomstick could carry him, Clark flew east. He turned over his shoulder: the gargoyles had disappeared, nowhere to be seen. He dared not stop.

Clark swooped into the dark tunnel, the wind whistling past his ears. Without warning, a gargoyle burst in between the rungs, hurling at him from the side like a bullet, and snapping and clawing. Clark ducked and rolled over, flipping upside down. He missed the demon as it breezed past his head and knocked off his hat, his back skidding against the pavement beneath him, and almost causing him to topple and crash off his broom. Clark almost wanted it to happen, to end the nightmare. The gargoyle's wing crashed into the median barricade instead, breaking off, and the gargoyle smacked and bounced with a sickening wail, and toppled into the East River. The splash echoed throughout those quiet streets.

The other gargoyle lunged up from the left, but Clark was not fast enough. It caught up to him in his slipstream, and with its ferocious claws, an open paw the size of a trash can lid, dealt a savage swipe, slashing at Clark's back. He uttered a guttural cry in pain. His vision went black. Clark was careening, losing focus and control.

He threw his body into the broomstick to a sharp right, smacking his back into the stone girder, which knocked the air out of him, and slipping out of the bridge and up to the top deck. Reeling, spiraling, he ascended along the highest cable of the highest tower, his back stinging in the cold night air. Only, Clark was slowing down: he realized he was fighting gravity, as the two gargoyles revealed themselves from below, beating their thunderous wings up, higher, and higher, gaining on him with ease. Together, they uttered that booming roar that filled the entire dark city: a kill roar. They encircled him fast.

At the top of the spire, the gargoyles lunged with their arms and their claws outstretched. Clark held the broom with his bad shoulder, and with the other, just as the gargoyles closed in on him, he grabbed the rung and spun, slingshotting out of harm's way. The two gargoyles swiped and snapped with one another, colliding and crumpling in a heap of tangled limbs and wings. With a deadening, booming, echoing cry, they fell to the bridge with a crash of glittering rock and smashed into the river below with a deadening splash. Clark dared not stop on his silent flight along the river, back to Astoria, and to home.

As he approached the unlit RFK Bridge, he veered east until he saw the tracks of the subway. He was close. That's when he heard another one of those battle cries that sent a pang through his chest and made his stomach flip.

He grunted from the cut on his back but turned just the same: to his dismay, a single gargoyle was flying straight towards him, its wet, beating wings glistening in that false light pollution of the dark New York sky, somewhere over Roosevelt Island.

Clark dipped low, hoping to lose it amongst the hodgepodge of squat Astoria rooftops, darting around the alleyways and in between buildings he knew so well. In one tight, dark alley, Clark peered up, and heard the beating of the gargoyle's wings flash above him. He listened to it howl as it dove into a street a few blocks away.

Somewhere south of home, at what must have been Astoria's Broadway, Clark ended up swerving into the underbelly of the subway tracks. He flew fast and homebound. All was quiet. Clark could only hear the whistling of the wind in his ears. He took a breath. That's when the gargoyle nosedived through the track's slats, spraying wood like shrapnel all around. Clark dodged. The gargoyle lunged straight for him, arm raised and claws out, and Clark dipped just in time for it to slash the back of the broomstick's bristles. Clark spiraled out of control. The back of his broom hit the steel train beam and ricocheted; the gargoyle clawed into the pavement and shot up at him; Clark screamed and kicked up on its head, sending it flying into the pavement and him up and over the railway up above, onto Newtown Avenue. Clark flew in a sharp left, then a right into an alley, and then north on his tree-lined street. He encircled his building, came upon its northern side with his fire escape just in view, when, to his horror, so did the gargoyle, coming straight for him.

Up his fire escape he sailed, in through the apartment window that opened for him, granting him admittance.

In bed, there was no Joey, no sheets turned down, only a still Clark, lying fast asleep as the broom launched him into bed and skirted into place—just as the last gargoyle came crashing in through his window with a kill roar that shook the air. The last thing Clark knew was the flying of glass, metal, and brick, blasting into him and his bed, and the gargoyle lunging at him from the frame, but by then it was too late:

Clark was startled awake and into reality, kicking and thrashing at nothing there.

When he awoke, Clark's watch had died, frozen at three a.m. He lifted himself off his bed and winced. His shoulder twinged and stung just as it had in his dream, and his bedsheet was spotted in blood.

He walked himself to the bathroom mirror and, sure enough, his cheeks were wind burnt, and there were three long, shallow lacerations on his right shoulder blade. Clark had never had an accident like this before, and he wasn't sure what to do. He couldn't go to Astoria Hospital just blocks away—and explain what, that he had narrowly escaped the bloodhound gargoyles of his boss? He dabbed the stinging cuts with toilet paper and returned to bed, covered in an old towel and lying on his side.

A single, penetrating, anxious thought kept him awake and his heart racing out of his chest: the terrarium had known it was him, that he knew too much. And if it knew, Charisma knew. And if she knew, he had to stop her before she stopped him . . .

Eventually, exhaustion overcame him, and finally, Clark passed out asleep.

At Charisma's that morning, Clark was a little late for the first time he could ever remember.

Clark went through the motions of errands and organizing. Not daring to wear color, Clark wore black, and for good reason: in a mirror, he could make out the glint of blood spotting on his back through his button-down shirt. He noted all the cameras and the corners in which they lurked, especially the ones in the Closet. Monica kept her distance, giving him the silent treatment he so did not mind.

Lorena passed him by and said, "You don't look so good. You're not going to get us sick, are you?"

"I'm fine," he replied, making sure to turn his back away from her. She seemed to avoid him the rest of the day anyway. It was Friday night and Joey had taken a night shift at work, so he wouldn't have to worry about explaining the injury he had somehow sustained in his dream . . . at least not yet.

Later that evening, as the night turned to eleven, Clark made his way back on the train and headed to Charisma's.

Clark had sent a text to Joey:

> (11:03 p.m. Clark Crane): Hey, Mr. Big, I just want to tell you that I love you. <3

> (11:31 p.m. Joey DiMuccio): I love you too =]! Is everything okay?

> (11:31 p.m. Clark Crane): Everything's great :]

At his last words and with a pang of guilt, Clark felt tears in his throat that wouldn't come up.

* * *

Before he left, Clark had made his arrangements at home. In his diary, he had left a note:

Witches are real.
This is not a fairy tale.
This is not a joke.
I didn't realize it until I was in deep. And now, if you're reading this, it's probably too late for me.
If you're like me, then you've read about witches or seen them on TV. These witches are worse because this is real life.
Witches don't wave magic wands.
They don't have green skin or warts.
They don't live in candy houses and eat children . . . as far as I know.
Witches hide in plain sight. Bad things happen to the people around them. I would know.
They do make deals. I've seen their clients.
Witches have money. Town cars. Assistants. And covens.
And they do like to wear black. A lot of it.
You won't know they're the villains because they wear couture. They are very rich and very powerful. They are amongst us. You can always tell a witch by their eyes. In some way, they always reveal themselves. They're not trying to hide. At least, not the ones I know.
Charisma Saintly is their queen, although a saint she is not. It's all a ruse.
Only, before I realized, I had no idea that big business around witchcraft could even exist, let alone a queen of all witches. She's the most powerful of them all. And if she or hers find this, I'm as good as dead. If you're reading this, I probably am already.
I did something not nice, and it fired back. Someone got hurt. I saw Charisma kill one of her assistants and cover the whole thing up like an accident. Charisma is the match and the fire, and she will make it look like an accident when she disappears me too. If anyone finds this, if I don't survive, please tell Joey that I love

him, I really do. Tell Patricia I'm sorry. Tell my family too, even
if I haven't talked to them in ages.
I'm going to stop her, if it's the last thing I do.

The feeling of that opened, unblinking Eye in his mind had not gone away; on the contrary, it had only gotten stronger. The same could be said for the ringing in his ears, which hadn't subsided for weeks, peaking to a shrill, deadening whine.

This time, knowing Charisma's nighttime security by name made getting upstairs easy, even if Charisma would be out on some kind of meeting. Clark opened the door, arriving again in a quiet, vacant home. He darted past the portrait in the front landing room to the stairs, up and up to the Closet.

With his back to that camera, Clark approached the terrarium, and tried to move or lift the glass enclosure—but it would not budge. He peered under the table to its pedestal leg: bolted. Clark questioned, *If they don't open it, how does it stay alive . . . ?*

Clark combed through the drawers in search of a tool—Ouija boards, hundreds of crystals, the hundreds of votive candles—until he found it: their restock of candle lighters he'd made sure to request.

With his back to the camera again, he clicked one alight, and to his bewilderment, the flame evaded the terrariums' frame within an inch as if repelled, just like the picture frame of Charisma's portrait in his dream. The worry dawned on him. *What if she doesn't have a weakness . . . ? What if she can't be stopped . . .*

He peered into the terrarium. The room was spinning, and Clark held his stomach, thinking he was going to be sick.

A gentle voice from behind him said, "I told you to get out while you could, baby." The pet name and words were like a hug; this time he didn't startle. Clark knew who it was.

"Hi, Miss Honey," he said, turning around.

"Hi, baby," she said.

"What do you know about . . . all of this?" Clark asked, reeling. "What haven't you told me? What haven't I been let in on?" His mouth was dry, and the small of his back was wet with sweat—or maybe blood.

"Well, baby," she said slowly, "what you see is what you get, and what you see is what I see. Witches gonna witch, you know what I mean?"

They stood in silence for a moment. His thoughts swarmed his head, and his heart began to race. "No. I don't know what you mean. I need some answers. Now. *Please*. Charisma is . . . Ugh, I don't even know where to begin," he said. "Is this terrarium . . . enchanted? Bewitched?"

She nodded.

"Is it . . . connected to her?"

She nodded again.

"What do you know about it? Is it . . . sentient?"

She said, "Why don't you ask it yourself, baby?"

Clark turned and put his hand on that glass enclosure. *How are you connected to Charisma . . . ?*

Sure enough, a branch faintly clinked against the glass, an "answer": like a download of knowledge, Clark knew the tree was an oculus, it was older than he could understand, its life force held in that glass container and . . . somewhere else.

A wave of shock shot through his body.

Clark turned to look at Miss Honey. "Does it sustain her somehow?"

She only met his gaze with those honey-almond eyes, and said, "I'm not sure, baby. It's tied to her . . . But how or to what end, I'm not sure."

"Can she be stopped?" Clark asked.

"I think if her talismans are destroyed," she said, motioning to the terrarium, "if her magic is subdued, then she could be. But I don't know."

"The deliveries . . . The notes . . . ? Is she some kind of drug lord mafia queen?"

Miss Honey chuckled gravely. "Sounds like it to me."

"And the Powers? The Order? Who are they all?"

She furrowed her brow. "That much I don't know. I came close though, before . . ."

Clark had a knot in his stomach.

"Before what? What else don't I know?" he asked. "Miss Honey . . . why are you here this late?"

After many moments, Miss Honey looked away and said, "I told you, baby, to get to steppin' if you know what's good for you. But you didn't listen . . . and now it's too late, you're in deep . . . you're in deep . . . and now she's coming."

Clark erupted into sweat. "Coming? Who's coming? What do you mean?"

But Miss Honey looked to the floor, and with searching eyes and labored breaths, began to wring her hands and rock from side to side. "You get too close and play with fire, you gonna get burned . . . You gonna get burned, baby . . . I tried to warn you but you wouldn't listen . . . Burned, I said . . . You . . . I . . ."

"Miss Honey . . . ?"

"She . . . she's coming . . . No . . . Don't get too close, don't . . . No, don't! DON'T! DON'T YOU COME ANY CLOSER," she shouted, her eyes wild, wet, and darting around. Tears began to streak down her face, and sweat dripped onto her forehead. "I SAID STAY AWAY. NO! *NO!* I SWEAR I MIND MY OWN, I DO MY JOB. I WON'T TELL NOBODY. *NOBODY!* STAY BACK! *STAY BACK!*" Miss Honey's body quivered harder and harder, and Clark was sure she would wake the whole penthouse.

"Miss Honey, it's okay," he pleaded in reassuring softness. "Please, it's just me. Breathe. Please, stop or they'll catch us—" But Miss Honey was not hearing him. She was looking at him but not seeing him, and Clark could tell, the look in her wide, sweet eyes . . . he had seen before: it was that of pure terror.

Clark inched closer to her and she took some steps back, shaking her head and waving her hands, the crying and the rambling worsening. She shouted through heaving sobs, "DON'T YOU COME ANY CLOSER!"

Clark stopped where he stood, just a few feet away.

"I DIDN'T DO NOTHIN', I SWEAR! PLEASE, LEAVE ME ALONE! *LEAVE ME ALONE!* NO! *NO!* BUT MY BABY! PLEASE, *MY BABY!*"

Clark watched in disbelief as Miss Honey put her arms up, shaking and sobbing. She screamed, *"NOOO!"* and in an angry flash, Miss Honey burst into a screaming fire from head to toe. The flame was so intense and close that it forced Clark back like an explosion, knocking him to the floor. Miss Honey fell to her knees, and when her screaming stopped, fell face down. Throat dry, ears ringing, clothes damp with sweat, and hair standing on end, Clark lay on his arms in a state of shock. The fire had licked the ceiling black and the smoke filled the room. A tear escaped onto his cheek. Another one, gone and dead to Charisma's madness. It must have been because of him, he figured. He had said too much, and Miss Honey had paid the cost.

After some time, Clark wiped his face and gathered himself off the floor. He approached with examining eyes, not daring to touch or get too close. Miss Honey's body lay on the marble floor, smoldering, silent, and still. An airplane flew by overhead, jarring Clark back to reality. He realized his shoulders were sore from being wound up to his ears, and the lacerations on his back had a horrible twinge. He held his breath—hanging in the air was the smoke and scent of singed hair and scorched flesh, and he knew he would never be able to forget it as long as he lived.

A dreaded voice came from behind him that made his stomach drop: "What is going on here?" It was Lorena in her nightgown, and standing next to her was Charisma.

"It's . . . Miss Honey, she . . ." Clark began, but what he saw next sent the room on a tilt: Miss Honey was nowhere to be found. Not her blackened body, not the ash of her clothes, nor the smoke in the air, nor the charred remains of her rubber tennis shoes—just the lingering smell, and the spinning room crashing all around him. Reeling and confused, Clark was dizzy and lightheaded.

"Come, darling," Charisma said. "Let's have a chat."

CHAPTER XI

The Powers That Be

Charisma, Lorena, and Clark in tow walked wordlessly down the stairs and towards the offices—Charisma in heels under her nightgown, no less, and Clark in the daze of shame from being caught, and a state of sheer, unmitigated dread. The portraits they walked past all seemed to say, *dead man walking* . . . As he caught his reflection he hardly recognized in a passing mirror—drawn, hollow-eyed, and hopeless—he thought to himself, *Maybe they're right* . . .

It was funny: Charisma was about the same height as Clark, yet she felt bigger, giant, broader even, as if Clark was always craning his neck to look up at her. The charge of the very air around her seemed to snatch at him in her wake, and he succumbed to it like prey to a predator. In the orbit of her gravity, Clark felt powerless.

The three walked past Lorena's office to a door Clark had not yet visited. Inside was nothing like Lorena's moody, film noir office: Charisma's had a regality, with fine silhouettes and classic lines, open windows, white-gold accents, and marble throughout, like the rest of her home. Behind the desk was a tall, gold chair on a platform of two or three steps. Her throne.

So this is where I'm going to die . . . Clark thought with dread. *Not bad . . . ! Could be worse . . . !*

"Sit," Charisma instructed, indicating the chair in front of her desk. Clark did as he was told.

"I knew the boy was trouble from the first moment I met him. I should've believed Monica when she—"

"I can take it from here, Lorena."

"Yes, but if only I could—"

"Lorena, go," she commanded.

"But, *Sissy*—"

"*Lorraine.* I said leave us. Now."

Clark watched Lorena's chest lift as if about to speak, and then, knowing there was no use in arguing, she turned on foot and left. The door drew shut as if on its own accord, clicking and closing them in, and then all was quiet. Just the two of them left. Clark turned in his chair to face her.

Here she was, the infamous woman still a mystery to him, whom he both delighted and disdained, sitting right in front of him, her eyes boring into his. Charisma was regal, beautiful, cool and calm, sitting there in her nightgown, her alabaster skin smooth and even in the warm lamplight and the city glow outside those office windows. Clark, on the other hand, was scared shitless. She smelled of her white-floral fragrance, and her green eyes were still her trademark smoky feline. Clark wondered if she slept in her makeup.

Charisma produced a fresh cigarette, put it to her lips, and inhaled as a small flame ignited the tip, seemingly out of thin air.

Clark knew he was caught, and about to pay heavily for it. *Be brave . . .* he kept telling himself.

"I don't believe we've been introduced yet, darling," she said.

"I'm Clark," he said.

"Like Kent?" She took a drag and smiled, and the hair on Clark's arms stood on end. "I know what your name is. Always a frog, never a prince, ay? Tell me, Clark darling: how old are you?"

"Twenty-four," he said.

"Twenty-four, I see . . . And, when is your birthday?"

Clark hesitated. He was a student again in the principal's office. "October twenty-fourth, a week before Halloween," he answered. She wore the most peculiar of knowing smiles on her alabaster face. Clark wondered if she had already known that much too.

"Ah, Scorpio on the cusp of Libra," she said. "Year?"

He answered.

"Taurus moon, Capricorn rising, and your Mars is in Scorpio: once you decide to do something, there is nothing that can hold you back—*ohh, how passionate.* Your Tenth House is in Scorpio, too . . . a truthseeker. Well, happy belated, darling."

"Thank you," Clark said. "You too."

"Thank you. Now, color me confused, but what is it that you think you are doing here exactly, in my Closet, in my home, in the middle of the night?"

"I, um . . ." But Clark broke away. This time, he was not sure what he could say that would get him out of this. "I . . . left something. In the Closet."

"And did you find what you were looking for?" she asked through narrowed eyes.

"Um . . . yes," he said.

She tilted her head, and giving him a side-eye, with that smile that didn't quite reach her eyes, said, "*Ah ah ah,* one mustn't ever lie to me. No no, that would be a grave mistake. A very grave mistake to make indeed . . ."

What do I say . . . ? What can I say . . . ?

Charisma said, "You can start by saying the *truth.*"

Clark flushed red and his stomach flipped. The violation he felt was akin to being intruded on in his own privacy, as if being walked in on in the restroom.

Charisma spoke with sharp finality. "You are here tonight because . . . ?"

"I thought you would be . . . out," he said. He was unable to stop himself. Despite his best wishes, he *wanted* to talk.

"Out where?"

"Out with . . . the Powers."

"With the Powers?" Charisma laughed and the sound was like bells. Clark's stomach twisted into knots. He hated that he liked her voice, liked the sound. "Whatever do you mean?"

"I know about the Powers," he said. "I know about the Order. I know about the terrarium. I know all about you. I know you killed Melissa, I know you killed Miss Honey, and many, many more."

She broke into a smile and chortled into her cigarette while Clark sat quiet. "That's what I love about you working-class New Yorkers . . . so much *gumption*. It was you who intercepted my note, wasn't it? I figured as much. Since you know so much, you do know what happened to the last person who intercepted my notes, don't you? If not, I'm sure you can imagine . . ." She took a drag and the ember sparked. Slowly, she exhaled a puff of smoke.

Instantly, he knew he'd made a grave mistake. Clark shifted in his seat; he wanted to disappear right then and there.

"Now, look, it's one in the morning. Let's cut the bullshit, shall we? Tell me, what is it that you want?"

"Answers," Clark said almost automatically, the word seeming to escape his mouth before he could even stop it. Clark was sure that he was being witched.

"But," Charisma said with a smile, "you just told me you know all about me. So which is it, darling? You know all about me, or you want answers?"

Clark realized, far too late, that he had no clue what he was doing. That this was it. He had gone too far. That he was as good as dead.

"I, uh . . ." Clark began. "Umm . . ."

"What's the matter? *Froggie* caught in your throat?"

Clark's blood ran cold again.

"Frogs . . . how very interesting of you. Frogs symbolize abundance—*and fear*. Didn't you know? Riddle me this, then: you were here that night of your birthday when we took down the moon. Why?"

"I . . . heard about the eclipse ritual," Clark said. "I had a little liquid luck and, um, I wanted to see what it was about. To see if you all are actually witches, who do actual magic." The words escaped him almost against his will—it felt so good that he was relieved to say them, ashamed to like it even. "I'm sorry," he added, blushing. He hated himself for it.

Charisma sat there giving him a studying look. She said, "Taking down the moon is one of a witch's most sacred rituals, and on the night of an eclipse no less. When we accepted the moon into our aura, yours mingled with ours, big and bright. I'll admit, I haven't seen one like that in quite a while. While I can't blame you for being *curious*, curiosity did kill the cat, you know . . . Speaking of, mine got you pretty good, huh, darling? The gargoyles."

At this, the slash on his back twinged. Clark couldn't believe this was happening. She spoke with a smile, but what she was saying was pitiless. He had a feeling of dread in the pit of his gut that was making him ache all over.

"How did you do that?" he asked. "The gargoyles in the dream? The cut . . . Was it a dream, or was it real?"

"As my good friend once said, of course it was a dream, darling, but why would that mean it wasn't real?" She spoke with a coy smile. "As for the gargoyles, consider them a precaution, a security system of sorts. That was quite the feat, your little broomstick chase. It took some willpower to summon one of my brooms and accomplish that. *Bravo*."

"And the Powers? The terrarium?"

"The terrarium is an ancient magic. One could even say it *speaks for itself*. As for the Powers That Be, well, some *powers* are outside of the realm of a witch's control, *be that* as it may. Everybody answers to somebody, even me . . .

"Some magics are so powerful, in fact," she continued, taking a drag and billowing out smoke, "one needn't wave a magic wand or recite an incantation, especially when that magic is a glamour of the mind. When the mind refuses to See, the glamour cast is a cloak of invisibility one puts on by their own ignorant volition. And as you may be well aware, *mon petit justice complex*, the truth is as loud as the superhero underwear you surely don . . . and always reveals itself. One need only be willing to look and listen."

"I'm sorry but I don't understand."

Lift the veil, darling . . . Look again . . . Charisma said to him in his mind. On "look," she tapped on the middle of her forehead as his began to prickle. She bored into his eyes with the most carelessly invasive gaze, and Clark sank back into his seat, locked in her stare. He had the feeling he was looking into someone's eyes he shouldn't be.

This time, it was like there was a double memory living in his recollection, unknown to him before, as if some kind of déjà vu, a memory of an experience that had always been there but not quite recalled. It was as if the radio in his mind had dialed to a frequency in between.

It was his interview with Monica, when not a word could be heard outside of his table. Clark was listening so intently, so nervous, wringing his hands under the table, that when the waiter appeared soundlessly from the kitchen, Clark choked on his water. Only, Monica didn't take the sound bubble with her—Clark had been the one to mute the world around them.

"I did that?" he asked. Charisma did not reply.

Another memory came to him: It was his first day again, and Clark was standing in Hell's Entrance, Miss Honey before him, delivering that warning. Except, he realized there was no one sitting at the table. He was talking to thin air.

Another memory: Melissa was confessing to leaving the Coven in that elevator, but this time, and to his horror, he was Charisma, listening in on them as she reviewed the security footage.

And another: drawing the circle and gabbing with Emily on his birthday in the Tower—but this was not from his memory or the security footage. This he was overhearing from the terrarium. And again, on that same night, Clark watched himself from above and out of body, conspicuously standing at the lip of that iron staircase, spying on the Coven: there one moment and gone the next, his aura enveloped him in a distorting cloak, rendered him almost imperceivable. Then, he watched his aura, indigo and periwinkle blue, grow under the eclipsed red moon and meld with the Coven's, giving him away. His showed brighter than any of theirs, and Charisma took notice.

Next, Clark saw through their four pairs of eyes simultaneously, the gargoyles looking up at his blue-aura-ed silhouette in that dark New York, and in unison swan-diving through the air, bobbing up and down with the beat of their wings, and lunging after him as he shot into the darkened street below. This made his head hurt so bad, he thought he was going to vomit.

And then, Clark saw himself through the eyes of Charisma's portrait, darting past the landing room earlier that very night as he snuck into the penthouse. He saw himself through the eyes of the terrarium, trying to lift its container and test its flammability. He watched through his own eyes as Miss Honey burst into flames all over again, as she had that night; and then again, he watched himself through Charisma's eyes, being blown back as if by nothing, crying for a body that was not there. Recollecting those memories was as if the television of his mind's eye had switched to a movie he had seen so many times he had come to know it by heart, only to realize that he had never watched it in English until that very moment.

Charisma broke her focus with a roll of her eyes. Clark blinked and came back too. She put out her finished cigarette and lit another. The room was spinning.

Clark said, "Miss Honey is . . ."

"*Dead,*" Charisma finished. "Dead, dead, dead. And has been for quite some time. She used to work for me, some years ago."

"But . . ." Clark began but stopped. *Is she a ghost . . . ? A figment of my imagination . . . ? Am I going crazy . . . ?*

Darling, haven't you been paying attention . . . ? she said, speaking to him mind to mind. *We are all a little mad . . . You have to be to do what we do. Eventually, you will learn that crazy is a compliment . . .*

"Why? Why did you kill her?"

"Why? Because, she knew too much, that's why. I had caught her snooping around, just like you, and when she became a problem, I had that problem eliminated. How she infiltrated my defenses and appeared to you is another matter entirely . . ."

"I'll expose you," Clark blurted out. "I'll tell the whole world about you and what you are."

At this, Charisma laughed, and he regretted it instantly.

"And who would believe you? Who in this great wide world, in this city that is mine, would believe someone like you?"

Clark was at a loss for words.

"Besides," she added, "you signed an NDA."

Clark thought back with regret to his first day, when he had most certainly signed himself away. What would it take to break his word? To break a witch's contract? Clark saw the answer in his mind's eye, a thought alien to him, intruding on his own:

He went up in screaming flames, then and there in Charisma's chair—fired in immolation, just like Melissa, and just like Miss Honey. In a blink, the scene flitted from his mind as quick as it had come, and Clark was left staring at the person who he knew had imprinted it.

Charisma spoke with a smiling coquettishness: "If all of what you say is true and I'm the *Big Bad* you say I am, why then did you stay?"

Clark looked back, perplexed. "I didn't have a choice. I dropped out of college, I went down to weekends at the coffee shop to support myself. I . . . I—"

"You can lie to yourself all you like," she said, "but one always has a choice. You chose not to return to school, and you chose to interview. You chose to drop in hours, knowing full well you could go back to your old, boring life whenever you wanted. But no: you chose to get ahead. You chose to crash my party, knowing there would be consequences. You chose to pit Monica and Melissa against each other, knowing they would tell on one another. You chose to sacrifice them, Melissa especially—offered her up on a platter, even, for your own personal gain. And then, you chose to stay. You have always had a choice, my darling."

"What . . . ?" he said breathlessly. "I didn't think that—I just wanted to take the heat off of me, to distract them. I . . . I didn't choose to . . . to 'sacrifice' her . . . How could you even say that?"

Charisma took a drag. "Sweetie darling, I just finished the job. *You* did the hard work for me. You turned the tables, for no one else but yourself. And here I underestimated you, thinking Monica would be your demise like every other junior's before you. Maybe she's met her match. Maybe we needed a male witch after all."

Clark's eyes widened. "Wait, I'm not a . . . You think I'm a witch?"

"I told you never to lie to me, boy," she said. "I know what you are. You can fool the others with your act, all unassuming and innocent and naive-like. But I know better. I've known it from the first moment I laid eyes on you."

Clark was speechless. Him, a witch? All his life he had dreamt of being special, of being unique, but he never thought it possible. Not for someone like him. Not this way. He'd thought news like this would make him feel a sense of elation. All he could feel was horror.

He searched for the words and looked up at her. "Am I evil?"

"That depends on your definition," Charisma said, waving his worry away. "Morals are relative, wouldn't you say?"

Clark asked, "Are *you* evil? Do you work for the Devil?"

Charisma smiled. "My my, aren't you an assiduous little witchling." They looked at one another for a moment before she answered, "No more evil than anyone else. No more evil than *you*. As for *her*, well, she doesn't need our help."

Clark said sternly, "I'm not like you."

"You're right. You are not like me. You are nothing like me . . ."

As Charisma spoke, the walls began to lean in as the world fell silent and still, even the very air, to listen: "I am the Sovereign, the Witch Queen, reigning supreme in this world. In my time, they have called me many names: Hecate, Medea, Lilith, Circe, Morgan le Fay. I am the one all your beloved stories are written about. The first and the last of the Original Witches. I have always been here, and I always will be.

"You, on the other hand, have acted like a fool. Your aura is permeable. You live in fear of other people, and of yourself. You care too much about what other people think and feel. It makes you easy to read, easy to probe, poke, and toy with. It makes you weak."

His night terrors of being ridden flashed before his mind's eye. His cheeks flushed with indignation. "I'm not weak," he said meekly.

Charisma raised up in her seat as Clark sank lower into his. "*Never* forget that the price for your insolent choices is the loss of a finger, a hand, a limb; your loved one, your mind, *your life*. Never forget that tonight, I showed you mercy, and that could change at my whim and mine alone. In the old days, I'd cut out your tongue myself, simply for talking too much."

I want this to be over . . . he thought. *For her to kill me right here and now, and be over with it . . .*

"Oh, but not to worry, sweetie darling, I'm not going to kill you. At least, not yet." She leaned back into her office chair and put her heels up on the desk, while taking a deep draw of her cigarette. "I find fear to be a powerful motivator, don't you?" She flashed her perfect white smile. "And besides: Melissa had to go, just like that wretched maid. It had to be done, and for that, I'll spare you. Just this once. And if you hadn't done it, I would have found a way. I had known for quite some time. Let's just chalk up your little indiscretion to 'exuberance of youth,' shall we?"

"You . . . knew she was going to leave?"

"Oh yes. And that witch-bitch Monica was getting a little too big for her britches, too. You know what I think? I say job *well done*." At this, Charisma giggled. Her eyes turned to Melissa's, burnt and dead, staring at him in the Tower.

"I didn't do to her what you did. I could never do that. What you did to Melissa I would never do . . ."

"Oh, for fuck's sake," she said, putting her cigarette out into the ashtray in front of her. "*You already did.* You can play dumb to yourself all you like, darling, but not to me. Never to me. You think you are my moral superior? Think again! Did you get *buddy-buddy* with my staff to make friends? No. You asked Lorena how we operate here, how witches are hired into my coven. You did it to infiltrate. You asked to become more involved, and then, Emily had you draw the circle—*your* circle. You were jealous of the witches, of the interviewees, and all the nice things that working for me can afford them, weren't you? You did away with Melissa. You shifted the tables when you upended Monica's tirade and finally stood up for yourself. It was either them or you, and you picked your petty little self. You knew what you were doing the entire time. In my house, I see all. And some things are so loud, *they scream*. You have been acting out your unconscious needs and desires in everything that you do. You, who have lived so disconnected, a voyeur to your own power—in this existence? How? Good *Goddess*, for the City That Never Sleeps there sure are a lot of sleepwalkers! Time to wake up, darling!"

Clark was speechless. He realized his mouth had been agape, and running dry, and he quickly shut it.

"And now, on this night, here you are sitting in *my* chair, in *my* home, taking up *my* time, and waiting for what, some kind of Dumbledorian wisdom to be bestowed upon you? What is it that you are looking for? Pardoning? Permission? You have been an entitled little brat the entire time you've been here. So what exactly is it that you want here, if you are so above us? Money? Power?"

"I'm . . . not sure," he said.

"Get up, boy. Answer me."

Clark's legs carried him as if with a mind of their own. In front of the almost wall-length, gold mirror, framed in hieroglyphs, they stopped. There seemed to be a whisper coming from inside the mirror. There he saw himself: average and awkward. A boy and not a man. Charisma stood behind him, looking at him too. Atop the frame was an Egyptian ankh and Eye of Horus peering down at them.

"I don't know," Clark said finally.

"You know," Charisma spoke into his ear, leaning in, more calm and yet more grave than ever. She wore that sly smile. "Do not make me ask again, witch: what is it that you want?"

Then and there, the words that had been boiling just under the surface for months made themselves known, breaking in a bubbling instant as if he had known what to say all along, as if he had already spoken them. The words came to him effortlessly.

"I want to be like you." His cheeks flushed pink as he let it all out. He turned to look at her. "Make me a witch like you. Make me the new assistant."

The release was so sweet he almost shed a tear.

There was a long pause as Charisma folded one arm under her elbow, and with her free hand took a drag from the cigarette that was hanging from her lips. Her venomous green eyes narrowed in on his own twinkly brown.

Clark worried, *What is she thinking . . . ?* The expression on her face was not surprise, he decided, but more so, *Is it . . . satisfaction . . . ?*

Charisma uttered a short *hmm* before deeply inhaling her cigarette down to its lipstick-covered filter. She turned him slowly back to the mirror.

There . . . she replied in his mind, looking at his throat. *Now doesn't that feel better . . . ?* Clark realized that the sore throat that had plagued him for months was gone. Cured. "Yes . . ." he said, reaching up to touch it. "Thank you."

"Good," she said, as her office door slid open as if on its own. "Have a good night."

CHAPTER XII

Happily Ever After . . .

$\mathfrak{I}$ust as he feared, Clark was somehow still employed at Charisma's. He was worked like a dog the rest of December by a disdainful Monica. He could tell by the way she treated him that she was fulfilling her own personal form of revenge . . . and cooking up something else. Whatever she was planning, Clark couldn't be so sure. The night terrors had thankfully stopped cold turkey. That almost worried Clark, who had begun to wonder if Monica was behind them to begin with.

Joey didn't probe Clark about the lacerations when they had been discovered. Clark had explained it away as a slip at work, a "corner of a cabinet" gone rogue, but he knew that Joey wasn't buying it.

The next thing he did know was that Christmas had arrived to the city. With the fashion and witching industries quiet and on hiatus, the Saintlys and the Henceleys all abroad in London for the next couple of weeks, and no other business to attend to until the new year, Clark embraced a very short, and very welcomed, break from work.

The day before Christmas Eve, his first day off, he caught up on sleep for almost the entire day. He awoke in the middle of the evening to a series of texts:

(3:33 p.m. Emily Manitis): Merry Christmas, babes! See you
in the New Year xoxo

(4:50 p.m. Patricia Hartford): Merry Christmas Eve, Clarky!
Love you!

(6:16 p.m. Maria): Merry Christmas, pumpkin! I'll fly you
down to visit, just let me know the dates. Don't forget to call
your father. I love you— Mom.

Clark's face turned a little pink at Emily's text. He replied to the
first two, and to the third, he wrote:

(8:45 p.m. Clark Crane): Merry Christmas, Mom. Okay, a
visit would be nice. Love you— Clark.

Joey invited Clark to his family's for the holiday, spending it with
his parents and sister, and all the many, many cousins and aunts and
uncles (who adored Clark and whom Clark, to his relief, fit right
in with). They spent their time in and out of Joey's large basement
room, full of records and record players and old-timey cameras and
antiques. In the daytime they played board games and video games
and watched movies with the kids, and in the afternoons and evenings, they drank wine and talked politics with the parents at the
adult table.

One day, they even went out ice skating at Bryant Park, and just
like Joey had mentioned on their first date, enjoyed roasted chestnuts on a cigarette-smoke-filled New York City sidewalk. Other than
maybe at Patricia's, Clark couldn't remember spending a more loving
Christmas. His hollow under-eyes volumized, his smile returned, and
there was a warmth to his complexion he hadn't seen in a long time.

Clark got Joey a couple of vinyl soundtracks of witch movies he
loved, one from the 1940s and one from the '70s. Joey got Clark a
weeping fig tree that Clark could've sworn grew massive overnight.

"That means it's working," Joey said. "The lady at the market said it's like a money tree, but for abundance, or something like that."

A couple of nights after the holiday, when all the cousins had made their way home, and Joey's work schedule called, the twosome made their way back to Astoria to Clark's little papier-mâché apartment, returning to their nights cuddled in bed with marijuana and movies. They were watching a black-and-white, one Joey had seen a million times, when he paused to speak to Clark.

"Hey, baby, I want to ask you something, and please don't think I'm crazy," Joey said.

"What? You know you can tell me anything," Clark said.

"I've been thinking and—I know it's soon, but I love you, I really am crazy for you, and I've thought it through long and hard, so I want you to think about it and get back to me when you're ready . . ."

"You're not about to propose to me again, are you," Clark asked facetiously with a smile. Joey giggled. "Because this time, I want a ring."

"Good to know. But no, not that, not yet . . . I've just been thinking a lot about work, and where we're at—thinking about us—and I wanted to ask you if you would want to . . . maybe, move in together?"

Clark looked at him perplexedly. "To your parents' place . . . ?"

"Gawd no! Not to my rents'. I meant, out on our own, here in Astoria or somewhere closer to work, on the Upper East Side or Murray Hill or wherever. We can figure it out. Make a new home, together. I'm just so crazy about you. I've seen the sacrifices you've made, how you've come out strong from some dark moments . . ."

Had he?

"I admire you so much, Clark. I think this is the right move. You don't have to make a decision right away. Just . . . what do you think?"

"Wow, Joey, I admire you so much, too." They leaned in for a kiss. Another quick move, so soon after Coney Island. Joey seemed to be making all the moves in their relationship, and while Clark was down for the ride, something pulled at his heart all the same. "You're so beautiful, and strong, and sweet. You're like a dream. You're my Mr. Big, the *Chrysler Building to my New York, baby* . . . but do you really think we're ready for it?"

"Yes!" Joey said. "I do. I think we're ready for the next step. Don't you?"

Clark looked him in the eyes, and then looked away. "Joey," Clark began, "there's something I've gotta tell you, something you've gotta know about me . . ."

Joey crinkled his eyebrows. "What? What is it?"

Clark cleared his throat a few times, unable to find the words. Joey grabbed his hand and held it in his. "Clark," Joey said, "just tell me."

"You're gonna think I'm the crazy one . . ." Clark said. Joey gripped his hand.

"Clark, baby, tell me. Please."

"Okay, okay. Fine . . . Joey, the thing about me you have to know is that I'm . . . I'm not a good person."

"What do you mean?"

"Um . . . I—I thinkImmuhwtch," Clark mumbled.

"Huh?" Joey raised his eyebrows.

Clark took a deep, sharp inhale, his shoulders practically up to his ears. He spoke fervently and fast. "I think I'm a witch," he said. "Only, my boss, Charisma, yeah—she's a witch. Emily, and Monica, and Melissa, the one who died, all of them are witches. Charisma's some kind of Queen of All Witches. There's a ton of them here in New York, an entire network. And not just here, but the entire world! When I interviewed, at first, I didn't understand—I had no idea! I mean, c'mon, what did I know? Would *you* believe it? Then, I snuck up to her penthouse on the night of my birthday—remember that night? Yeah, me too, except I didn't go straight home, not right away. I witnessed Charisma kill Melissa, only, she didn't have to lay a finger on her! You're looking at me like I'm insane but it's the truth! I'm telling you the truth! She just burned Melissa up to a crisp, right in front of us, as a sacrifice for betraying her—and she's done this before, and gotten away with it too! She killed a maid, Miss Honey, who tried to warn me, and I should've listened but I didn't, and, and—"

"*What?!* Wait, Clark, slow down . . ."

Clark told him all of it, from the train-wreck interview to the intercepting of the note to the night terrors and the gargoyle chase he couldn't shake, with the scars to prove it. Joey's big brown eyes were as large as the moon. Then Clark told him about Miss Honey going up in flames and disappearing into thin air like a ghost. He only left out the triangulating of Melissa and Monica (*he doesn't have to know* everything, *does he . . . ?*). Joey's face changed from warm concern, to raised eyebrows in worry, to something akin to gray and vacant and not at all there.

"The thing is . . . it's all my fault. I didn't realize! I made a wish after my interview, after how badly it went, that things would change for me, that I could get ahead in life—and then I got the job! Do you see what I'm saying? I *asked* for this to happen. I just didn't realize it would come true, not in this way!"

Joey grabbed Clark's face and held him in his hands. "Clark," Joey said. "Breathe. No. Just *no*. Listen to me: This isn't your fault. You got the job because you were *referred*. You were at the right place at the right time. You didn't ask for this to happen. You didn't ask for your manager to . . . die." Joey gulped. "The wish didn't lead you to get the job, *you* led you to get the job when you decided you wanted more than Astoria Coffee Shoppe. That's all."

Clark scrunched up his face. "But it is, Joey, it is all my fault."

"It's *not*, baby," Joey said.

Clark pulled away and downed the glass of water on his night-stand. He drank it so hard he sputtered and coughed, almost choking himself.

"And now I can't get out," Clark said, "and it's too late, and now . . ." Clark buried his face in his hands.

Joey sprang up and hugged him. "And now what?"

He came up for air, laughing. "And now, you're really gonna hate me. I snuck back into Charisma's to, I dunno, uncover her and her Coven and her weaknesses. When she confronted me, caught me snooping, in the end . . . I asked her to make me the new assistant."

Joey's eyes widened and he took a step back, holding Clark at arm's length. "You did *what?*"

Clark explained how he was finally caught snooping, confronted by none other than Charisma herself. When Clark was done, Joey skipped gray-faced and went straight to white.

"I've gone from, 'the master's tools will never dismantle the master's house,' to 'play them at their own game,' to 'if you can't beat 'em, join 'em.' Honestly, I don't know what the hell is wrong with me!"

Joey moaned, "Cla-ark . . . !"

"Oh, and, um, also . . . My first name isn't Clark."

"It isn't?!"

Clark shook his head and then buried his face in Joey's shoulder. "Clark is my middle name."

"Well, what is it then?"

Clark looked up at him. "It's Ryan, okay? My name is Ryan. Boring, plain-as-hell Ryan. I'm technically Ryan the Third, named after my father and my father's father. *That's* why Monica agreed to meet with me: Patricia must've given her my first name so that she would think I was a *girl* named Ryan."

Joey laughed, easy at first, and then a little too hard. After a moment, he took a deep breath. "I need a drink," he said finally.

Clark had never heard Joey say that, or seen him take a sip of alcohol for that matter. "Joey?" Clark asked. "Are you mad at me?"

"I'm not mad. *I'm concerned.* And you haven't been totally honest with me. You've kinda been living a . . . a double life practically. Why didn't you tell me all this sooner?"

What do I say . . . ? Clark thought. *What can I say . . . ?* He bit his lip.

I can start with the truth . . .

"It's not a different me. It's the same me," he said. "And I was afraid! Afraid of what you would think, of what would happen if I told you, afraid you would leave . . ." Clark meant that in more ways than one, thinking about Charisma's NDA. "Please don't be mad at me, Joey," Clark said, looking into his crestfallen eyes. "You're all that makes sense right now."

"Hey, babe," Joey said, holding him by the shoulders. "We're gonna figure this out. I love you."

"I love you, too," Clark said. They kissed. They looked at one another, Clark into Joey's big teddy bears, and Joey into his twinkly browns.

Thump!

From the fire escape outside the windows, there was movement and a thud. From atop Clark's ancient window AC unit, two glowing, vertical yellow-green eyes stared back. Clark and Joey screamed. They both jumped back in shock, holding one another close, before Clark realized exactly what they were really looking at. He walked to the eastern window, and despite Joey's protests *("Clark, wait!")*, he opened it.

A black cat leapt inside off the fire escape, and meowed. It peered around the studio, its head bobbing up and down, tasting the air with its mouth agape. Then, it rubbed on Clark's legs, looking up at him while purring.

"Aww!" Clark said, petting her. "Daddy, can we keep her?!"

They argued back and forth for some time while the cat explored the apartment. "You can't keep a stray! She's feral! What about fleas?!" Joey reasoned.

"It's winter! She's cold!" Clark protested. But the cat, a small, skinny runt, had climbed onto the foot of the bed and made herself at home. She looked up, kneading biscuits and purring loudly, and the decision had been made for them, end of discussion. Soon, the two were off to sleep with their new friend snuggled up in the middle. The cat would show up every night thereafter, for a can of dollar-store tuna, a snuggle, and a sleep, and leave in the mornings, always to return the next night.

One of the following nights, when Joey was at work, and it was just Clark and the cat, Clark got around to asking what he and Joey could not decide on. "What should we call you, cutie? Pumpkin maybe? What's your name?"

They locked eyes, unblinking. The noise of the world around them seemed to turn down to mute, and Clark understood with relief that the yellow-green eyes haunting his dreams were the very ones looking up at him then, from the fire escape all along. Clark had that telltale tingle in the middle of his forehead. Almost instantaneously, a single name came to mind. He scrunched his nose.

"Wait, really? Hmm . . . I've never heard of a cat named Jessica, but okay!"

Eventually, the temperature would plummet to below forty degrees, a proper New York winter's cold, and Jessica the cat would refuse to leave. Joey and Clark agreed that she needed a checkup, and so, after a visit to the vet, Jessica became the third member of that tiny papier-mâché Astoria home, and of their family. Clark didn't have to worry about cat sitting anymore, or Joey being upset with him. In a way, Jessica had brought them even closer together.

Clark spent the rest of Christmas break picking up shifts at the coffee shop, some longtime weekday patrons happy to see his face again before their workdays, wondering where he had gone. There was a familiarity there that he had forgotten how much he missed.

New Year's Eve came, and Clark and Joey spent it at Northlight's bar. They rang in the New Year with the big ball drop at Times Square on the TV screens, his management too busy to notice or care when they stole a kiss at midnight.

By January second, Clark was back to work bright and early at seven a.m., just like every shift before. All of the Coven had been back, only arriving a day prior, and having assembled that morning in the main kitchen, including Lorena. Clark was all aglow, and nothing they could do could get him down.

"Good morning, ladies," he said, not one of them except for Emily happy for his cheeriness. "I'll make us a coffee run. What can I pick up?"

"Why? We can use the coffee maker here," Lorena said. She pointed to the coffee machine in the corner of the kitchen he had never noticed.

A resounding ping and buzz sounded off from all the occupants' phones. They paused, all bent over in reading—and then, in shock, all eyes were raised and rested on none other than Clark. Emily clapped her hand to her mouth in laughter.

"What?" he asked. "Why is everyone looking at me?" *Am I finally fired . . . ?*

Before he even had time to blink, all the ladies had launched up at him, talking at once.

"Oh my GAWD!" Emily jumped up to hug him. "Congrats!"

"What did you do?!"

"How did you do it?!"

"How could she do this?!" Monica demanded. The room fell silent. "How did you convince her—*you*, of all people!"

"Hey!" Emily said. "This was Charisma's decision. Respect her choice!"

Monica asked Lorena, "Did you know?"

"I had no idea!"

Alicia said, "Clark's not going to accept, he's not ready for such a big responsibility . . . right, Clark?"

They all stared at him unblinkingly. "What's going on?!" he asked.

"Clark," said Alicia, "Charisma just announced the new assistant effective immediately. The new assistant is *you*."

All that holiday cheer and glow quickly drained from his face. His knees felt weak. He wanted to jump for joy and throw up and cry all at the same time.

"What?!" Clark gasped.

"And he's just twenty-four!" Emily exclaimed. "You'll be the youngest coven member in the country, maybe even the entire world."

"Please," Monica said doubtfully. "He won't last a day."

Clark had no words. *Did she just promote me . . . ? Is this really happening . . . ?*

"Congratulations, darling," Lorena said through pursed lips. "Now that you're an . . . employee, we'll get your paperwork started."

"Paperwork?" Clark asked.

"Yes," Lorena said. "You want to be paid, don't you?"

I'm going to be paid . . . It's happening . . . ! It's all finally happening . . . !

Clark broke out into a big, beaming smile.

* * *

Life moved fast for Clark that New Year.

The news came Thursday. By Friday, as if his own personal PR team making an announcement, Clark posted to his social media that he was promoted to "the new fourth assistant to the personal team of Charisma Saintly."

It happened quickly: the reactions and the comments piled in by droves, his phone on one continuous chime, from people he hadn't talked to in years, showering him with blessings and praise.

"That's my friend! So proud of you," his friend Krystal had commented.

"So *that's* where you've been?!" Justin had written.

The new followers came in by the hundreds, of course, and by the next day, were in the thousands. *All because of who I work for . . . ? If only they knew . . .* Clark decided he could hate it, or roll with it, and decided that the latter would be much easier in the long run.

That weekend, the day he knew was coming (but which had come sooner than expected) had finally arrived. Now that he was being promoted and going to be paid, Clark did the hard thing: that Saturday, he put in his notice for the last time at the coffee shop.

Gloria, of course, was weepy. As a send-off, she handed Clark an envelope and a card full of well-wishes from her, her husband Eduardo, their two little girls, and the rest of the Astoria Coffee Shoppe's team. Inside was a small sum of cash. "I saw it on your social media," Gloria said. Clark reflected on how he could've used that money earlier while hungry and housebroke, but was grateful regardless. The gesture brought him to tears.

That night Joey and Clark celebrated with a big Chinese takeout meal. Having a weekday work schedule and the weekends off for the first time in years gave Clark a little space to breathe, and a little hope for his future.

That Sunday morning, however, things took a turn when he received a group text message from Lorena.

(6:00 a.m. Lorena Henceley): We are flying for LA
tomorrow morning at 8 a.m., sharp.

Clark was quick to text Joey the news: "Babe! Oh my gawd, babe, guess what?!"

Emily texted him separately. She told him to pack a bag: the night before any early travel, the Coven would sleep at Charisma's in her many guest rooms, and fly on her private jet. Clark was so ecstatic he threw up a little in his mouth. What would he wear? He had never been west of Florida, let alone to the west coast. Clark left Astoria Coffee Shoppe a little earlier than scheduled, not knowing it would be his last time there.

That evening, he packed in a frenzy and made his way to the penthouse. One of the night maids, Luz, took his bag up and not the other way around for once, as the Coven gathered in the dining room for dinner. It all felt like a dream. Could this be real life?

"Just be yourself," Emily had told him. "Sit back. Watch. Listen. Jump in on the conversation when you can. But above all: be yourself," she said to him. "You've earned your seat at the table . . . no matter what you might have done to earn it." She couldn't hide the suspicion in her voice. Clark didn't notice.

The ladies were discussing their itinerary for L.A. when he and Emily entered.

"Seems like Felicity is halting film production. She's refusing to leave her hotel room," Alicia had shared. "Charisma's being called to step in. To see if she can coax her—"

"Oh my GAWD!" Clark exclaimed. The women stopped to look at him with raised eyebrows. "Sorry, I mean, I'm practically gagging. Felicity?! I'm such a HUGE fan of hers. What a star! And we're going to L.A. to see her? This is crazy!"

As Hollywood's most sought-after and highest-paid A-list actress, singer, and dancer, Felicity was in the midst of a media storm of harassing paparazzi, a divorce, a custody battle, and a sudden conservatorship that had rocked the media with controversy—all the while being pushed into work on a major blockbuster. Clark had been following the case for years, and even living under a rock, was truly an admirer.

"Noted. Don't let him near the client," Monica said sardonically to the air, "lest he *gushes* her to death."

"Now, now, Monica," Lorena said, "let him get it out now . . . while he can . . ."

Alicia, Lorena, and Monica exchanged looks with one another. Emily gave them all a look too, one of reproach and disapproval. Clark was too happy to care.

That night, dinner was filet mignon *(These women love their steak . . .).* Lorena let the fork scrape against her teeth, which Clark found to be entertaining and irritating at the same time, as she was. The red wine flowed (*"thenk yew,"* Clark began to say).

After dinner that night, when they retired to their rooms on the second floor, Clark heard a knock on the door: Emily had come for a visit, her long hair back and dressed down in sweats and a hoodie. Clark thought her so impossibly beautiful, out of black and makeup as she was, he blushed out of nervousness.

"Hey, babes," she said. "Thought I'd come to say hi and . . . share a drink?" She was holding a thermos. "It's spiked hot chocolate."

"I'd love some!" Clark had almost thought she had come to break the news that the jig was up, this was all a big joke, and he was to go home never to return, but nope. They clinked and drank.

"I feel like I haven't gotten a chance to talk to you alone. How are you feeling?"

"So excited," he replied. Clark shared with her everything he could: he told her about the night terrors leading up to the gargoyle chase, Miss Honey and the terrarium, the portrait, showed her the faint scar on his back even, but left out the part about intercepting the note, as well as the triangulating Melissa that led to her getting fired, just like he had with Joey. He shared all that he could remember from his confrontation with Charisma, how he couldn't believe she had promoted him after all, how he was going to L.A. for the first time, and that meeting Felicity was like a happily ever after.

"Yeah, it's all a huge deal," Emily said. "You should be proud! Of course, everyone in the witching community already knows. Once Monica knows, everyone else does. You're the talk of the town."

"Really? And my ears have been *burning* since Thursday," he said.

"Yeah, I bet. That's a sign," she said. "You're making a lot of people mad, and I say *good*. Fuck 'em! Charisma was right about something, though—be careful with whom you trust and talk to from here on out. You never know who has bad intentions for you, now that you've got a mark on your back. When we return from L.A., I'll have to teach you some defense magic, like how to close your aura and protect yourself."

"You're gonna . . . teach me magic?"

"Duh!" she said. The way his face brightened, she clearly couldn't help but smile back. She looked away and refilled their drinks.

"Oh! Hey, I'm remembering something, now that you mention it: on Halloween at Charisma's party, there was a woman who approached me. It was really quick and kinda strange. She knew my name and I swear she talked to me telepathically. She handed me her card and told me something about when I'm ready for a real coven, to call her. What do you make of that?"

"Did you get her name?" she asked.

"No. But she told me to call her Mother. Isn't that odd?"

Emily's jaw dropped. She looked around and spoke just above a whisper. "No . . . ! Mother was there?"

"So you know who she is?"

"Shhh . . . ! *Of course* I know who she is, everyone in and out of the witching community knows who she is. Mother is after Charisma's throne."

"Oh, no," Clark said.

"Look, Clark . . . That's not good. There is no coven that proselytizes. You come to them. Every witch on a coven asks for admittance. Maybe she's been watching you . . ."

"Oh, no . . ." said Clark again. Still, there was a small feeling of flattery lurking about his mind. "And Emily?"

"Yes?"

"Who are the Powers and the Order?"

Emily's tone changed to a low, grave, barely audible whisper. "How did you find out about that?"

"I, um . . . overheard them being talked about."

She gave him a side-eye. "I'm not buying that. Tell me how you know, and I'll tell you what I can."

"I don't like those odds," Clark said. "But alright . . ." He explained after all how he had intercepted a note of Charisma's, and how she'd confronted him on it at their midnight meeting.

Emily gasped. "You did not . . . !"

"I did," he said.

"*Clark . . . !* She could've—oh my gawd, I can't believe you!" She buried her face in her hands and looked up at him with astonishment. "You have a death wish, I'm convinced."

"Maybe . . ." he said. He hoped she didn't believe that either. "Do you know who they are?"

Emily sighed. She spoke so low that Clark had to lean in and watch her lips to understand. "The Order is a sect of oligarchs that control . . . everything, the entire world. They, in turn, answer to the Powers That Be, an order of beings not on this plane of existence, but . . . Clark, you have no idea what these people are capable of."

Clark pressed on. "Is that whom Charisma answers to?"

"I . . . can't say. She's planning . . . *something*. First, New York; next, the world. That's all I can say, for now. I bet she's keeping you under her thumb. That's why she promoted you. Whatever you do, please, don't get involved with any of their business. It could spell major bad news for you . . ."

The hair on Clark's arms stood on end. What did the Powers want with this "Order"? How was Charisma involved? No matter the case, it would have to wait another day.

They talked about other, lighter things for a while, what shows they were watching, what they were reading ("So much in common!" Clark had said), about Joey suggesting they move in.

Emily squealed. "Charisma can probably put you up in one of her apartments! She's lended them to assistants before."

"Really? You think she'd do that?"

"You're in, babes. Why wouldn't she?" As the clock neared eleven, Emily said, "Well, time to get to bed. Before I turn back into a pumpkin. I'll, um . . . I guess I'll see you in the morning, Clark."

"See you in the morning!" he said. Clark wondered why the hesitance. Regardless, to him it was like they were going to an amusement park when they awoke.

At the door, Emily turned for a moment to look back, with that sad smile in her eyes. "And Clark?"

"Yeah?"

But after a moment's pause, she said, "Nothing. Sleep well, babe."

"You too. Goodnight, Emily!"

"Goodnight."

Clark finished up the thermos and buzzed around the room. It was what he had imagined staying at a five-star hotel was like. Out the window, the city of New York twinkled. He looked out to the east side, Queens and Brooklyn. In the distance and over the East River to Astoria, the RFK Bridge winked at him—only this time, he was winking back, on the other side of it.

Clark resolved that he was going to get some answers. There was the matter of the terrarium and her weak points, Charisma and her empire to be dismantled, much of which was still a closed book to him then, just the same as ever—but there would be time for that. He was in, and that's all that mattered. He knew that everything would be all right. Clark felt like he had won. There, from that penthouse room, Clark felt like he was on top of the world.

He brushed his teeth in the room's attached bathroom, set his alarm, and climbed into bed. On that bed of silk pillowcases and satin sheets in an iron bed frame, his belly full and his heart even fuller, Clark fell quickly into the most delicious sleep he had ever known.

That's when they came for him. In the middle of the night, as he was sound asleep, they snatched Clark right out of bed, gagged and bound.

ABOUT THE AUTHOR

A. T. Napoli went from starving artist to celebrity makeup artist before writing his Bitchcraft novels. Having studied English literature and women & gender studies at Marymount Manhattan and Hunter College, he now boasts over a decade of experience in fashion and beauty. Napoli has worked with world-renowned entertainers such as Halsey and Lizzo as well as the editors of *Allure*, in which he is frequently mentioned. Like Clark in Bitchcraft, he often tries to save the day. Napoli is a first-generation American who resides in his native Astoria, New York.

DISCOVER
STORIES UNBOUND

PodiumAudio.com

Printed in the USA
CPSIA information can be obtained
at www.ICGtesting.com
JSHW021053190724
66718JS00005B/5

9 781039 469273